MOON OVER EDISTO

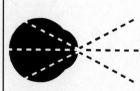

This Large Print Book carries the
Seal of Approval of N.A.V.H.

MOON OVER EDISTO

BETH WEBB HART

THORNDIKE PRESS

A part of Gale, Cengage Learning

GALE
CENGAGE Learning®

Detroit • New York • San Francisco • New Haven, Conn • Waterville, Maine • London

© 2013 by Beth Webb Hart.
Scripture quotations are taken from THE HOLY BIBLE, NEW
INTERNATIONAL VERSION®. NIV®. Copyright © 1973, 1978, 1984, 2011
by Biblica, Inc.™ Used by permission of Zondervan. All rights reserved
worldwide. www.zondervan.com
Thorndike Press, a part of Gale, Cengage Learning.

LIBRARY OF CONGRESS CATALOGING-IN-PUBLICATION DATA

Hart, Beth Webb, 1971–
  Moon over Edisto / by Beth Webb Hart.
    pages ; cm. — (Thorndike Press large print Christian fiction)
    ISBN 978-1-4104-5687-8 (hardcover) — ISBN 1-4104-5687-0 (hardcover)
  1. Large type books. I. Title.
PS3608.A78395M66 2013b
813'.6—dc23
                                                    2012051208

Published in 2013 by arrangement with Thomas Nelson, Inc.

Printed in Mexico
1 2 3 4 5 6 7 17 16 15 14 13

For Edward

For it is in giving that we receive.

FRANCIS OF ASSISI

CHAPTER 1
JULIA BENNETT

New York

When the bright red delivery truck from Gravy parked halfway on the sidewalk by the doors of the Kent Risen Art Gallery on Prince Street, Etienne winked at Julia and went out to pay the delivery boy.

"Po'boys," she said as she glided back through the gallery's thick glass door while lifting the greasy paper bags high. The smell of fried seafood filled the narrow space as Chih-Yang put down his wire cutters and rubbed his hands together. "I'm starving."

"Can't." Sanchez removed a nail from between his lips and began to hammer a hole in the black wall where he was planning to hang his 3-D "found objects" portrait of Bill Clinton, whose hair and eyebrows were made out of bubble wrap and crushed Diet Coke cans.

Etienne rolled her dark eyes. Sanchez had ordered them all the macrobiotic platter from Caravan of Dreams the night before, and Etienne had spat out the bland mixture of tofu and sea vegetables before lecturing them on French cuisine and how sad she felt for anyone who didn't regularly partake of butter or cream or mussels or red meat. Then she'd marched down the block and purchased a burger combo from the Fanelli Café that smelled so good even Sanchez asked for a french fry.

"In honor of our Southern belle," Etienne said as she unwrapped the shrimp po'boys piled high with large fried prawns and creamy coleslaw.

Julia winced ever so slightly. "What?" Etienne said. "I've read your bio. I know you grew up catching shrimps down in South Carolina."

"Sorry, Etienne." Julia pushed her glasses up on her nose. "I just can't do imported shrimp."

Chih-Yang, who had already taken a heaping bite of a po'boy, began to chew slowly. Then he shrugged and swallowed. "Mealy Asian prawns with salmonella are my *favorite.*" He took another bite as Sanchez shook his head and lifted his portrait up. Then Chih-Yang hunched over for a rather impressive pec flex. (He was the youngest, fittest artist in the group.) "My body thrives on toxins."

"Well, how about some fried chicken then?" Etienne opened the second bag, which contained a bucket of wings and legs as well as a basket of biscuits.

Sanchez was trembling as Julia reached for a wing. "Don't worry, Joseph," Julia said to her old friend from art school. "Do you think a restaurant this pricey would serve anything other than free range?"

Sanchez fanned himself with one of the gallery's brochures. "I think I need some fresh air." Then he slid on his organic hoodie and headed out the door as Julia imagined throwing the cast net off the bow of her father's old johnboat. And how, on a good day in late June or early July, their casts yielded nearly half a cooler full of the small, succulent tidal creek shrimp that her mother would boil up and serve with a bowl of melted butter at the end of their rickety dock on Store Creek on the south side of Edisto Island.

"So how often do you go back?" Etienne tore open a biscuit, and Julia was mesmerized by the steam rising from it and the comforting smell of flour and butter. "To eat the nontoxic shrimps in South Carolina?"

"Rarely," Julia said. She hadn't thrown

the cast net, hadn't stepped foot on the old dock, in nearly two decades, and she had no intention of ever doing so again.

Two hours later Julia rounded the corner of Fifth Avenue onto East 92nd. The hall entrance light was on at the bottom of her brownstone, which sat four doors down on the opposite side of the street. Well, it wasn't actually *her* brownstone. It belonged to her old friend Bess, who was married and had four children. There were a psychiatrist and a chiropractor on the first floor. Bess lived with her family on the next three floors. Julia had the fifth floor, the "penthouse," really just a large studio apartment with a nice-sized rooftop deck. Julia painted and gardened there by day, and by night she stretched out on the old Pawleys Island hammock beneath her potted ficus trees and stared at the sky.

On a clear night she could see the moon. She would have felt like the luckiest woman in the world — a gainfully employed artist with a charming significant other and a rooftop view in the middle of one of the world's greatest cities — if it weren't for the forlorn look on the moon's face. *This will not end well,* the face seemed to say. *Buzz off,* she said back to him sometimes.

East 92nd between Fifth and Madison was nearly noiseless this time of night. It was a little after ten and most everyone in this little section of Manhattan was bedded down, sleeping deeply before the predawn wake-up call that catapulted them out of bed and into their designer suits and private school uniforms.

Almost all of her colleagues at the college lived in either Brooklyn or the East Village or Harlem or the Bronx. Sometimes she felt a little silly living in the posh Carnegie Hill neighborhood on the Upper East Side, a stone's throw from Central Park. Wasn't an artist supposed to live in the real world? The earthy, gritty one where you were regularly intersecting both depravity and danger? Didn't pure art spring from facing the grit and gristle head-on, and not only that, but from immersing oneself in it? Ah, well, she had done that. For over a decade she had done that, and it hadn't proved to be nearly as inspiring or romantic as she'd hoped. In fact, it had left some scars as well as some steep therapist bills.

So when Bess and her husband, Graham, bought the building a couple of years ago and invited Julia to check out the penthouse, she didn't think twice. She was through with life-on-the-edge. She was a tenured professor in the art department of Hunter College with health insurance and a retirement plan. Within the next year she was slated to become department chair. She had finally entered into a season of balance and security on nearly every level, and she was not going to let anything keep her from her own little piece of Manhattan sky.

Julia crossed the quiet street toward home. As she got closer to her building, she spotted a figure just beyond the glass-paneled street door who had not yet been buzzed into the main entrance. The figure's back — it appeared to be a woman — was to Julia, and she was leaning against the wall, head and all, as if she had fallen asleep standing up. The woman was slightly hunched over in a thin beige raincoat. Not nearly heavy enough for this crisp March evening.

Probably one of Dr. Hu's patients, Julia thought as her high-heeled boots steadily clapped the street before she slowed down and took a cautious step onto the sidewalk. She dug through her bag for her cell phone. She'd better wake up Graham, who was surely snoozing in the master bedroom on the fourth floor. She hated to bother him, but she didn't need to be wrangling with a mental patient on an unpeopled street this time of night. *Why a psychiatrist's office in*

14

my building? she thought as she dialed Graham's number. *Why not an optometrist or a dermatologist? Why not* two *chiropractors?* She might have called Simon too, but he was an ocean away in England visiting his sons. She missed him.

As Julia waited for Graham to pick up, the figure slowly turned around. Julia pressed End and dropped her phone in her bag as her heart caught in her throat. Beneath the fluorescent light the familiar face looked as though it had aged twenty years. The last time she had laid eyes on it was at Julia's father's funeral four years ago. Her thick mane of rich, brown hair had thinned substantially and was streaked with gray. Her sharp azure eyes, blue like the center of a flame, were now sunken into a thin, weathered face. Her gaze met Julia's. She looked almost fragile or elderly — like a deflated balloon or a carved-out jack-o'-lantern left out on the stoop too long. She was forty, just one year older than Julia, but she might as well have been in her late fifties.

Julia ground her teeth, willing the familiar symptoms of her panic attacks to subside: sweaty palms, racing heartbeat, constricted throat. Once you'd had one panic attack, your greatest fear was having another — it

15

was even greater than the fear of what might trigger it. *No,* she said to her pounding heart. *Stop, stop, stop. Please stop.* She breathed deeply and blinked several times, hoping the stars she was seeing would fade away. *Lord, have mercy, have mercy, have mercy,* she prayed. She had all but abandoned her childhood faith, but somehow this old prayer her Aunt Dot had taught her (when she was six and afraid to go to sleep because of some vivid nightmares involving Doberman pinschers) helped to stave off a full-blown attack. *Christ, have mercy.*

When her heart slowed a little, the woman came back into focus. Then the thought crossed Julia's mind: run, run down the street, hang a right onto Madison, and zip over to Zinnias for a nice glass of pinot noir. And maybe another. Though, truth be told, she hadn't had a second glass of wine in years.

Against Julia's better judgment, against every signal from her tense and trembling body, she found herself slowly walking toward the door. This was her house, her life. Had she not learned anything from her therapist? She knew exactly what Dr. Johansen would say: don't let anyone invade it.

She set her jaw, and the woman shifted

her weight and reached to the wall to steady herself. "This ought to be rich," Julia muttered under her breath. Spite was the second best fuel she'd found to battle the panic attack symptoms, and as she bridled it in her gut, she could already feel her heart slowing down further, her throat muscles relaxing slightly. She took a deep breath and then found her key, shoved it into the hole, and turned it with a flick of her knobby wrist.

As the door slammed behind her, the glass rattling in its pane, the woman slowly cocked her head.

"Julia," she said. "We need to talk."

Marney held a handbag that looked as though she had dug it out of some Dumpster in the textile district. She'd never had much taste. Much style. Much sense of fashion whatsoever. And that hadn't changed. It was the eyes that she had. And at one time, curves in all of the right places and a full face with even fuller lips. Most of all, she had gall. Or maybe it wasn't so much gall as it was ferocity. (Julia had received years of counseling regarding the subject of Marney.)

They rode the cramped elevator up to the top floor of the small, narrow building together. Julia turned her face away from the antiseptic smell coming from Marney. Like she'd just come from the doctor's office or a medical supply store. Marney wrung her dry, weathered hands, and Julia noticed that she still wore her wedding band. She wouldn't have put it past Marney to remarry right away, to have someone waiting in the wings, but it was the same one from before, the simple gold band with the fig vine engraving. Marney's husband was dead. Deep in the grave. Why did she still feel the need to wear it?

The elevator opened right into Julia's apartment. There was the tightly made bed in the far right corner, the studio in the far left beside a panel of windows, and around a curve in the wall there was a galley kitchen, which opened up onto the deck where Julia had recently planted tomatoes and lemons in several large terra-cotta pots along the far right edge where the sunlight was best.

The moon was nearly full and the sky was clear. Julia had an eerie feeling. As if the moon were winking at her. *Told you,* it might have said. She nodded to the little sitting area, two chairs and a small table, in the center of the apartment. "Okay," she said. "Have a seat. I'll put on some tea. Then you can tell me how you are going to ruin my life today."

"I'd rather have water." The woman's voice was faint and groggy. She took out a yellowed men's handkerchief and blew her nose.

"Sure."

Julia poured two glasses of water from the tap. As she carried the glasses toward Marney, she thought of an old Bible verse Aunt Dot used to read to her. Something about loving your enemies. Feeding them a big meal. Maybe something about offering a cup of water. Oh, she'd fallen out of the habit of going to church sometime during college, but that stuff still stuck. It surfaced unexpectedly like a porpoise fin rising out of the dark water.

Julia handed Marney the glass and took the seat opposite her. "How are the kids?"

"Surviving, I guess." The woman cleared her throat. "I have a son now."

Julia nodded in as civil a manner as she could muster. She remembered how big Marney had been the day of Julia's father's funeral.

Julia's father was buried in the Bennett family plot at Magnolia Cemetery outside of Charleston on a sweltering hot day in late August, and Aunt Dot was worried Marney might go into labor right there at the graveside service. She'd been having contractions. Her feet and hands were swelling. Her blood pressure was all over the map.

Marney always seemed to be the center of attention. Just by existing. Even at a funeral. Her husband had been well one morning, catching and cleaning trout for a late breakfast, and dead by dinnertime. He'd keeled over in a plastic chair on the dock next to his acrylic tubes and easel, the canvas showing the beginnings of an egret hunting at low tide on the far marsh bank of Store Creek. And wouldn't it have taken the cake for Marney to deliver the dead man's fifth child, his first son — Julia's half and only brother — on the day that he was being lowered into the ground?

But Marney didn't deliver the baby that day. No, Charlie Foster Bennett III was not birthed at the funeral of Charlie Jr., age sixty-six. Julia was on a plane back to New York late that afternoon, and to this day she had no idea how or when the baby actually arrived. It was her own mother who called to invite her home for Thanksgiving, who mentioned the baby's birth some weeks later. And then she'd received a birth announcement with Aunt Dot's handwriting and a photograph of the infant in a bouncy seat flanked by his two older sisters on the old Edisto porch of Julia's childhood summers. Aunt Dot, trying to patch the family together. Trying to be the glue of Julia's father's mistakes. Always the big sister, Julia supposed.

Marney was picking at a string on her raincoat. She had picked at things in college too. Julia had been paired up with her for a roommate her freshman year at the University of Georgia, though she had requested a room of her own. It was a cruel twist of fate brought about by the UGA computer system (or whatever demon inhabited it), but Julia didn't realize it at the time.

In fact, she had adored Marney, who smelled like cloves and was both older and street-savvy, yet very fragile. Marney's father had left her when she was just a young girl, and her mother had a prescription drug addiction that had landed her in and out of rehab over the course of Marney's childhood. Marney had seemed so alone. So on her own. Like a compelling protagonist in a young adult novel. Like the character about whom you think, *How or why does she go on?* And yet you can't look away because you want her to survive. You want her to thrive. She'd managed to get a scholarship to the university, and she was studying biology. She'd wanted to be a veterinarian.

So Julia had been compelled, compelled to bring Marney home during their college summers because she had no place to go. Each year they'd head to Edisto and wait tables at Dockside and spend the days lounging on the beach or taking the johnboat out into the tidal creeks and waterways. Marney had grown up in a concrete suburb of Atlanta, and Julia showed her porpoises, alligators, foxes, bobcats, and even a copperhead slinking across the orange and dusty dirt road. She taught her to fillet her first fish with a rusty boat knife and how to peel the heads off of a cooler full of shrimp too. Julia's mama, who was an amazing gardener and cook, would prepare big meals for them. Fresh-caught shrimp with plenty of butter for dunking, fried flounder and trout, tomato pies, okra soup, sweet corn on the cob, fresh-baked biscuits, and lots of creamy grits to go with everything. Julia's younger sister, Meg, was always there with a friend or two from town, and so was Julia's father, who took nearly all of the summer off from his law practice to do what he loved best — paint.

The last summer between their junior and senior year, Julia had been invited by her art professor to spend eight weeks touring the art museums of Italy and France. She jumped at the chance. Her parents invited Marney to spend the summer at Edisto, as usual, if she'd like. And she did. At the same time, Julia's maternal grandfather had a massive stroke, and her mother moved back to Charleston to care for him. Meg went back too. She was seventeen, and she had a crush on a South of Broad boy who taught sailing at the Carolina Yacht Club, so she spent the summer taking lessons from him. She would marry him seven years later.

By the time Julia returned to Edisto from Europe mid-August of that summer, she noticed some strange things: Marney taking a sip of her father's late-afternoon gin and tonic and setting it down beside him, Marney folding her father's clothes and delivering him a cup of coffee on the dock every morning as he painted, and once, when they must have thought Julia was still asleep, Marney putting her arm around Julia's father, and him doing the same, pulling her close for whole seconds as they stared out at Store Creek at the rising tide, wide arcs pushing toward the inmost part of their little salt marsh nook.

Now Marney cleared her throat and Julia woke back up from the memory. "I have cancer in my left lung, but my oncologist thinks they've caught it early enough." Marney pulled the beige string out of the lining of her jacket and let it fall onto Julia's hardwood floor. "I need to have surgery next month to remove it."

Julia exhaled slowly. She swallowed hard. "I'm sorry." Sorry Marney had torn her family apart, crushed her mother's heart, exhausted her father with an entirely new second family, and now was battling a wicked disease. Messiness heaped upon messiness. Julia did not like messiness. What she really wanted to say was, *So what does this have to do with me?*

As if Marney could read her mind, she straightened up, met Julia's gaze, and said, "I need you to come home in May and take care of the kids. The recovery will take a month or two."

CHAPTER 2
MARY ELLEN DUVALL
BENNETT

Charleston

Dressed only in her nightgown, Mary Ellen poked her head out of her piazza, bent down, and made a quick reach for the newspapers on her stoop just beyond the little wrought-iron gate that led to the street. The *Charleston Post and Courier* and the *New York Times.* She scooped them up in their little plastic baggies and ducked back into the house and then out through the kitchen to her little backyard garden where her coffee was steeping in the mini French press. She smiled at her china bowl of cereal topped with slivered blackberries and pecans glistening in the morning sunlight. It was already warm on this mid-March morning in downtown Charleston. The thick smell of roses from her neighbor's garden made her inhale deeply. Her own garden blossomed with azaleas, wisteria plumes, and pale green hydrangeas, each a perfectly rounded bouquet unto itself. But the roses seemed to trump them all with their rich, syrupy sweetness.

It must have been at least seventy-five degrees already, and she could almost feel her hair frizzing. She patted it down as she watched the mourning doves flitting back and forth between the palmetto trees and the cable wires before letting out their five long melancholy notes.

There was a window of temperate weather in Charleston where you could enjoy the outdoors nearly all day long. It was the time between the winter chill and the sweltering summer heat that brought with it enormous mosquitoes, aptly nicknamed the state bird, and the potential threat of hurricanes flung off of the west coast of Africa like enormous, razor-studded Frisbees. When that window opened, somewhere between February and early June, Mary Ellen liked to take as many meals as she could in her little back garden. Fresh air and sunshine did her soul good. And it lifted her spirits.

She poured herself a cup of well-steeped coffee, took a sip, and then pulled her *Times* out of the plastic sleeve and flipped right to the Arts section. Soho's Kent Risen Gallery was featuring five young New York artists in its latest exhibit, and there on page two in section B was an article about the show with a decent-size photo of the artists on a slick leather sofa in the center of the large warehouse-style room. Mary Ellen's eldest daughter, Julia, was on the far right side of the sofa. She was the only native-born American and the only Caucasian. "I'm the token white girl, Mama," she told Mary Ellen over the phone just yesterday. "Nonsense, sweetheart," Mary Ellen had scoffed. She had never been comfortable with her daughters beating themselves down — she had dreaded seeing them fail or knowing their hearts were wounded.

Tonight was the opening of Julia's exhibit, and tomorrow there would likely be a review in the Arts section. Mary Ellen's stomach did a little flip just thinking about it. Her child was far away, and had been for years, but she still felt deeply connected to her. To both of her daughters.

Julia's art — the one she had seemed to settle on after graduate school — wasn't something Mary Ellen fully understood or appreciated. Julia painted shapes — simple shapes — in neon colors, and had done so for nearly the last twenty years. Mary Ellen ran her fingertips across her daughter's face on the printed page. She could still picture her with the easel set up right here on the

Savage Street sidewalk or out at their little family vacation home on Edisto Island — beneath the oak-lined dirt road that led to the salt marsh creek, beside the rows of sunflowers and tomatoes, and, of course, on the dock as the tide and the sky and the waterfowl and sea life altered the canvas moment by moment. More often than not, Charles was painting right alongside her.

Now Mary Ellen could hear a little rustling in the pittosporum bushes just behind her. Her nightmare neighbor, Nate Gallagher, had more activity over there than usual. Jane Anne Thornton, who kept everyone on the street well informed on all matters, reported a few days ago in passing at Burbage's that Nate's grandson from New Jersey was staying with him for the week.

Of course, hardly anyone on all of Savage Street was speaking to Nate Gallagher. He hadn't exactly assimilated into the South of Broad culture gently, what with his rantings at the downtown neighborhood association meetings, his frequent calls to the city to request the towing of neighbors' cars who parked an inch over the line in the space in front of his house, or his enormous beast of a dog that he walked in the early morning — without a leash — and allowed to run down the driveways of the neighbors' houses where he left shockingly large and smelly surprises in many a back garden. Mary Ellen's son-in-law, Preston, was an attorney. She'd had him threaten Nate with a lawsuit after he'd repeatedly blocked the sidewalk in front of her house instead of his own with the debris from his backyard trimmings. He'd yet to look her in the eye after she slid the letter in his mail slot one night last year.

Mary Ellen put her linen napkin in her lap and leaned in for a bite of her cereal when something bright orange and rubbery plopped right into her china bowl, splashing Grape-Nuts flakes and bits of blackberries and pecans all over her face and her hair and the front of her pink seersucker robe.

She grabbed her linen napkin and gently patted the milk off of her nose and eyebrows. Then she turned back to see a full-cheeked, freckled face staring back at her from a little hole in the bushes. A boy, maybe eight or nine, with a scrunched-up nose. He cocked his head rigidly. "Can I have my ball?"

She wiped the ball off with the bottom corner of her robe and tossed it back over the thick wall of green to him. Then she stood, refastened her belt, and walked back to the house to clean herself off and get a fresh bowl of cereal.

As she sliced more blackberries, she watched the boy out of the window. He was tossing the ball against the back side of Nate's house. *Thud. Thud. Thud.* He had a shock of orange hair and a ruddy complexion, and he was sporting black jeans, black high-tops with orange trim, and a black T-shirt that said "Kick Buttowski" on the back. He caught the ball nearly every time. As she watched him she was struck with a longing to see her three grandchildren, so she called her daughter Meg.

"Hi, Mom." Meg always sounded breathless on the phone. As if she'd just run a mile in an all-out sprint.

"Hi, darling," Mary Ellen said. "Would you all like to come over for dinner tonight? I've got the day off. I can make shrimp creole and maybe a strawberry cobbler."

Meg sighed and then muffled the phone to gently scold one of the children. Mary Ellen wondered which one it was. Probably Cooper. He was her favorite, but he knew how to send Meg into a tailspin.

"Can't," she said. "We've got a basketball game this afternoon, then we've got midweek church."

Mary Ellen's heart sank and she was surprised by the sudden sting in the corners

30

of her eyes. "Oh."

She could hear her daughter exhale. "We need a good week's notice, Mom, okay?"

Mary Ellen swallowed hard. Meg had told her this once before. "All right, Meg. I forgot."

"Margaret," the exasperated voice on the other end said back to her.

"Yes, of course," Mary Ellen said. "Margaret." She wanted to say, *I miss you. I miss the children. Please let me see you. Please invite* me *over if you can't come over here.* But she did not.

There was a squeal and then a large clatter in the background at Meg's. "Gotta go, Mom. Check the Facebook page for info on the game if you want to come."

Facebook, Meg had told her mother, was the best way to keep up with their goings-on. It was a one-stop spot to connect with them. They didn't have time to call or e-mail the extended family. But the more Mary Ellen checked their page, the more distant she felt from them. It was as if their lives existed on an entirely different plane, and she was only allowed momentary glimpses via a camera lens and some sort of smart or sassy quip.

"Yes, I'll do that." Mary Ellen started to

say good-bye, but Meg had already hung up.

When Charles left Mary Ellen, everyone she loved seemed to scatter: Julia, Meg, and many long-term friends to whom she was connected through Charles, the native Charlestonian. She was an outsider, born and bred in Savannah to a shy but loving mama and a bighearted father who was a third-generation Episcopal priest. She lost Charles, of course. And that had broken her heart. But in a sense, she lost them all. Julia was off in Rhode Island obtaining her master's, Meg was off at her freshman year at Wofford College, and Charles — the man to whom she'd been married for more than half of her life — was starting a new life at their vacation house on Edisto with a woman half his age. One moment she had been busy taking care of everyone. The next there was no one around. One summer she was tending to her dear father on his death-bed, and by autumn she was alone in the big house on Savage Street with only the cat and Jane Anne Thornton to keep her company. She became deeply depressed those first years, so much so that she hardly remembered portions of them. She let her garden go. She stopped cooking. She crawled up in the bed and slept and slept for weeks on end.

Oh, it was a cliché. An old story told time and time again, one that fit right under the opening verses of Ecclesiastes. *What has been will be again, what has been done will be done again; there is nothing new under the sun.* But somehow Mary Ellen never imagined it would be *her* story. She had thought she and Charles had a happy marriage, that they could count on one another in spite of the undulations of life. She was wrong.

The second spring she looked at herself in the bathroom mirror and finally said, "You have to start all over again." It was the only way she could survive — by building a new life under the roof where she'd loved her husband and raised her daughters. She was taken in by a group of divorcées and widows about town. They jokingly called themselves Collateral Damage, and they sipped wine every Saturday night and took day trips to try lunch or tea in a new setting. Every now and then they ventured to the mountains or to New York City, and once they invited her to a tour of Austria and Germany, but she'd had to decline. She couldn't bear the thought of an overseas flight. Some fears she just wasn't yet willing to face.

Mary Ellen went to work at an antique

restoration shop on King Street, and she gained a reputation about town for being the master of antique frame restoration. Her employers were a couple who had relocated from Brooklyn, and while they were a bit on the solemn side, they appreciated Mary Ellen and she was grateful to have the chance to use her hands and whittle out her own little niche.

It had been almost eighteen years since Charles sat her down and broke the news to her. She'd been on a few dates early on, during those first several years, but then she started declining invitations, and finally no more were extended to her. That was that, she'd supposed. Good-bye romance. Hello to the second half of life. The solitary half.

She'd felt an odd blend of sorrow and satisfaction when she heard that Charles's law practice went down like the Hindenburg shortly after the divorce. All he wanted to do was live out on Edisto and paint and hole up with his new, young love. Thankfully, Mary Ellen had inherited a little something from her family after her mother's passing just a year after her father's, and while she was by no means wealthy, she could certainly live comfortably enough with her salary and her little inheritance.

She stood at the kitchen sink, looked out

at the newspaper on the table in the garden, its pages lifting slightly in the gentle breeze, and the thought crossed her mind: *I could buy a ticket and fly up to Julia's show tonight. To surprise her.* But, again, she hated to fly. Every time she'd been to see her, she'd taken the train and it was a good whole day's trip. *Maybe I could just go. Be there by early evening.* She finally had a computer and knew how to use the Internet. Preston had set her up with one so she could keep up with them via Facebook. There were sites where you could just go buy a ticket and be gone the same day. She could pop a Valium (she had a few left over from her root canal) and just do it, couldn't she?

As she stood at the kitchen sink watching a blue jay in the birdbath in her garden, one of the small panes above her sink shattered. Mary Ellen shrieked and jumped back. She looked down to find the orange rubbery ball in the same cereal dish she had placed in the sink. And there were shards of glass all over her windowsill and countertop.

She put her hands firmly on her hips and marched right over to Nate Gallagher's house and rang the doorbell.

He took a step back when he saw her. She must have been a sight — frizzy hair and bathrobe stained and splattered with berries and breakfast, white eyelet bedroom slippers.

"Now look here, Mr. Gallagher." She presented the ball to him and forced him to meet her eyes. "That child on your premises has dropped his ball not only in my cereal bowl while I was eating in the garden but *through* one of the glass panes of my kitchen window."

She could feel the perspiration on the back of her neck. It suddenly felt as muggy as an August afternoon.

Something clattered to the floor in the back recesses of Nate's house and he turned back for a moment before facing her again with his jumpy, bulbous blue eyes. Was he suppressing a grin? She could feel a hot redness rising on her neck. Why, the nerve!

He scratched the back of his neck and squinted. "I . . . uh." She had never known him to be speechless before. Still, his tone was loud and clipped. He called over his shoulder, "Sky! Get over here."

The boy dragged himself to the front door, stopping short of the threshold. He stood behind his tall grandfather and peered out from behind the old man's elbow where his own hand was cocked on his hip. The child seemed to be trembling. Suddenly, Mary Ellen felt both ridiculous and a little sorry for the chewing-out the kid would receive. "Did you knock out Mrs. Bennett's window?"

He shrugged his shoulders.

"You don't know, eh?" He shook his head and pointed up the stairs. "Get on up there, and I'll deal with you in a few minutes." The boy turned and trudged slowly up the staircase.

Nate Gallagher took another look at her and started to chuckle. She turned in a huff and walked back toward the sidewalk, calling out to him, "I'll send you the repair bill."

"Fine!" he said. "And I'm sure you'll threaten to sue me if I don't pay it, right?"

Mary Ellen stopped in her tracks. She could feel her temples pulsing. She took a deep breath, refastened her belt, and turned back for a moment. "Perhaps I will," she said, glaring into his pock-marked face with fury.

As he slammed the door, she huffed back to her wrought-iron gate. Just as she was unfastening it, Jane Anne Thornton came power-walking down the sidewalk in her wide-brimmed straw hat and her hot-pink running suit, with her little apricot poodle, Daisy, at the end of the hot-pink leash.

"Why, Mary Ellen," she said. "You look like a wreck. What in the world have you been doing?"

Mary Ellen shook her head and muttered that she couldn't talk now, then she marched back into the house where she caught a glimpse of herself in the foyer mirror — purple-blackish-splattered bathrobe, droopy brown eyes, no makeup, and frizzy gray hair.

"My word," she said aloud. "Who in the world is that old woman?"

CHAPTER 3
JULIA

"Of course . . . you can't go." Simon's voice was fading in and out of her cell phone. She ducked into a quiet alleyway off of Prince Street and stuck her finger in her ear to hear better. Simon was in London visiting his two teenage boys, and she'd been playing phone tag with him for a couple of days.

"I know." She swallowed hard and felt her ears pop. She was dizzy from hardly eating anything since Marney's visit. Or maybe it was her nerves about the opening night of the exhibit. She just hoped there was no panic attack in sight. It had been a year since she'd had one.

"You've got your Fulbright, we have our trip to Istanbul." He exhaled and she could tell he was smoking, a habit he seemed to fall back into each time he ventured to London. "It's impossible, Jules. And frankly, the farther you stay away . . ." He faded out for a moment. "Southern gothic dysfunction . . ." Then he was gone. Call disconnected.

She stared at her iPhone, at Simon's image on the screen. He was feeding the mallards in Central Park with his poplin suit pants rolled up to his knees and his canary-yellow bow tie with thin blue stripes untied. He had a kind of spiked, just-rolled-out-of-bed, salt-and-pepper hair she adored. He was looking at her out of the corner of his eye, grinning through glossy red lips as he threw a bread crumb toward the murky water.

Her phone quacked. It was the ring she'd selected for him.

"Hey." She tried to hide the weariness and fear in her voice. Simon didn't seem to respond very sympathetically to weariness, and he'd never seen one of her full-blown attacks. She had told him about them, but he didn't really believe her. He claimed she was the one and only artist who had her act together, who was sane and — even more astounding — adept at both order and self-control.

Plus, she'd issued a fairly clear ultimatum before he departed last week. "Propose by the first of the year or it's over." And she didn't want to add weary and panicked on top of pushy. Especially since he was an ocean away surrounded by well-coiffed prep school moms and young female artists vying for his attention at every turn. Simon was an art dealer — a very successful one as of late, as he recently landed an exclusive relationship with the pop artist David Hockney — and every aspiring artist longed to catch his eye.

Julia knew Simon wasn't sold on the idea of marriage. He'd ended a particularly nasty one over a decade ago and was still licking his wounds. Plus, he could hardly keep up with his nearly grown sons and all of their school and sports events. He Skyped every Sunday night with each of them at their separate boarding schools, and she could tell he felt saddened and guilty about the literal and figurative distance between them.

But Julia was ready to settle down. She was thirty-nine. Her clock had been ticking for years and now more than ever she wanted a lifelong, committed companion and — dare she say it — a child.

"Your art is your child." Simon had thrown the remark out a few months ago like an inexperienced fly fisherman, hoping for a lucky snag.

She'd taken a deep breath and stared him down with her serious green eyes. "Okay," he'd said. "You're not going down that easy, are you?" He'd shaken his head and muttered in his charming British accent, "Blasted maternal instinct."

Marriage and children weren't things she'd always wanted. Her parents' split had spooked her good, and she took great pride in the fact that she'd been able to make it on her own in one of the most elusive fields in one of the most cutthroat cities in the world. But there was a desire she just couldn't shake — a desire to be a part of something more than just her individual life, to be a member of a family, to be a nurturer — and time was running out. Time was one of the few factors in life she had very little control over, and she knew when she had to yield to it.

Simon had wrinkled his thick brows during one of their first marriage/baby conversations, batted his long eyelashes, and narrowed his pale blue eyes. "Ah, Jules, *really*? I'm too old for all of that diaper changing and stroller lugging. I'd never make it."

"You're forty-nine," she'd scoffed. Then she listed the new families she knew with fathers over fifty. She came up with three, but one of the men was in the hospital getting over a back operation to repair a crushed disc, so that didn't really help her case. "I'm sure you'll survive."

Simon, on the other end of the phone on the other side of the ocean, cleared his throat. "I'm sorry I can't be there tonight."

"It's okay," she said, but her stomach tightened while she rounded the corner toward Prince Street where the gallery sat two doors down, the enormous paintings in the front window casting square and rectangular shadows on the sidewalk.

"Call me as soon as it's over and tell me all about it."

"All right. I'm walking in the door now," she said. "Tell the boys hi for me."

"I will, my love."

When Julia crossed the threshold into the mod warehouse space, she noticed dozens of white calla lilies around her portion of the exhibit in the far left corner.

Her phone quacked. It was a text from Simon. *Like them?*

They were her favorite. *Yes,* she texted back. *TY.*

He quickly responded, *I love you. I know it will be a great night.*

Despite her stomach knot, she smiled at the long lilies like giant celery stalks with white, papery teardrops on the ends.

"You have quite the admirer," Ava said. She was the assistant to Kent Risen, who ran the gallery, and she had that typical young, supermodel-fresh-off-a-Milan-catwalk look: jet-black hair pulled back in a sort of 1920s low bun, short silky dark dress, a sort of black and deep purple combination that highlighted her shockingly long legs, high black heels that crisscrossed the Achilles' and buckled around the ankle.

Julia felt like an unsleek midget next to Ava. She wore her golden hair down and hadn't bothered to dye the few gray streaks that had recently surfaced, and she sported her maize-colored, off-the-shoulder cowl-neck dress with a thin, gold chain belt. She should have worn higher heels, but she knew she'd be standing all night, smiling until her cheeks hurt, laughing at patrons' jokes and answering questions. She went with a slightly scuffed pair of olive-green round-toe boots she'd bought in Paris in her twenties. She just hoped they were so old that they'd come back in style again.

The art exhibit was titled "Young New York Artists." She didn't consider herself a *young* artist anymore, and she certainly wasn't a Manhattan native. She was sharing the gallery with four other artists. The two youngest would surely be getting the bulk of the patrons' and the media's attention. Etienne's paintings were surreal — tall men with peacock feathers and French pastoral vistas with bread loafs and chickens and false teeth and missiles coming at the viewer in an almost 3-D effect. Chih-Yang was Taiwanese, and he painted only with black ink on rice paper — his images were of the human body always morphing into some sort of concrete object: a rocket, for instance, or a smartphone. Compared to them her neon geometrical shapes were uneventful. The other artist, Joseph Sanchez, was an old grad school friend and he had made his mark creating 3-D images from found objects. In his current exhibit he had several portraits of presidents. There was an Obama with a bicycle wheel for a head, a George W. Bush with a nose made out of little plastic army men, and a George H. W. Bush on a Lite-Brite screen with a head full of shining little yellow bulbs.

Julia — quite by accident — was a little bit of a legend in the Manhattan art world and so she wasn't entirely surprised to be invited to participate in this exhibit. Her legendary status wasn't so much because of her artwork but more because of two events that were passed around by word of mouth from one struggling artist to the next: Peter

Tule, a notoriously successful artist in the early nineties, had tried to force himself on her in his studio (as he had a reputation for doing to his female minions). Julia crashed a large, wet canvas over his head, then stormed out of his studio for good. Tule had to call a friend to help him extricate himself.

But most notoriously, she had been leading a group of students with another professor on a bicycle tour of lower Manhattan the morning of September 11, 2001. It was a photography class she had taught for a couple of years at Hunter with her good friend and award-winning photographer Jack Ball. They were on Vesey Street near the intersection of Broadway when the first plane hit the tower. She had immediately stopped, rounded up the students she could, and sent them pedaling back uptown toward campus. Jack stayed to photograph the images, the fire and the hole in the tower, like a bullet through the city's face, and then there were the people who had no other choice but to jump. She remembered Jack screaming when he saw the first one leap. He ran toward the scene but was held back by a fireman. When the second plane hit, they both noticed a straggling student staring up at the two holes in the buildings as if in a kind of trance. Jack handed Julia his camera and ran for the boy as the second tower — the first to fall — came down and the plume of dust started to fill the streets, blinding everyone in its path for several blocks.

Julia had turned then, surrounded by the thick white dust. She abandoned her bike and ran up Broadway, her hands outstretched, feeling her way around the warm hoods of cars, parking meters, and one street post after the next until she tumbled over a fire hydrant and hit her head on the corner of an old newspaper vending machine.

She stood for a moment, her heart pounding in her ears, the pain reverberating down her spine, and then she staggered before collapsing in a building doorway, hitting her head once more on a glass door before she was completely out. She woke up some time later — maybe hours — to the sound of screams and sirens. The haze had dissipated somewhat and she could see through it enough to know which way was north. She stood up and staggered up Broadway and away from the inferno until a cabdriver pulled over, took off his jacket, and wrapped it around her head before delivering her to Bess's old place on the Upper West Side.

She found out the next day that the

student, a daydreamy boy named Antonio Carmine, made it out, but Jack never did.

Within an hour the gallery was full of patrons, fellow artists, friends, colleagues, and a couple of critics. Bess and Graham were there. Graham brought some friends from work. Some fellows from Goldman Sachs who thought it might be interesting to do the art scene on a Friday night before having a few appetizers at Nobu. Bess brought some friends from the school board and the Junior League. Julia had painted some of their children's portraits when she first came to the city and was strapped for cash. They all seemed to be trying hard to act interested.

"I've bought *Ice Cubes,*" said Bess's friend Elise. "I'm going to put it in the children's playroom."

Julia looked again at the painting of four rounded squares, one on top of another, in a tall glass. She was glad to see the little red sold dot by the painting's title. The other artists had already sold a few before the event even started, but she hadn't. She smiled and chuckled a little. "That's great. I hope it works for you there." Julia had envisioned the painting in a funky living room or foyer of a modern office building, but she'd been around enough to know that the people who liked her paintings and the places they intended to hang them were almost always a surprise.

Her boss, Max Dial, the chair of the Hunter College art department where she taught, shuffled over to her. They both turned to look at her neon-pink painting of a hexagon. "Looking forward to Budapest?"

"Yes." She turned to face him. He was a gentleman — not so much like a father figure but more of an older brother. She said what she knew he was thinking. "I know I need to find something new."

He nodded kindly. Her work was stale. They both knew it. And she couldn't spend the second half of her life painting neon-colored geometrical shapes.

He patted her back gently. "You'll find it, Julia. I have complete faith in you."

She smiled at him.

"Just don't let the administrative stuff bury you the way it has buried me." He was ready to retire, and he was sure she would become the department chair, though there would be a fight as a couple of other professors really wanted the position.

He put his arm around her. "The poets are right, you know? Time really is a thief."

She looked into his watery eyes, and he

stepped away, pulling his handkerchief out of his pocket and patting his face. He had lost his wife in a car accident a few years back, and he had yet to come out of his grief. He pointed to a group of critics around one of her paintings toward the back of the gallery. He nodded that way as he stepped toward the door. "Go see your admirers."

Julia was making for the group when she realized she was too starving to say another word. She dipped discreetly to the back of the gallery where there was a little kitchenette to pour herself some ginger ale and gobble down a little cheese and fruit so she wouldn't faint. While she was back there she overheard Juan Weims, the *Times* art critic who was staring at another one of her paintings, a circle within a circle within a circle in bright yellow, orange, and green.

He was murmuring to someone who seemed to be his assistant because the other fellow was young and taking notes on his iPad.

"Nothing new from her in *years*." He shook his head. "To tell you the truth, I'm not sure she ever had much to begin with."

The young fellow nodded and typed something.

Julia swallowed hard. The art scene in

New York was brutal and flippant, and she was well aware of that, but something about what Weims said got her right in the gut and sank its teeth in hard. Was it the truth? In this moment she believed that it was, and now she was certain that she was a complete fraud. Suddenly she felt a little dizzy. A cracker caught in her throat and she realized it was tightening.

She prayed, *Lord, have mercy. Christ, have mercy.*

She swallowed hard and saw a few stars and hoped the attack would pass over like a few quick-moving dark clouds. She stood there for twenty minutes until Bess popped her head into the kitchenette.

"We're heading out," she said.

Julia beckoned Bess over and pointed to her chest where her heart was beating wildly. Her friend looked her up and down. "It's happening, isn't it?" Julia nodded. Bess ran to tell Graham what was going on, then she came back, found a door in the back, and they stepped out into the alleyway. A cab happened to be pulling over to a lounge on the other side of the dark street and Bess waved her arms. She tucked Julia into the cab, then held her hand all the way home. Julia could hardly breathe. "Should I call Dr. Johansen?"

Julia shook her head. "I just need an Adderall. I'll be okay." She closed her eyes as her heart pounded and her throat tightened. She bit the heel of her palm hard and blinked back the stars as the cab flew up Fifth Avenue toward Carnegie Hill.

Back in the apartment, the Adderall producing a calming effect, she closed her eyes and saw a face she'd tried to block out for a long time. Her father. He had called her just a few weeks before his heart attack to see if he could come up for a visit, but she'd said no. "It's not a good time, Dad. Maybe after Christmas."

"I miss you, Julia," he had said. *Me too,* she had wanted to say, but she hadn't.

When she woke up the next morning, Bess and her daughter, Chloe, were knocking on the studio door. They had the *Times* and a pot of coffee and her favorite spinach and feta cheese omelet from the little diner around the corner on a tray.

"A nice review," Bess said. Weims had a way of trashing you without trashing you, so she was curious about how he had put it. Of her work it read, "While Bennett's paintings bear a strong resemblance to the work of her last several exhibits, she remains an institutional presence in the New York art community with a voice and vision that are both well practiced and comprehensive."

Her cell rang. "Hi, Mama."

"Congratulations, love. Tell me all about it."

Her face reddened. She felt like a little girl again. A little girl who wanted to please her parents. But that was silly. Her father hadn't really loved her, their family had been a sham — probably — all along. But her mama needed to feel like a mama sometimes. This much she understood and was willing to give. "It was a fantastic evening." She winked at Bess, who took Chloe by the hand and tiptoed out. "It started with an enormous calla lily delivery and then . . ."

Chapter 4
Etta

I'm a secret keeper. A pretty good one. And there's a lot of stuff I know that I'm not going to tell. But I will say this. Our mama loves us. Not like the mothers in books and on television and on vacation at the island where we live, but it's not bad, and I know we are the reason she gets up and out of bed every morning. Our daddy loved us too, but he was gone before Charlie was born.

Here's a secret: There are enemies out there. Enemies who mean to do us harm. My older sister, Heath, knows who they are. And so does Mama. Charlie doesn't know, and there's no need to tell him right now. It'll become clear enough to him if they strike again, but maybe they won't. Maybe they will forget about us and leave us alone. We are fine, but I bet there are other kids out there in the world who aren't.

There's also sickness, which is a different kind of enemy. Not the kind that drives down the long dirt road and knocks on your door when you're in the middle of drawing a bouquet of yellow snapdragons. There is sickness in Mama's lungs. The doctor showed it to her on the X-ray when we spent the day at Aunt Dot's. Heath was watching cable TV and Charlie was playing with Aunt Dot's old fire truck, the one her son used to play with, when Mama came home from the doctor. She and Aunt Dot ducked into the kitchen, and I crept up quietly to the doorway and listened.

An operation can fix the sickness. The doctors can cut it out from inside Mama like cutting off a rotten spot from a peach. She said it's no problem. It's a done deal. But by the look on Aunt Dot's face when she walked us to the car and by the way Mama stops to stare at us sometimes when we're on the porch passing the milk for the cereal or doing our schoolwork, I'm not so sure. I think there are some unknowns. Some secrets our own bodies keep from us. Secrets that grow in dark places when no one is looking. And sometimes we don't know what the secret is until it's too big and too late.

Take my father, for instance. His body kept a secret from him. There was something called plaque in his body, and it built up year after year in an important place near his heart. One day the plaque burst without warning, and it formed a wall that blocked all of the good blood from getting to his heart. A heart without good blood begins to die. It's true. I saw it with my own eyes just a week before my fifth birthday. Heard him cry out in the chair before he fell forward onto the dock, his legs bucking then twitching like a fish out of water. That's another one of my secrets. But I've got more.

Aunt Dot has a bad hip, but she will take care of us when Mama has to have the operation. Heath and I will help Aunt Dot. We can pick up Charlie and give him a bath. We can feed him. We can chase down Phydeaux, our crazy old dog that Daddy found on the side of the road the year before the plaque burst and built its wall. We can feed him and give him his worm medicine. All we have to do is bury it in peanut butter and plop it down in his bowl.

Mama will be in the hospital for three weeks. Then she'll be back, she'll get stronger, and we'll have the end of our summer to do the things we like to do: make Velveeta sandwiches for a picnic and swim to the little island that forms in our creek at low tide, get ice cream at the movie store on the beach, ride around in our old Suburban with our flashlights at night hoping to stop some deer in their tracks, watch the sunset at the sound, and pick fresh tomatoes in Skeeter and Glenda's garden.

Then homeschool will start again, even though Heath wants to go to a real school and meet boys and girls her age. Heath is real smart. She's only twelve, but she's skipped three grades in homeschool. Mama tried to get her a scholarship to a private school in town, but it didn't work out. I think the enemies had something to do with it, but I'm not sure.

I just like to draw. Still lifes are my favorites, but I do portraits too, as well as landscapes. Daddy worked with me when I was little, and I still remember what he taught me — how to divide the face into three parts, how to shade the nose, how to create a shadow beside the basket of oranges or a shadow of the rising moon on the water. I don't show Mama or Heath my drawings. I only show Charlie, who doesn't know how lucky he is not to have known my father. Not because Daddy was mean or bad, but because he doesn't have to miss him the way we do.

I know a lot of other stuff that people don't think I do. I know that Daddy had a whole family before our family. His wife and daughters were beautiful. I found the picture in his handkerchief drawer, a picture of them all in front of a pretty Charleston house in their Sunday best, but I didn't tell anyone. This means we have two half sisters. Heath seems to know that much of the story too, but I don't think she's seen the picture. One of the sisters could be an enemy. She came here once after Daddy died, and screamed at Mama. The other one is a famous artist who lives in New York City. Daddy used to show me articles about her in the newspaper. She's pretty and stylish and serious looking. Her eyes, even in the grainy black and white of the newspaper, look like they can see right through you, into your secrets. Her name is Julia, which is a name that reminds me of dew on a flower petal. It's sweet and melodic. She went to college with my mama. But that's another secret too. One only she, Mama, and I know. And her mother and her sister, of course. But not mine. Heath doesn't like knowing that kind of stuff. She's like Mama in that way.

I don't know what happened. How my daddy came to be with my mama instead of Julia's mama. And anyway, I've probably said too much already.

"Eddda!" Charlie's feet slap the hardwood

floor. "Where's my remo contro helcopter?"

Much of my life is spent finding Charlie's things.

He stands in the doorway, his eyebrows furrowed. He's pretty cute even though he's demanding. He looks like a miniature version of my daddy, deep brown eyes and lots of golden curls.

"Come on. I'll show you." I walk past him, brushing my arm against his shoulder.

Aunt Dot says it's not good to act exasperated. She knows a lot of stuff that seems right because it makes my heart feel better. Mama says she doesn't believe in the stuff Aunt Dot does, but she also says it's okay if I want to. She says maybe it will help me and my condition.

I do want to believe in what Aunt Dot believes in, but I'm not going to tell Mama or anyone else. It will be another secret, though I might tell Aunt Dot or someone else when I grow up and leave our little house on Edisto Island.

Heath says there is a whole world outside of this one, but it is hard to imagine. Maybe I will go live with my half sister in New York and we will be artists together. Maybe she believes the thing I want to believe. The thing Aunt Dot believes. Maybe she has secrets too, and we can share and trade

them like Silly Bandz or baseball cards or
Lifesavers. You don't have to look at her
picture in the paper too long to know she
has some. Sometimes you can keep a secret
so long that you forget it's even there. And
it's not until everyone around you starts
talking that you realize what you've hidden.
But it's not all bad. There is a kind of
strength in silence. A kind of power. It can
be dangerous, I know, but it can also protect
us from the enemies.

CHAPTER 5
JULIA

She was sitting at her office desk in the art department entering the final semester grades into the computer system when her phone rang.

"Juuuuul-yah?"

"Aunt Dot!" She instinctively grinned when she heard the soft, warbly Southern accent of her father's older sister. She hadn't talked to the woman since a phone call over Christmas. "It's been too long — since, what, Christmas? How are you?"

"Well, I'm all right," she said. "If you count half-blind with a bad hip and a general tilting toward the grave as all right."

Julia chuckled. "Oh, it's not that bad, is it?"

"Of course it is, dahlin'," the woman said. "But no one wants to talk about that, nor do they want to talk about your half siblings and their ill mother."

Julia squeezed her eyes shut. She had a

feeling where this conversation was going, and she needed a way to stop it without upsetting her aunt. When she opened her eyes, Simon was standing in the doorway, leaning against it with his thin red lips forming a grin. He was back a day early. What a nice surprise.

She cupped her hand over the receiver. "Hey," she whispered. "Welcome home. I'll be off in a minute."

He nodded before striding into her office, where he slid a book on Cubism off of her shelf and sat down on the bright yellow love seat against the wall.

Julia cleared her throat as Aunt Dot continued. "Julia, I'm not going to beat around the bush. Marney needs you right now."

"Aunt Dot —"

"Now, I know you've been avoiding the woman and the situation for nearly two decades, and that's pretty impressive, I have to hand it to you, but something has changed, sweetheart. The woman is *not* well, not *at all.* She needs help with those kids for a little while until she can get on her feet again, and I'm in no condition to lend a hand right now."

Julia exhaled. "What about friends? Neighbors? She's been in that community for a long time."

Aunt Dot clucked. "C'mon, Julia. Do you think Marney has close friends?"

"Well, even dreadful people connect with other dreadful people, don't they?"

"You're the last real friend she's had." Aunt Dot cleared her throat. "And that's the truth. And now she's alone with those three children, and in for a battle we all need her to win."

Julia went to open her mouth. Simon was watching her carefully. He had a kind of morbid fascination with the story of her family's demise, and he was watching like someone on a street corner who can't turn away from a car accident.

"Of course it's unfair to call on you," Aunt Dot continued. "And I know you've got that big career in the Big Apple your daddy was so proud of you for building." She lowered her voice as she had during Julia's childhood when she was about to reveal a family secret. "But those children are *fragile* and they've had some *struggles,* and whether you like to acknowledge it or not, someday you're going to come to realize that they are your family, and no amount of states you put between you and them can change that."

Julia raked her hands through her hair as Simon furrowed his brow and cocked his head. Southern gothic dysfunction was right. It was a freak show, and she was not going to be sucked into it.

"What about Meg?"

"I've tried." Aunt Dot cleared her throat and lowered her voice again. "Meg is in a worse place than you on all of this. She's not going to be any help."

Meg, Julia's younger sister, seemed to have not had anything to do with Marney or their father from the moment she found out about the affair. And there had been a distance between Julia and Meg ever since the divorce that seemed almost too large to bridge. They'd see each other from time to time over the holidays, but they never did more than talk on the surface. The landscape of their lives was entirely different. While they shared the same wound, a wound that neither one of them wanted to reopen, it seemed to Julia that for Meg there was a deeper seething beneath it all that she didn't fully understand. She'd have to summon the nerve to talk Meg into looking after the kids. She had kids of her own. Motherhood was her passion. It would be natural. But how?

Then it occurred to her. Meg had become more active in the church of their childhood. All of her Christmas cards featured her children in their pageant costumes, and her Facebook posts often featured some sort of parenting tip with a Bible verse to undergird it. Maybe Julia could take the orphans-and-widows angle, or the love-your-enemies one with Meg.

"I'm asking you to reflect upon it, Juuulyah. Search your heart. Pray."

Julia rolled her eyes, but she felt guilty as she did it. She did have at least a shred of faith left, and she owed that to Aunt Dot.

"You have a sweetness in your heart, dahlin'. Even though you talk like a Yankee now, and even though your artwork is as strange as all get-out. You still have Prince of Peace love in your heart. Don't ya, dahlin'."

Julia could feel her neck tightening and her heart pounding. She did not have a sweetness in her heart when it came to this topic. No, she did not.

Now Simon was tapping the top of the book with his long, manicured fingers, and instead of being reminded by Aunt Dot of the basic tenets of Christian theology, Julia wanted to hang up and run into her man's arms. She was still close with her mother — as close as one could be with a weekly phone call and the occasional e-mail — but Aunt Dot was about the only thing tethering her to her father and to her old faith.

Julia hated to think it, but the thought surfaced like a swimmer intent on coming up for air: she would be relieved when her father's sister was gone.

"I have to go, Aunt Dot," Julia said. "I hear what you are saying. And I'll talk to Meg."

"But, Juuuuulyah —" The voice started to crack. It was changing from warbly to stained glass with a blend of disappointment and protest.

"I have to go now, Aunt Dot. I'll be back in touch."

Then she hung up the phone and strode over to the other side of the desk where Simon stood and embraced her hard. "I missed you, love."

His thick British accent made her weak in the knees. It was an unfair advantage, but she adored it. Then she rested her head on his chest and took in the smell of cigarettes, airports, peanuts, and coffee. "Me too."

He pulled back and took her by the shoulders. "You can tell me all about your call to Aunt Dot tonight. I've got an eight o'clock reservation for us at Union Square. We're due for a nice night out, don't you suppose?"

She smiled. It was her favorite restaurant,

and they hadn't been there in months. "I do."

He rested his stubbled chin on her golden head. "I've got to drop by my office and then by the apartment for a shower and shave. Pick you up at seven forty-five?"

She nodded. "Perfect."

He walked out, grabbed his suitcase, and started wheeling toward the elevator, then he called back over his shoulder, "It's going to be a good night, Jules."

She smiled through her watery eyes. Why was she weepy? And then she looked back at the phone where she had hung up on her seventy-five-year-old aunt, her father's sister who had asked her about the Prince of Peace in her heart.

"I could use one," she called back, unable to keep her voice from cracking.

Julia spent the remainder of the afternoon practicing her phone call to Meg as she entered her grades. She would try her the next day. It was six forty-five when she finally finished her work and hailed a cab back to her apartment, where she jumped in the shower and then into her silky midnight-blue dress with a subtle roll neck. It was late March and the city was starting to thaw a little. It had almost hit sixty-five degrees today, and even though there would be a little chill tonight, she decided against a coat, put on some metallic pumps, and grabbed the crinkled silver handbag Bess had lent her. Bess and Chloe insisted on seeing her in her outfit and riding the elevator down with her to the foyer.

She was puzzled by all of their fuss. "It's just Simon," she said.

"We know." Bess made an effort not to meet Chloe's side-angled glance. Something was up. Chloe started to turn red and giggle just as Simon pulled up.

"Go on!" Bess pushed her out of the entrance door and into the street. "Have a nice time!"

They had a table by the window in a private little alcove, and by the time the entrée arrived, Simon's neck seemed to be turning red and he was tugging on his white starched collar.

"Are you all right?"

He took a small bite of his lamb chop before he put down his utensils and took a big sip of wine. Then he fished something out of his pocket and slid it across the table to her.

Her heart started to pound as she gently opened the velvet box. It was a large oval sapphire ring set in platinum from a British jeweler. Simple but stunning. And in her favorite shape.

"Well, I don't think I need to tell you where I've come down on your ultimatum."

She blushed and looked into his pale blue eyes. She noticed a vein in the center of his forehead. It splintered near the top and seemed to be throbbing.

"I'm terrified, Julia. But you're the best thing that's happened to me in a long time, and I'm not going to give you up."

He reached across the table, took the ring out of its case, and looked her in the eye as a little bead of perspiration rolled down his cheek. "Will you?"

Her heart was pounding like a large bird in a small cage, and she couldn't tell if it was elation or fear that she felt. Maybe it was just surprise. Shock. Somehow she hadn't really expected it of him. She nodded slowly and extended her left hand. He slid it slowly onto her ring finger where it promptly fell to the side. He had overestimated her size, so he apologized and quickly asked the waiter for some masking tape. Then she took it off and handed it to him as he wrapped some tape around the bottom and slid it back on. They both admired it as it sparkled beneath the candlelight, casting every color of blue with its sharply cut prisms.

Soon enough the valet brought around the car and they were on their way to Doubles, a swanky little club beneath the Sherry Netherland Hotel where Bess and Graham were members.

Down the silky wallpapered stairwell, Bess and Graham and a few other couples from the art department and galleries were there to celebrate. Champagne was popped and poured and a few people made toasts. Simon seemed to have it all planned out — he favored a small Christmas wedding. Then they'd jet off with his sons to Buenos Aires and Uruguay where it would be summer, and they'd take in the beach. It sounded wonderful to her. Bess would help her with everything. She would make an appointment with her doctor next week and the family-making could begin in a few short months.

"Everything's coming together, isn't it?" Bess whispered in her ear. They rubbed foreheads and smiled.

Julia's caged heart kept pounding. It was almost as though she could hear it, and she still couldn't tell if she was happy or dumbfounded or terrified.

"You think it is?" She looked Bess in the eye hard. Her friend straightened up and looked back at her. She knew her well.

"Remember the ultimatum? This is what you want, right?"

Julia blinked back tears and nodded her head. "I know." They both turned to see Simon, who was laughing heartily with a couple of buddies from the ir77 gallery.

He caught her eye and lifted up his champagne flute. She lifted hers back and they both took a hearty sip together as Bess put her arm around Julia and whispered, "Nerves are par for the course."

Simon made sure she caught a cab home. He was going to smoke a cigar with his buddies and she had an early morning faculty meeting. Chloe was asleep on top of Julia's bed, clutching a handmade card that said "Best Wishes" in colored pencil with a drawing of a big blue ring on the front. Julia tucked her beneath the covers. She texted Bess to let her know where Chloe was. She was happy to sleep on the couch tonight.

Julia slipped off her pumps, put on her bathrobe, and went out to look at the moon. It was only a sliver, but it was set so low it almost seemed within reach if only the building had a few more stories. Should she call her mama right now? It was after midnight, and she didn't want to scare her.

Then the urge came over her quite suddenly. She wanted to call her father. She wanted to tell him. He would have been very excited. He would have been awake this time of night, always the night owl touching up his paintings after everyone else was asleep. Did she need someone to give her away at age thirty-nine? Well, Graham would do it, she supposed.

When a strong wind cut through the rooftop terrace, she decided to head back in. Before she knew it she was pulling out the shoe box where she kept old letters she couldn't seem to throw away. Near the top there was a letter from Aunt Dot shortly after her father's death. In the yellowed envelope there was that photo Julia had half-forgotten about. She slid it out and gazed at the image: Baby Charlie Foster Bennett III, in a white onesie with a pale blue blanket draped across the little bouncy seat where he sat. He was book-ended by two beautiful suntanned girls who looked like they hadn't combed their hair in quite some time. The younger one had lost one of her front teeth Julia noticed as she gazed at it for the first time in years. The other one kept her mouth shut tight and her hands on the seat as if she would guard the child till doomsday if

72

necessary. Julia did the math. They must have been about twelve, nine, and four by now. "Lord, have mercy. Christ, have mercy," Julia muttered. She wasn't having an attack, but her heart was still thrashing in her chest.

Tomorrow she would call Meg. Surely she would rise to the occasion and help Marney out. But could she ask that of her? Why had this suddenly become her problem to deal with? She scoffed, put the lid back on the box, and shoved it back in the drawer. Then she let her hands fall to the side and felt something slide off of her left hand and hit the floor. She looked down, but her engagement ring was nowhere in sight. Then she got down on all fours and crawled around the kitchen as she heard Chloe tossing beneath the covers, muttering something in her sleep.

After a few moments she spotted it, glinting against the dark surface of the baseboard by the dishwasher. She grabbed it, stood up, and put it down on the kitchen counter. Then she grabbed a wineglass and put it on top of the ring where she stared at it like an exhibit in a museum. She would be a bride, a Christmas bride. She would start a new family. Her own family in this city in this built-from-scratch life it had taken her years to construct. She would find her new muse in Budapest. She would become department chair. It was what she wanted, and everyone back home would have to sort out their own problems. It wasn't her bed to lie in. And she was very good at forgetting.

CHAPTER 6
MARGARET

Margaret stared down at her cell phone. The area code was 212. Julia. She was sitting in the carpool line on Chapel Street outside of Charlestowne Prep School where her husband was the chairman of the board. Summer was fast approaching, and she had been busy making all of her children's schedules: sailing, camp in the mountains of North Carolina, a week at Litchfield by the Sea.

This was the third time Julia had tried to get her. She only had about five minutes before school let out so she wouldn't have to talk too long.

She took a deep breath and pressed the green button. "Hello, Julia."

There was a pause. "Hi, Meg."

"It's Margaret, remember?"

"Oh, right. I apologize."

Margaret rolled her eyes. "So I hear congratulations are in order?"

"Yeah." Julia had all but lost the gentle lilt

to her voice. Her vowels were sharp and enunciated. She sounded like a stranger.

"December twenty-second is the date. I hope you all will consider coming."

"Send me the info on Facebook, okay? We will try to make it happen."

They wouldn't be missed. Julia had a whole life up there, and in truth there was no way Margaret was going to allow her family to forego all of their usual Christmas activities: the holiday program at school, the Christmas pageant at church, the *Nutcracker* at the Performing Arts Center, and brunch with Santa at the Yacht Club.

There was a silence between them. It was awkward. "Did you need something?"

"I'm calling about Marney."

Margaret could feel her temples pulse.

"You know she's sick, right?"

"No, I didn't," she lied. She had heard from their babbling Aunt Dot that she'd had an early stage of cancer, and she wasn't surprised. Bad lives yielded bad fruit. It was inevitable.

"She has lung cancer and has to have this major operation. There's no one to look after the children while she recovers."

The school bell rang, and the children started pouring out of the brick building and lining up on the street by the carpool queue. They were screaming and laughing and guffawing, the sun catching the crowns of their smooth, golden heads. She saw her youngest, Katherine, holding hands with her best friend, and then her two boys, Preston and Cooper. Preston was shoving a classmate a little too roughly, but she wasn't surprised. It was that annoying Simms boy who was a head taller than everyone else. Her younger son, Cooper, was in an indepth conversation with a couple of his friends, probably talking about Harry Potter. She wouldn't let him read past the third book, so he read the first three over and over, though he tried to get hints about what happened next from his friends who had been allowed to read further on.

"Hmm," Margaret finally said in response to Julia. "Well, Marney's resourceful. I'm sure she can figure something out."

Julia exhaled deeply. "Both she and Aunt Dot have asked me to help, but I've got this fellowship in Budapest."

"That sounds nice . . . Come on in, sweethearts." She didn't bother moving the receiver away from her mouth as she greeted the kids. Did Julia have any idea what a busy life Margaret had? And her work was far more important than painting and teaching and traveling to some offbeat European city.

Her work was raising young lives.

Margaret was not going to budge. Not going to give Julia an inch. If Julia thought for one moment that she was going to have anything to do with those children, she was wrong. If it were up to her, she would never cross paths with them again.

"Well, I don't suppose you'd want to watch her kids or know of someone who could?" Julia finally got to the point of her self-centered call.

Margaret cleared her throat. "The kids? No, I'm afraid not," she said as though she had been asked if she would like crumbled blue cheese added to her garden salad. "We've got a very busy end of spring and summer. I won't bore you with the details, but there is no way I can help." The kids tumbled into the car along with the other two neighbors they carpooled with. They tugged their backpacks in behind them and elbowed around and into one another until they each found a seat. Preston kicked the back of Margaret's seat. "Let's *go,* Mom."

"It's a really bad situation." Julia's voice was growing faint as Margaret pulled out of the carpool line. She knew she had gotten her message across.

"I'm sorry to hear that." Margaret turned back at the stop sign and made sure everyone was buckled in. "That's really too bad."

Cooper called out, "What's for snack, Mom?" over the backseat. Margaret lifted her index finger sharply to indicate she needed a moment more. "Best of luck figuring something out, Julia. I have to go." Then she clicked her phone off and turned back to her son, whose head was already back in his book. "The usual," she muttered.

The kids got home, and she made them a healthy snack: peanut butter on celery and sliced apples and organic milk. They quickly finished their homework and then they went racing out into the backyard where she watched her two sons and daughter chasing one another around, kicking the soccer ball, and then going in three separate directions: Preston on the trampoline, Cooper in the treehouse with his book, Katherine on the tire swing.

Just as she was preheating the oven for the chicken, her husband walked through the front door and patted her playfully on the backside. She stood upright, put her hands on her hips, and swiveled around.

"What's wrong?" he said.

She pulled the whole chicken out of the fridge and glared at him. "Guess what egotistical artist called me from New York today."

Preston stepped back and furrowed his brow. Then he pulled a canister of almonds from the pantry and started to munch on a handful. "How's Julia doing?"

Margaret clucked her tongue. "How's she doing, Preston? She's doing the same as always, hiding far away from the mess she left behind." Preston scratched the back of his neck like a thickheaded baboon. He never seemed to share her disdain for Julia, or anyone for that matter. In that way he was as obtuse as her father, unaware of the motives of women, unmindful of the trouble in the world, even though he practiced law. Though she was the one who was particularly involved at their church, for the sake of the children, he was the one who seemed as though a weight had been lifted every time he uttered the Confession during the Sunday service.

Margaret stuffed the carcass with onions and carrots. "And she had the gall to ask me if I could help or find help for Marney's children while she has her operation."

Preston selected a bottle of red from the wine storage cabinet and slid off the wrapping with a single pull as Margaret washed her hands thoroughly. He shook his head as he reached for the corkscrew. "*You* keep Marney's kids?"

He was the only one who knew what Margaret had done those four years ago when she realized her father had left the entire Edisto property to his second family in his will until the children were grown, dashing her hopes for having a vacation home out there.

She had called DSS. And she had not regretted it. She saw how Marney kept house, and anyone in their right mind would have done the same thing. Somehow Marney had weaseled her way through the system and had the kids back within a few months. In the meantime, Preston had been promoted to partner at his law firm and Margaret gave up the dream of an Edisto home and conceded to several acres on a lake in Williamsburg County, which they purchased with the plan of building a nice cabin in a few years.

"But why is Julia involved with Marney's illness?"

Margaret reached for the pepper grinder and began to spin its knob above the chicken.

"Because Julia wouldn't know a snake if it bit her on the hand."

Preston chuckled as he poured two glasses of red. Then he opened the glass door for Katherine, who was knocking gently on it.

"I need to tee tee," the little girl said.

"Okay." Preston leaned down and pointed to his cheek, and the child gave him a kiss before continuing to the bathroom.

"I guess you're right, honey." He came over and gently massaged Margaret's tight shoulders. She relaxed for a moment and leaned back into him.

When the oven buzzed, she turned away and shoved the chicken in. There was only one person with whom Margaret was angrier than she was with Marney and her father. And that was Julia.

She went over, picked up her wineglass, and took a hearty sip as Preston went out to greet the boys and kick the soccer ball around with them. Then she sat down at the computer at the kitchen table, its glow calming her along with the wine as she selected her Facebook page on her favorites so she could check the comments regarding the photo of Katherine at her ballet recital, which she posted just before picking up carpool. They read "Adorable," "What a beauty," and "She's growing up so fast." She "Liked" them all, then she clicked over to the ticker page to see what the rest of her friends were up to.

CHAPTER 7
MARY ELLEN

On Mary Ellen's way to work, she took the neatly folded window repair bill, walked gingerly up Nate Gallagher's old brick walkway, and slipped it through his tarnished mail slot. Relieved that his enormous beast, a chunky English mastiff, hadn't stirred, she quickly pivoted in her navy espadrilles only to find Nate and his beast returning at a lively pace from their morning walk.

The mastiff barked loudly, then broke away from Nate and began pawing at the L.L. Bean canvas bag Mary Ellen always carried to work. It included her bifocals, her notebook, her newspapers, and her lunch. She and the Collateral Damage girls had eaten out at Hall's Chophouse the night before to celebrate Jane Anne's sixty-fifth birthday, and Mary Ellen had packed the last half of her rib-eye and a container of the leftover creamed spinach for lunch.

"Order this creature off of me!" she said.

Nate chuckled and said halfheartedly, "Down, Luther."

Mary Ellen patted the dirt from Luther's paw off of her canvas bag. He had smudged her celery-green monogram.

"So what's the damage?" Nate lumbered toward Mary Ellen.

"Well, he's dirtied my bag."

Nate sniffed loudly. "I don't mean that, Mrs. Bennett."

She cocked her head as it dawned on her. Then she straightened her shoulders. "Four hundred and twenty dollars. They had to replace the entire window, and it took them a couple of hours."

He shook his head as Luther continued to sniff around Mary Ellen's bag, rubbing his wet nose inside the slit of her long linen skirt.

She pushed him away and straightened her linen jacket.

"Ridiculous," he said as Mary Ellen made her way briskly toward the sidewalk.

She stopped just after passing Nate, pressed her painted pink lips together, and turned back. "You ought to know by now that repairing anything in these old homes is expensive."

Nate leaned down to pick up his newspaper, and as she turned to leave, Luther snarled and lunged at her bag once more.

Just as she was about to drop it, Nate called harshly, "Halt!" And the beast stopped just inches away from Mary Ellen, who took the opportunity to race down the sidewalk toward Broad Street.

She got to the studio in the back of the Berkowitz Antique Shop before Jeanne and Gene Berkowitz shuffled down the back fire escape of their above-store condo and opened the showroom.

Their location on King Street was a prime one, right between Fulton and Clifford Street, in the three-block heart of the antiques district. The store specialized in the conservation and restoration of seventeenth-, eighteenth-, and early nineteenth-century European furniture and art. It had a 2,500-square-foot showroom divided into categories: case pieces, tables, seating, decorative objects, silver, and artwork. Their period lighting pieces were scattered all around the showroom, some chandeliers hanging so low in certain sections that one needed to duck to get around them.

Mary Ellen's specialty was recasting the molds of damaged frames and regilding them. She was the best in town, and occasionally other dealers would visit her home in secret and ask if she would restore a particular damaged gem they had acquired.

She was loyal to the Berkowitzes and always asked their permission before she took on outside work. They were usually amenable, though they had a few enemies in town, and every now and then Gene would look over his bifocals, clear his groggy throat, and say, "I'd rather you not, Mary Ellen. But of course, it's up to you."

The Berkowitzes hired Mary Ellen a year after her divorce, and in many ways she experienced the restoration of her heart in that back studio, working with her hands, taking something old and broken and making it beautiful again. She loved history and the smell of antiques, she enjoyed the colorful customers who made their way in and out of the store from around the world, and she liked bringing home a steady paycheck each month. And even though Gene and Jeanne were demanding in many ways (they only gave her five vacation days a year, the same amount they took themselves), they seemed to appreciate her work and her loyalty, and they often invited her upstairs or out for dinner after a long day.

By midmorning, she was well into her

project for the week: the restoration of the body of an old seventeenth-century harp Jeanne had found at an estate sale in New Orleans. She hardly noticed when Gene knocked gently on the studio door, a client holding two small paintings right on his heels.

"Here she is," Gene said as he directed the woman toward Mary Ellen, who was on a stepladder, scraping off the mold on the top side of the harp.

She rubbed her hands on her work apron and walked over to meet the customer.

The woman put the paintings on the counter and extended her hand. "I'm Winifred Kitteridge. It's so nice to meet you, Mrs. Bennett."

Winifred Kitteridge. The name didn't ring a bell. And yet the woman seemed as if she knew Mary Ellen. She took the two small paintings and turned them around, and Mary Ellen instinctively put her hand over her mouth.

"Father/Daughter Dialogue #9," she said.

"Yes," Winifred eagerly agreed. "They belonged to my great-aunt, and she left them to me in her will. I'm going to hang them in some special nook in my new home at Kiawah, and I was hoping you could tell me the story behind them."

Mary Ellen blinked several times before walking over to study the paintings. They were of the little island that formed on Store Creek at low tide. And there were figures on the island, she and Meg, crabbing.

Charles used to set up Julia's miniature easel, the one she got for her seventh Christmas, right beside his. Together they would watch and watch and watch some more before dipping their long, narrow brushes in the clumps of acrylic paint on their palettes. Often, Mary Ellen and Meg were featured in the work.

Eventually a local gallery that showed Charles's work offered to display Julia's as well. They usually painted the same vista and the gallery would set their paintings side by side on the walls. They titled them "Father/Daughter Dialogues." Julia sold her first painting at age twelve — it was a painting of two sunflowers in the field — and by fifteen she had her first commission, the angel oak tree on John's Island, which a man wanted for his son who loved to climb it. Charles had been mighty proud of her. He would work with her on the weekends and all summer long, and she was teachable. She listened. She understood and she tried her best and she had the gift. She applied what he had to say and made something of her own that was both original and pleasing to the eye.

"My ex-husband. Well, he's dead now anyway, but we divorced before he died. He was an artist —"

"Yes, Charles Bennett," the woman said. "I've researched him on the Internet, and I read the little biography the Joggling Board Press published about him."

The vista was like a dream to Mary Ellen. How she had loved that spot on Edisto Island. How she had enjoyed swimming out there with her daughters and her husband, catching enough crabs for the evening meal, sunbathing, or watching the porpoises feed along the mud banks. It had been her solace for decades.

She pointed to the other painting. "And this one is by my daughter."

"Julia?"

"Yes. She painted alongside her father from age seven on. I think she painted this one around age ten or eleven."

"Amazing," Winifred said. "I researched her too. But her art is so *different* than this."

"Yes, it is," Mary Ellen said. "To tell you the truth, I don't even think her father understood her art over the last few decades."

The woman lifted both the paintings up.

"I heard that you build custom gilded frames."

Mary Ellen nodded, and Gene patted her back in a brotherly way as he answered the call of a handful of cackling tourists who had just entered the showroom. "I do from time to time."

The woman smiled and leaned in. "Do you think you could build some for me? For these? I'll pay you whatever you ask."

Mary Ellen looked at the two gems. She thought they had all been bought by a collector in Florida, and she didn't think she'd ever see one again. She could take them home to her little upstairs studio by the laundry room and build something over the weekend.

"I'd be happy to," she said.

Winifred clapped her hands and then promptly sat down on a stool, took out her checkbook, and asked Mary Ellen to name her price.

Around five thirty in the evening, Mary Ellen walked home with the small paintings in her bag. Possessing them for these few days somehow unlocked a fresh container of memories of a season of life she had yet to stop longing for, a season about which she had yet to stop wondering how it had all fallen apart.

She thought of how Julia's high school art teacher encouraged her to apply to Interlochen, a fine arts boarding school in Michigan, when she was fifteen, but Mary Ellen and Charles said no to that. The eighteen years of childhood went fast, and they weren't going to give a one of them up. They loved being parents to both Julia and their younger daughter, Meg. Maybe something in both of them sensed that it would all come crashing down soon.

"Plus, Julia needs something to fall back on," she remembered Charles telling her as Mary Ellen nestled in his thick arms on the old porch swing after supper. Charles made his living as an attorney. The art was his love, his hobby, and occasionally it brought in a little side income that went into the college or the Edisto house renovation fund. When Julia got a full scholarship to the University of Georgia's studio art program, she studied English literature as well. Then she went to the Rhode Island School of Art and Design for an MFA and then on to study with that wicked Peter Tule before landing a tenured track position at Hunter College.

"She's actually making a living as an artist," Mary Ellen had said to Charles. It was one of the last times she saw him before his sudden passing a few years ago. She had taken the train up to New York for one of Julia's exhibits and she was surprised to see him there as well. They were standing in front of an eight-foot painting of a hexagon in neon-yellow set against a neon-orange background. It was titled *Unbearable Lightness.* Though Mary Ellen and Charles lived less than fifty miles from one another, she hadn't seen him in years.

He had looked over and his barrel chest filled with air. He narrowed his brown eyes and met hers with what she sensed was a thick mix of sorrow and guilt, though she could never know for sure. Had she ever really known him? He reached out to touch her forearm, but she flinched and took a step away. He exhaled and turned back to Julia's painting. "Yes, she is," he said. "And I'm not surprised."

Now as Mary Ellen rounded the corner from Broad onto Savage Street, she spotted her porch and Jane Anne sitting there the way she always did when she had something really juicy to share. She smiled at the sight of her neighbor, who lifted a bottle of wine and something wrapped in tinfoil. Jane Anne was a widow and they enjoyed many impromptu meals together. Cooking for one was ridiculous.

Mary Ellen picked up her pace. She couldn't wait to show Jane Anne the paintings. It was as if a precious relic of her old life had been excavated, and if she could stare at the images long enough, maybe she could make more sense of the turn she never saw coming. Jane Anne would help her with this.

As she crossed Nate Gallagher's drive, she held up her bag to indicate the treasure within, and as she did the English mastiff leapt out of nowhere, his paws reaching for the bag, toppling Mary Ellen over as the paintings slid out and onto the sidewalk.

"Get off of her!" Jane Anne raced off of Mary Ellen's piazza, her own little poodle barking behind her as Mary Ellen opened her eyes only to have Luther lick her face with his giant, wet tongue before pawing her chest.

Nate was on the sidewalk by this point. He pulled Luther away as Jane Anne helped her friend up. Mary Ellen searched for the paintings. They were facedown. She broke away from her friend and picked them up, paying no attention to her skinned knees and her torn linen skirt.

An edge was slightly frayed on one and a

little paint along the side had been scraped off the other, but other than that, the paintings were fine. She clutched them to her chest as Jane Anne gathered up the rest of her belongings and Nate muffled an excuse about Luther's enthusiasm. He ordered Luther into the house and then extended his arm.

"No, thank you," Jane Anne said, then she pointed right to his chest. "The next time that dog gets out of line, Nate Gallagher, I'm calling the pound. Do you hear me?"

Nate nodded as Jane Anne's poodle left her own little surprise beneath his tea olive bush, then she offered her little arm to Mary Ellen, who took it without so much as looking Nate in the eye as she hobbled to her front piazza, the paintings carefully tucked beneath her arms.

Once they were inside, Jane Anne helped Mary Ellen wash off her knees and bandage them.

"I'm fine." Mary Ellen shooed her away. Then she brought out the little bamboo trays and warmed up some okra soup she'd left thawing in the sink as Jane Anne sliced the Vidalia onion pie she had brought over.

Once they were settled with their trays on the back screened porch overlooking the

94

garden, Mary Ellen turned and said, "Now, what's the scoop? I know you've got something good to share."

Jane Anne sipped her soup from the silver spoon. "You're the best cook in town," she said to Mary Ellen. "I do believe this okra soup is better than the one at Alice's Kitchen."

"Spit it out, Jane Anne," Mary Ellen said.

Jane Anne took a sip of her white wine and looked at Mary Ellen head-on. "Marney Bennett has lung cancer." She sucked her teeth and narrowed her eyes. "It's bad, I hear."

Mary Ellen exhaled slowly. She pictured the two daughters she had seen at Charles's funeral and then the photograph of the little boy on Dot's refrigerator when she stopped by to check in on her old sister-in-law as she did from time to time.

The irony was not lost on her. Here she was — healthy as a horse — and Charles's young wife, as young as Julia, had cancer. How many more twists to this story were there going to be?

The thick scent of roses from Nate's garden sifted through the screened porch. Some days were heavier than others, and this one was starting to feel like a ton of bricks. She felt a little dizzy. Or maybe that was just from her sidewalk fall. Either way, sometimes life was so unpredictable it took her breath away.

"That's awful," she said. "That's awful news."

Jane Anne raised her eyebrows, indicating there was more.

"Go on," Mary Ellen said. "Spit it all out, gal."

"Well, guess who — according to Dot — she asked to help take care of the children while she undergoes surgery?"

Mary Ellen knew exactly who Marney would have asked. She knew it instinctively. She became aware of her heart pounding. It resounded in her ears.

"And what did Julia say?"

"She said no, of course." Jane Anne took a hearty bite of her onion pie and shrugged her bony little shoulders. She was petite, but she could clean a big plate fast, and she was almost always a second-helping girl.

Mary Ellen looked out over her blooming garden. From the trickle of her fountain she could almost hear the voices of Julia and Marney, home from college on the occasional long weekend. She had loved cooking for Marney, who was always so appreciative of a warm meal at the dining room table. She was a second-helping girl too, and Mary Ellen made sure to bake Marney's favorite, coconut cake, every time she knew Julia was bringing her home.

Jane Anne put down her empty plate and picked up the last crumbs of the pie with her index finger. "Well, that's the scoop."

"I'll say that was a doozy." Mary Ellen suppressed the immediate urge to call Julia and ask her all the details of Marney's astounding request.

Jane Anne reached down to pat the top of her poodle's head. "Now what were you clutching so carefully?"

Mary Ellen inhaled slowly and put down her tray. "Some paintings I thought I'd never see again."

"Well, show me. I need a little breather before my next helping."

Mary Ellen stood and nodded. "Come on into the dining room and see."

Jane Anne oohed and aahed over the paintings and then, overcome with sleepiness, took her second helping home in a little plastic container. Just as Mary Ellen was watching her friend cross the street, Nate Gallagher popped his head around her privacy door and she jumped back.

"What now?" she said. "I don't think I've crossed paths with you this many times since you moved in."

He rolled his eyes and held up a check. "Well, since you'll probably be slapping me with a doctor's bill after your scuffle with Luther, I thought I better go ahead and pay for the window."

She smirked and held out her hand, but he didn't give it over. He cleared his throat. "I was hoping I could take a look at the job that was done. I've got a crack in my living room window, and I might have no other choice than to call these thieves."

"All right," she said as she led him into her home, through the dining room, and to the kitchen.

He stopped in the dining room to admire the paintings.

She looked back and waited until he glanced up at her. "These are both signed Bennett. Do you have some artists in the family?"

She nodded. "I did. My ex-husband painted one and my daughter painted the other."

"They are beautiful," he said.

She watched him gazing at them and she puffed up her chest. "Well, come on in the kitchen."

He looked up and followed her. He studied the job and nodded approvingly. Then he glanced her way. "It sure smells *good* in here." He nodded at the pot on the stove. "What is that?"

"Okra soup."

He made a face. "Too slimy."

"You're missing out," she said. "Okra is a low-country delicacy."

Nate grumbled, handed her the check, and then turned around. "See you around the neighborhood." He flapped his hand and closed the door behind him.

"Hopefully not," she mumbled to herself. And she did not watch him make his way home.

CHAPTER 8
JULIA

The weeks went by quickly as Julia secured the venue for the wedding and reception, strategized her department chair bid, organized her fall classes, and packed for her Budapest summer. Her passport was renewed. She ordered the supplies she'd need to paint and had them shipped ahead of her to the apartment she rented from a professor there. She bought a new Nikon camera that cost her nearly half of her monthly paycheck.

Bess and the kids had packed up and headed for the Hamptons for the summer and Graham joined them on the weekends. Bess was going to handle any of the other imminent wedding arrangements that came up during the summer. And she was going to track down the perfect little flower girl dress for Chloe, the only other member of the wedding party beyond the matron of honor (Bess) and the best men (Simon's two sons, Philip and Colin). Simon was off to England for Philip's graduation from Eton. He'd meet Julia in Budapest in two weeks for their romantic getaway to Istanbul.

Every now and then the idea of Marney and the cancer growing in her lungs surfaced in Julia's mind, but the fact that no one else had called her about it made her sure someone had stepped up to the plate.

She prayed as she still did from time to time when the world around her stopped and she felt alone and yet not alone. Her prayers were quick and one-sided, not like the ones she used to have in her mother's sunflower garden after Aunt Dot told her that God sometimes talked back if you were willing to hear beyond audible words. She prayed Marney would fully recover — it was a selfish prayer, of course. She prayed it because she didn't want anything to tie her to the woman and her family. She wanted to go her whole life without having to face Marney or her half siblings.

The day Julia was headed to the airport, she couldn't find her passport. She had tucked it away in a safe, obvious spot, only she couldn't remember where. It finally appeared in the zipper of the old brown leather jacket she always wore on flights because it was light and smooth as butter and made a wonderful pillow when rolled up tightly. She made it to LaGuardia with hours to spare, got her boarding pass, and was standing in the line of the international flights terminal when an unrecognizable number with a Charleston area code flashed on her screen. With time to kill and a concern that it could be her mother calling from work battling her old anxiety about Julia flying, she answered it.

"Juuuul-yah."

"Aunt Dot?" she said. The old woman's voice sounded faint and a good deal frailer than it had a few weeks ago. "Are you all right?"

"If you count being carted to the hospital with a fractured hip as all right, I guess I'm dandy."

"What?"

"I slipped and fell in the bathroom at Marney's last night and now I'm at Roper Hospital awaiting surgery. Going to get that hip replacement a little sooner than I expected."

"Oh no. I'm so sorry."

"Me too. Marney just had her operation two days ago and she's hardly even coherent according to Dr. Young, her surgeon.

Anyway, I had to get your daddy's old friend Skeeter to come watch the kids while they hauled me off in an ambulance, but he can only stay until sundown because he still works nights as a flounder gigging guide, so if you can't hop on an airplane and get down here, I'm going to have to call Mary Ellen and ask her to take off some time from work and help."

"My *mother*?"

Aunt Dot clucked her tongue. "Yes. I'm out of options, Julia."

Now Julia's heart pounded like an angry fist in her chest. Her mother hadn't been out to Edisto in eons. Could she even withstand a trip to that house with her husband's second family and all of the old memories? She'd been doing so much better.

"But Meg."

"Meg's not an option. She just isn't. You have to trust me there."

Julia exhaled slowly. She was starting to see spots, and she blinked hard as a man behind her cleared his throat dramatically, indicating that the line was moving forward and she needed to keep up.

She turned back to the man, gave him a grumpy look, and hauled her suitcase and carry-on bag forward as she balanced her cell phone between her shoulder and her ear.

"Julia. You know what you need to do, don't you?" Aunt Dot said as Julia came to a halt behind the woman in front of her.

Julia bit her lip as she watched the woman in front of her take off her boots and tuck them beneath her arm as the muffled security guard called through a crackly megaphone, "Take out all liquids and place them in a separate scanning container."

There was a pregnant silence on the other end of the line. Julia knew Aunt Dot was still there, waiting for a response. She tried to swallow, but her throat was too dry. She pictured her mama driving out to Edisto, holding back the dread and the fear of facing the loss she'd worked years to put behind her. Plus, there was the reality. Her mother's employers were kind but demanding, and how would they feel about her suddenly taking off a week or two to look after her husband's children? Yes, Julia's mother needed that job for the extra financial security, but more importantly, she needed it for the steady routine, for a sense of being useful, and for playing a role outside of the hundred-year-old walls and slanted hardwood floors of 10 Savage Street. Could Julia stand herself if she was hopping around

Budapest painting the banks of the Danube with her mother's emotional state and work life falling apart back in the States?

"I'm on my way home," Julia said, surprising herself.

"Good girl," Aunt Dot said. "I knew you would be." And the old woman hung up the phone.

Now Julia stepped out of the line and rolled her luggage down the corridor and back to the ticket counters for domestic flights. She walked over to the Delta counter. "I need a ticket to Charleston, South Carolina."

As the woman's long, silver manicured nails clicked on the keyboard, searching for direct flights to the low country, Julia texted Simon. *I know it's crazy, but I'm going home.*

By eight p.m. Julia turned off of Highway 17 onto Highway 174 in a small red rental car. 174 was an old two-lane highway that led to the bridge that connected the mainland to Edisto Island. She hadn't traveled this road in a long, long time and she was shocked by its lack of change — a church every couple of miles, trailers set on cinder blocks, rusted mailboxes leaning this way and that, an old barn nearly swallowed by kudzu. An unexpected lump formed in her throat as she drove over the tall bridge that connected the mainland to Edisto. The sun was beginning to set, and the way it glistened on the river and the green marsh and the mud banks was shockingly picturesque.

She knew she was not prepared to face her old home and her half siblings, but she didn't realize the visceral assault that the beauty of the South Carolina coast could have on her. It was heart wrenching not only because it was scenic but because she was only now realizing how much she had longed for it.

She couldn't deny it at this moment as she hit the crest of the bridge — she had missed the magical, soulful home of her childhood, her happy childhood, the setting where she'd hooked her first spot-tail bass, thrown a cast net, driven a johnboat, pulled a seine, caught a blue crab, harvested vegetables, fired a rifle, kissed a boy, and painted a sunset. She rolled down the window and breathed in the smell of pluff mud and the salty air thick as a wool blanket. She blinked back tears. It was almost too much to take.

Lord, have mercy, she said to herself. And then, *Get a grip, Julia. Get a grip.* The phone in the pocket of her leather jacket vibrated and she answered.

"Julia, what is going on?"

It was the first time she'd heard from Simon since she'd texted him back at La-Guardia.

She found her voice beyond the lump in her throat just as her car touched down from the bridge. "I'm on Edisto Island."

"Are you insane?" His voice was slurred and high pitched. It was one in the morning there and he must have been out celebrating his son's graduation or carousing with old Eton friends.

"Yes," she said. "Yes, I'm insane. I don't know what I'm doing, but my aunt was keeping the kids and then she fell and broke her hip. It was either me or my mother, and I couldn't let my mother shoulder this, could I, Simon?"

He cursed under his breath. Then he inhaled slowly, surely taking a drag of the cigarette he relished every time he went back home. She had never actually seen him smoke.

"I'm sure it will just be for a couple of days. A week at the most. Until I can find someone to take over."

"Our trip to Istanbul is in thirteen days."

"I'll make it," she said.

She could imagine him shaking his head in disbelief and annoyance. "I really can't believe you're walking directly into this backwoods nightmare. Don't expect to come out of this without scars."

Her heart raced with dread and she thought about how to respond. *You're probably right,* she wanted to say, then she realized she no longer had service and Simon was suddenly an ocean away and would be until she drove back over the bridge to call him again.

The road darkened as the sun quickly set, shooting dusty beams of soft white light through the live oak trees, the Spanish moss, and the scrub palmettos. The oaks formed a tunnel over the old road like an open mouth that was growing darker by the moment, swallowing her and her little rental car whole. She passed an abandoned gas station, a tomato farm, the old Presbyterian church, and then a field with a burning trash heap. How strange it was to see smoke rising and not feel the need to call 911.

After she passed the Old Post Office restaurant and then Store Creek, she turned onto Peters Point Creek Road, and the road narrowed further. She passed Cousin Bertram's house, the Seabrooks, the Reids, the Quattlebaums, the Belsers, the Walters, Red House Road. Finally, toward the end of the gravel drive she saw the old mailbox she and her father had secured into the ground when she was eight or nine years old. She had stuck the glossy silver stickers with the numbers on herself and the letters that went down the stake that held the mailbox. BENNETT.

As she pulled into the driveway, a girl in a long, white nightgown and bright red rain boots ducked back into the pine trees beyond the long dirt drive. She rolled down the window to speak, but the girl was hiding and she didn't want to force her out. These kids were probably as nervous about getting to know her as she was them. Then again, maybe they had no idea she was coming.

She pulled on down the road. It was dark now, and the mist from the cooling earth was lifting itself up in eerie ribbons she sliced through with the nose of her car. Eventually she saw the house set several yards back from the salt marsh creek with its rickety old dock and the plastic molded owl — meant to keep pesky gulls and varmints from congregating — still at the top of its post.

She parked the car next to an ancient Ford pickup truck that must be Skeeter's. She took a deep breath. Her heart was pounding, but she was too tired to get all worked up. *Lord, have mercy. Christ, have mercy.*

"Well, lookey here." Julia heard the screech of a screened door in need of WD-40 and then spotted Skeeter in the back doorway with a little boy with tufts of blond hair and huge brown eyes eyeing her suspiciously. The boy shimmied out from behind Skeeter's leg and darted toward the north side of the house, shooting Julia as he went with some sort of imaginary gun.

"Warm welcome," she muttered.

"Julia Bennett." Skeeter hobbled over to her car with his cane and spread his arms wide. "Haven't seen you since Charlie's funeral, and even then you were gone before I had a chance to get a good look atcha."

She inhaled. Skeeter smelled like he had when she was a child. Like the earth and like a slow-roasted hog. He had a toothpick in his mouth. His skin was leathery, a well-worn hide. He'd slimmed down a good bit and had more of a forward lean than she'd remembered, as if his shoulders were just too heavy to hold him upright anymore.

He must have been in his early seventies by now and looked too frail to guide a flounder gigging expedition. But then again, her father had always said he was one of the best fishermen around.

"Get over here, son," Skeeter said when

the boy peered around the house and aimed for Julia's chest.

Charlie sauntered over. "This here is Julia. Your daddy's eldest. Now, reach out your hand like Dot taught you."

"How do you do?" The boy was stunning. Even more so than the vista over the bridge. He had long dark lashes and a little birthmark on his right cheek as if a sculptor had seen fit to give him one little smudge so he could appear believable. "Nice to meet you."

"Nice to meet you." Her voice was hoarse. How could a boy be so striking? Looking at him was a kind of torture.

A light lit up the porch and in seconds two moths were encircling it. There was a girl, maybe eleven or twelve, standing there. She was the spitting image of her mother when she'd been young and healthy. Thick mane of hair, full lips, and sharp, deep-blue eyes. The girl blinked slowly. She appeared to be biting the inside of her cheek.

Julia had met the girl briefly at her father's funeral, but she reached out her hand. "I'm Julia," she said. "And you are Heath, the oldest, right?"

The girl nodded and cautiously extended her hand. Julia had to take a few more steps to meet it.

Then Heath raised her head and looked

out at the woods behind the house where a twig had snapped. Julia followed her gaze. She didn't see the girl she had seen when she drove in, but she knew she was out there. Etta was her name. The middle one. She turned back to Heath and their eyes locked.

"Are you the enemy?" The question came from Charlie, but it was the same one that was written all over Heath's face.

"Enemy?" Skeeter laughed and slapped his thin thigh. He bent down to look Charlie in the eye. "She's not the enemy. She's a relative, boy. And you better be good 'cause she's going to be taking care of you for the next few weeks until your mama gets back."

Julia's eyes widened. *Oh no, no, no,* she wanted to say. *I'm not here for a few weeks. I'm here for a few days until I can beg, borrow, or hire someone to take care of these kids.*

Charlie was narrowing his eyes toward Julia, and she could practically feel Heath's gaze boring a hole through her skull. She thought she'd better be quiet for now.

"Well." Skeeter patted her shoulder and ambled back toward the screened door as Heath stepped back into the shadows. "Let me show you around, and then I have to scoot. C'mon, Julia."

CHAPTER 9
JULIA

Julia woke to the smell of bacon. She'd had a fitful sleep in the guest cot at the top of the stairs, and her arms and legs itched like they never had before. Now she felt something light on her hand and she slapped it instinctively. The white morning light beamed through the window, and when she pulled back her hand, pinched the black speck between her fingers, and held it up to the pane, she realized it was a flea. Fleas!

She leapt up and threw on a pair of running shorts and ran downstairs to find Heath at the kitchen counter spreading peanut butter on toast with little Charlie by her side bouncing on the balls of his feet.

"Chocca chocca milk." The little boy tugged on his sister's T-shirt. He had a crazy bed head with a tuft of tangled curls in the very back that resembled a bird's nest. He started to scratch the tuft and she could only imagine what a field day the fleas might have in there.

"In a minute." The girl handed him the plate, and he ran to the screened porch where he turned on an old portable television and sat down in a well-worn rocking chair to take in a fuzzy version of *Curious George.*

Julia surveyed the old kitchen of her childhood summers. It looked as though it hadn't changed or been upgraded at all in twenty years with the exception of a pink microwave in the far right corner beneath the cabinets and an icemaker beneath the island that appeared to be leaking and had been for some time, considering the mold lining the baseboard beneath it. She noticed that no one had bothered to replace the far left windowpane above the sink, still cracked from where her father threw a football at it when he was teaching Meg to catch back when she was in middle school. The windows didn't look like they had been washed in decades either, and the appliances were worn out with rusty handles and layers of grime. Julia noticed a large cockroach clicking out from a crack between the dishwasher and the counter. It scurried down to the ground and across the linoleum floor where Heath stamped and nodded approvingly as it crawled beneath the oven.

"CHOCCA MILK!" the voice from the porch hollered.

Heath rolled her eyes, pulled out a plastic cup from the cabinet, and poured two heaping spoonfuls of powdered Nesquik into it before pouring in a little tap water and stirring it with her finger.

She shrugged and muttered, "We're out of milk." But this remark seemed more addressed to the window overlooking the dock and the salt marsh creek than to Julia. "He can't tell the difference." The girl walked the cup out to the boy and set it on the wooden floor beside him. When she returned she took an overripe banana, sliced it, lathered it in peanut butter, and walked out toward the dock where she sat down on a bench, the light breeze picking up the strands of her thick brown hair.

Julia took in the scene in the morning light. The dock framed with live oaks, Spanish moss dripping from its limbs like a Dali painting, the almost iridescent late-spring green of the salt marsh, the creek water pulling outward, always pushing and pulling itself one direction or another, and the sun piercing through the scrub palmettos and pines on the little spit of land beyond the creek. As she noticed a pale gray heron alight from a tree and settle on a nearby mud bank, Julia swallowed back a wail somewhere deep in her gut. She couldn't tell if it was a cry of grief or of longing, of beauty or of horror. What in the world was she doing here? How had she allowed herself to be cornered into this?

"More chocca milk!" The high-pitched voice was both warm and demanding.

Heath ignored it, so Julia walked, as if pulled by the same force of the tides, out to the porch, picked up the plastic cup, and filled it with water and two scoops of powdered chocolate. She found a spoon in the drying rack and stirred it.

"I want Mama." He didn't look at Julia but instead fixed himself on Heath, who had walked quietly out onto the dock with her rotten banana.

Julia found her voice. "I'm . . . I'm not sure when she's coming back." She noticed the dirt beneath his fingernails as he licked his thumb and pressed down on his plastic plate to pick up the last crumbs of his toast. "But I'm going to try to find out today."

Then he turned to face her. "How do you know me?"

It's the first time that he'd let her gaze into his rich brown eyes. She noticed the curve of his chin and his furrowed brow. Though his hair was a lighter shade, she was unable to ignore the resemblance. Looking at Charlie was like looking at pictures of her father as a young boy, barrel-chested, sharp-jawed, bright-eyed. He was handsome. He was angelic. He was filthy.

He glanced toward Heath, who had propped herself on the dock railing. "Etta said you're my sister." Then he met her eyes again. "I didn't know I had you."

She exhaled deeply. "I'm not your sister the way Heath and Etta are." She shrugged.

"Why not?"

She bent down and looked him in the eye. "Would you like to take a bath?"

"In Mama's room?"

"Sure."

He glanced at the television. "After *George*?"

She nodded. "Okay." Now Julia turned to look at the dock. She feared if she walked out there and took in the whole vista, she might break down. So she went back to the kitchen, ate a rotting banana, found some instant coffee, and made herself a cup. On the refrigerator was Marney's surgeon's number. Apparently he had a place on Edisto and was going to stop by with an update, which was good because Julia didn't think she could just call up a hospital — a stranger — and check on a patient. Even if she had somehow found herself caring for the patient's children.

Julia's scalp began to itch. What was she going to do about these fleas? As she scratched, she felt a presence behind her. She turned around quickly only to see the hem of the girl's nightgown as she darted up the stairs, each step creaking as she went.

So Etta talked, but not to Julia. She didn't even want to be seen by Julia. Oh well, she'd get hungry eventually and need to show her face. Julia started taking an inventory of what the kitchen needed: milk, eggs, fruit, vegetables, bread, meat.

She opened the pantry's cockeyed door and spotted the old ice cream churn on the top shelf. The one in which her father always made fresh peach ice cream every Fourth of July. Her mother was a great cook, but her father liked to make dessert, especially ice cream. He'd check on it all day, filling it with salt, churning it, turning it over and over. And everyone's mouth would be watering for it by nightfall.

They'd had it the first summer Marney had stayed with them. They all sat on the wicker porch and watched the fireworks being shot off at the docks farther down the creek.

Julia suddenly remembered something

Marney had said to her that night. She didn't allow memories of Marney to surface, and she wanted to push it back, but it was up and running away from her before she could catch up to it. "You have a real family. You're lucky."

Julia had taken in the scene through Marney's eyes. She saw her mother chuckling over something Aunt Dot had said and her father agreeing to fire off a few roman candles with Meg and two of her friends from school who were staying with them.

"I guess so," Julia had said. She had never really thought about how fortunate she was. Then she had turned back to Marney, who picked at her cuticles, something she did when she was reflecting or fighting off a down spell.

Now Julia looked at the brown banana and tossed it in the plastic trash can that looked as though it had been around and hadn't been washed for years. When she turned back, Charlie was naked as a jaybird standing right in the center of the kitchen. "I'm ready!" he said, proud and free in his birthday suit as he came over and took her hand. "Bath time!"

CHAPTER 10
JED YOUNG

Jed's coffee was resting on the dashboard of his old Land Rover. The steam rose up toward the windshield, leaving a perfect circle of condensation. He lifted his arm from his elderly black Labrador, Rascal, who was snoozing in the passenger seat, his head resting on the center armrest. Jed reached for the mug to keep it from toppling as he turned off of Highway 174 onto Peters Point Creek Road.

On his way to the dilapidated creek cottage he still couldn't believe he'd purchased, he had to swing by the old Bennett place and report to whoever was staying there how Marney Bennett was doing. He supposed it would be Skeeter or maybe Meg, the local daughter of Mr. Bennett's first marriage. And he was glad he had relatively good news to report.

Jed's neck and shoulders ached. It had a been a long night at the hospital — a five-hour lung surgery on an elderly man whom Jed wasn't sure could withstand the physical trauma, though the man's daughter had insisted they go ahead. The man, Mr. Wannamaker, had woken up from the anesthesia and his vitals were not too weak, though he had that look on his face that Jed knew all too well: the dark sunken eyes, the colorless cheeks, the weary jowls that said, "How much longer do I have to go on?"

Mr. Wannamaker's daughter — a rotund woman in her fifties with brightly painted orange lips and a lavender sweater with butterflies stitched across the shoulders — fired question after question at Jed when he checked in before heading home. "When will the catheter come out? How long until we can stand him up? When will he recognize me? When will he be ready to go back to the nursing home?"

Jed took a long look at the patient and then gave a side-angled glance at the seasoned nurse, Juanita, who was often getting herself into trouble for saying too much. Her lips were buttoned up this time, and Jed took a deep breath and said, "We're going to have to take it one day at time, Mrs. McCrary. But I can't imagine him sitting up, much less standing, for a good four or five days, and I don't want to push him."

Marney Bennett, on the other hand, was progressing better than expected. He hadn't had to remove as much of her left lung as he'd originally anticipated, and all her vitals had remained strong after the procedure. She was already sitting up and had eaten her first meal on her own last night. She was alert and seemed to understand what was going on. Yes, cancer was a wily, unpredictable beast, but if Jed were a betting man, he'd guess they caught hers in time.

Now he turned onto the familiar dirt road two down from his. When he was a kid, before his dad was hired to head up the genetic testing department at MD Anderson and he and his mother reluctantly moved from Atlanta to Houston, his family had spent a number of happy summer vacation evenings with the Bennetts, whom they met after Jed's rented johnboat ran out of gas near the Bennett dock one afternoon in early July. They were one of the most hospitable families he'd ever known, and he had fond memories of Mr. Bennett teaching him how to throw the cast net so adeptly that he once caught enough creek shrimp for dinner at age fifteen. He also remembered playing hours of poker on their screened porch, stealing glances at the eldest daughter, shooting off fireworks in their backyard, and, of course, devouring Mrs. Bennett's fried flounder, deviled eggs, and tomato pie from the heirlooms she grew in her bountiful garden.

None of the women in his life could ever really cook, so in the end he decided that if he ever wanted to taste food like Mrs. Bennett's, he needed to teach himself. And so after his move back to Charleston two decades later, he enrolled in classes at both the Maverick Kitchen and Alice's soul food joint, where he taught himself how to fry chicken, sauté okra, simmer creamy grits, bake corn bread in an old iron skillet, and roll out his own piecrust for his own cheesy tomato pie. The Bennetts' dinner table on Edisto had been his inspiration, and while he'd yet to cross paths with any member of the family since his move back to the low-country, he hoped that one of these days he'd see Mrs. Bennett and ask her if they could compare recipes and methods. He also remembered hearing about the nasty divorce through his mother when he was in med school, and he must admit that the first thought that crossed his mind was that Mr. Bennett must be insane. How could a man ever let a woman who cooked like that go?

But Jed knew better than to imagine relationships in such simple terms. And marriages seemed as unpredictable as cancer to him. Even more so, really, because you couldn't even track their path to destruction. He had learned this lesson the hard way after his beautiful new wife, Priscilla, an ER nurse at the Medical University, up and left the year they lived apart during his fellowship at Sloan-Kettering in New York. Within less than eighteen months of matrimony, she took off with one of his closest friends, Brandt Russell, who had just started his plastic surgery practice in Hilton Head. Brandt had been a groomsman in their wedding. He had given a heartfelt toast at their rehearsal dinner, and Jed was left wounded and scratching his head, wondering, *What went wrong?* when Brandt answered Priscilla's cell phone early one morning.

Of course, Jed crossed paths with the couple every now and then, and each time Priscilla looked different than before, a new nose one year, cartoonishly full lips the next, so that Jed began to wonder if she was even real. Or if she had been a figment of his imagination all along.

It had been a quick romance during his residency and an even quicker engagement, sped up for the reason that many nuptials are: Priscilla was expecting. She miscarried shortly before they wed, but Jed assured her that his love for her was real and that they would try and try again until they had a houseful of kids, and he meant it. He was a glass-half-full kind of guy. Always had been. So what had gone wrong? Priscilla never did have children. Maybe that was the last thing in the world she wanted. He'd never really know.

Truth is, short marriages were not atypical of the surgeons and researchers on his particular tract who seemed more married to their work than anything else. He felt his supervisors were pleased when they learned of the news, as if it was some badge of honor to his profession. This sickened Jed so much that he refused the job Sloan-Kettering offered him at the end of his fellowship and took a much less prestigious post at the Medical University of South Carolina because the lowcountry was the one and only place he felt at home. And he was not going to let his ruined marriage or his career keep him from that love.

As he turned into the soft dirt road of the Bennett driveway, the morning sun piercing through the pines and live oaks, he was struck by a longing that the island had evoked in him ever since he was an adolescent. It felt too primal to be nostalgia. But then again, he was tired and weighted down by the suffering of his patients and the stalwart disease that thrived inside their bodies. He had a weakness for Edisto, and this weakness clouded his judgment from time to time. It had moved him to find his way to an auction of a crumbling old vacation cottage last year and place the winning bid. And this purchase had already sucked an inordinate amount of his time and resources.

Now Rascal stretched and yawned and Jed wondered, as he had from time to time since his adolescence, where the Bennetts' eldest daughter, Julia, was and how she was doing.

As the dirt gave way to gravel, he pulled in beside a little red rental car with Tennessee plates and Rascal started barking, eager to get out and roam and chase rabbits and raccoons and any critter that moved with Phydeaux, his pluff mud buddy.

Little Charlie opened the door. He was in his birthday suit, a nice coating of talcum powder on his little barrel chest, and he was grinning from ear to ear. "It's the doctor!" he called back over his shoulder to a woman running toward him with a towel.

The woman covered the boy up and picked him up in her arms. She was petite and thin with golden, silver-streaked hair.

126

"Hi, I'm Julia Bennett," she said as she propped the boy on her hip and extended her hand.

Jed couldn't contain his smile. She cocked her head and narrowed her eyes, waiting for a handshake. Then he could see that it was dawning on her.

"Jed?" she said.

"Yep." He wiped his sweaty hands on his scrubs and met her handshake with a warm squeeze.

The little boy was looking back and forth between them. "You know the doctor, Jewel-a?"

"I used to," she said as Jed continued to grin into the gaze of her deep green eyes. "A long, long time ago." Charlie squirmed his way down her leg. "I'm going to put on my Spider-Man outfit."

"Okay."

She turned back to Jed. "Last I heard, you were in Texas."

"Twenty years ago." He rubbed his hands together and nodded toward the creek. "I bought back the old Saunders cottage. The one we used to rent? It's in pretty rough shape, but I come out and work on it when I have a chance."

"So you're Marney's physician?"

"Well, Maria Tamsberg is her oncologist,

but I'm the guy who operated on her."

Julia smiled. "So you followed in your father's steps?"

"Yeah, I guess so." He nodded. "Ironically, it was cancer that got him a few years ago. Pancreatic."

He watched her furrow her brow. She was more beautiful than ever. So real-looking with her gray streaks, her unmade face, her high cheekbones, and her jade eyes. What a woman she had become. He swallowed hard and hoped his face wasn't turning red. This was ridiculous. He was a thirty-eight-year-old man. A ladies' man by some folks' standards. He shook his head and instinctively slapped at his calf. Something had bitten him.

"This place has a flea infestation." Julia scratched her head and motioned for them to step outside where the two dogs were fighting over a well-worn chew toy. He leaned against the grill of his car, and she crossed her arms and raised her delicate eyebrows. "So how's Marney doing?"

He put on his serious surgeon's face out of habit and straightened up. "She's doing better than expected. We took out a fair-size portion of her left lung, but it wasn't as much as I thought we'd have to. Her vitals are strong. She's coherent and has just started to eat on her own. I bet within the next couple of days she'll be able to stand."

"Good," Julia said. She looked out toward the dock and back to him. "I'm supposed to be in Budapest on a fellowship that's pretty critical to my career. I need to get there as soon as possible."

Jed nodded. "Well, my guess is, she'll be released within the next three or four days and then she'll need some care for the next two weeks following that."

"Hey there!" a voice behind them hollered. Skeeter ambled over with his cane and his own frisky little dog, a scruffy Jack Russell named Maude.

"What's the report, doc?"

"Yeah, I want to know too," Heath said as she walked toward Jed with her finger in her book. "When can we see Mom?"

Jed shook the old man's hand and then patted Heath on the back. "I was just telling Julia that she's doing better than expected, and I'm sure she'd love a visit from you as soon as you can get there. My guess is she'll be home by Saturday. However, she's going to need a lot of help for a few weeks after that."

"Well," Skeeter said, "Glenda and I can help some. I talked to Dot last night and she came through her surgery all right as well, but it's going to be a long while before she can run after little Charlie. Glenda was going to go see her this morning, and I'm sure she wouldn't mind taking the kids to see Marney."

Heath smiled and nodded. "That would be great."

"Yeah!" Spider-Man appeared in the doorway, mask and all. "I want to see Mommy and Aunt Dot!" Then he jumped down and ran over to the big dogs, who wagged their tails and followed him into the woods.

"I can stay for a week," Julia said to Skeeter. "Then I've got to head out."

"We'll figure something out between now and then." Skeeter sniffed at the air before scratching a welt on his arm. "In the meantime, we've got to do something about those fleas. That house is full of 'em, from the dog, I reckon."

"Guess we better set off a bomb," Jed said. "I'd offer my house for you all to stay in, Julia, but the only thing working is the kitchen. I sleep on a little mattress by the refrigerator when I'm out here."

"Y'all can come on over to my place for the night, Julia." Skeeter scratched his chin as he thought. "I've got two extra bedrooms, one with bunk beds for the grandkids, so there's plenty of room." Then he turned to Jed. "Boy, if you've got a little time midday, maybe we can pick up all the furniture and set off a bomb. In the meantime, Julia, you can do the laundry and . . ."

"Clean the house?" she said.

"Yeah," Skeeter said. Then he leaned in toward both of them. "I've never seen such a mess, have you?" He looked around to make sure the kids weren't within earshot. "Marney knows better, but I guess she's felt too bad to do much about it. We've got to help her because even out here, there are eyes on this place."

Jed wondered what Skeeter meant by that. Eyes on this place? It couldn't be more removed from the world. But Skeeter was right about one thing, it was in sorry shape.

Spider-Man and the dogs ran by. Spider-Man was holding up a large palm frond that the canines were leaping at. They all collapsed beneath a live oak tree, and Spider-Man laughed a hearty superhero laugh as Rascal and Phydeaux yanked the frond out of his hand and pulled on it like a wishbone.

Julia leaned in toward Skeeter and Jed. She smelled sweet, and with the morning light on the strands of her long hair, Jed had to step back and catch his breath. "I haven't even met the other girl." Jed admired her delicate jaw as she turned to Skeeter. "She seems really shy."

"Oh, she's shy, all right. And she doesn't speak, except to Spider-Man over there." Skeeter shook his head, looked around to see if she was in earshot, and then said, "I haven't seen her say a word to anyone other than him since your daddy passed."

"How does that work with school?" Jed asked.

"Marney homeschools." Skeeter lifted his furry eyebrows and shrugged his shoulders. "But I've told her all along I think they need to be around other kids."

Jed watched Julia's eyes widen. "So should I be *teaching* them this week?"

"Nah." Skeeter batted at the thick air as Rascal dropped the better half of the palm frond at Jed's feet. "They're smart as whips. She'll make up for lost time later in the summer."

Skeeter examined his watch. "I bet Glenda will want to head out within the hour."

Julia clapped her hands once. "Okay, I'll get them bathed and dressed and deliver them to you by ten."

Skeeter nodded. "Sounds good. And I'll go to the store and get us a few bombs."

Jed patted Rascal's head and looked to Skeeter and Julia. "I'll help move the furniture after the cleaning is done. And in the meantime, I'll put together some sort of meal for us to have tonight. Y'all can all come over to my place for dinner."

"Okay. Great," Julia said. The enthusiasm in her voice was like a fresh wind to him.

After Jed got himself and Rascal back in the Land Rover, he stopped for a moment to watch Julia as she walked toward the outbuilding that housed the washer and dryer and cleaning supplies, as if on a mission. Her gait, the toss of her hair — it was coming back to him like an old song he still knew by heart, though he hadn't heard it for years, and as he started the engine, he had to shake himself out of the trance. He had a lot to do between now and dinnertime.

CHAPTER 11
JULIA

Julia walked back into the house where Charlie was watching *The Cat in the Hat* on the grainy television on the porch. Heath was curled up in a chair reading a Harry Potter book that looked thicker than *War and Peace.* Every now and then she reached up to scratch her scalp.

"So," Julia said, hoping to get the adolescent to look up. "We're going to do something about the fleas." The girl repositioned herself in the chair, glanced up at Julia, and then back down to her book where she deftly flipped the page.

"Why?" She continued to stare at the words.

"Well, because we can't live with fleas. It's dangerous and unsanitary. Fleas carry typhus, which can make us really sick. Plus, it will drive us mad."

Heath shrugged. "Yeah, we've had them before, and they did make Charlie sick. Phydeaux's been wearing that same collar a long time." Then the girl looked up at her and glared. "You aren't going to tell anybody about the fleas, are you?"

Julia furrowed her brow. "Nobody other than Skeeter and Jed . . . Why?"

The girl stuck her nose back in her book and shook her head. Then she started to rub at a bump on her chin.

Julia stepped carefully forward. "So when you had them before, did you use one of those bombs?"

The girl looked out of the window. She seemed to detest meeting Julia's eyes. "Dad used to use those, but Mom just put this powder around last time and put all of the mattresses out in the sun. That seemed to work okay."

Julia stared at Heath until she looked to her. "Well, I'm going to give this place a good cleaning and then Jed and Skeeter are going to set one of those bombs off this afternoon, so we need to pack an overnight bag — after I do the laundry — since we're going to stay at Skeeter and Glenda's."

The girl gnawed at the inside of her cheek. "Maybe I could just stay with Mom at the hospital. Dr. Young said she was better."

Julia could feel her neck muscles tightening. Of course, *better* meant raring-to-go to a twelve-year-old, but she sensed that Heath knew better. She remembered when her own mother had a hysterectomy back when she was eleven, and she got so tired of the beanie weanies her dad fixed and the odd rotation of babysitters and relatives, she was aching to go to the hospital and stay with her mom.

"She's still too weak." Julia took another step closer to the girl, whose back seemed to go as rigid as an irritated cat's. Julia tried to speak gently. "But you can call her if you want and tell her y'all are on the way."

The girl began to exhale. "Mom said we could only use the phone for emergencies."

Julia crossed her arms. "I don't think she would mind you giving her a call to let her know you are coming."

Heath softened her back slightly and cracked the faintest smile. "Okay."

"And I'll try to round up Charlie and Etta, who I haven't even gotten a good look at yet."

The girl stood. She had that gangly, awkward look of a girl between childhood and womanhood. She wore baggy clothes — a loose Bell Buoy Seafood T-shirt and baggy pajama bottoms. She had some sores on her face, a few pimples on her forehead and chin, and she seemed to carry her head down a little bit as if she didn't want to look anyone head-on. Or maybe that was just Julia.

"Good luck with Etta," Heath said over her shoulder as she went to the kitchen and dialed the number of the hospital written down on a little pad by the landline.

Julia went upstairs and rummaged through the pile of clothes on Charlie's bed since his drawers were bare. She didn't know if the pile was clean or dirty. She would wash it all, but she would do the overnight bag stuff first. She picked out two pairs of shorts, two pairs of underwear, two T-shirts — one with a bulldozer and another with a monkey swinging from a vine — and threw them in the hall. Then she found a little duffel bag in his closet and carried it to the bathroom, where she found a Spider-Man toothbrush, which looked as though it hadn't had much use in a while, and a tube of Thomas the Train toothpaste, and stuck them in the bag. Then she turned toward the only closed door upstairs, the one that had to be mysterious little Etta's.

She knocked gently on the door. "Etta, can I come in? We need to wash clothes for an overnight bag because we're going to Skeeter's after you visit your mother at the hospital this afternoon."

137

No response.

"Okay, I'm going to open the door now. I hope you can hear me."

She slowly turned the old brass knob and cracked the door. Still no response. When she worked up the nerve to open the door, her heart caught in her throat. The child's small room was wallpapered with sketches and paintings. They hung on every available space on the wall. There must have been at least two hundred of them. There were pencil sketches of the marsh and portraits of Charlie and Heath. There were watercolors and even a few acrylic paintings on small canvases — paintings of wildflowers and the cypress swamp, an alligator sunning on a mud bank, a johnboat tied to a dock, an osprey nest, a low full moon, a tire swing tied to the limb of an enormous live oak tree, a cracked bird's egg on pine needles, tomatoes on a vine, a field of sunflowers, a bowl of peaches. And there were some that were surreal: an open mouth with some sort of dark figure dancing beneath the tonsils, an eye with a dagger in the center of a pupil, a claw that was half human/half beast. In the center of the claw was a pile of faces, some screaming, some scowling, some weeping, and what was flying up from the faces and between the fingers of the claw were seagulls. They were flying out of the hand, through every open crevice and then up toward the sky. Remarkable and haunting.

Above the child's bed Julia noticed a small sketch of a man. She walked over to it and touched its curling edge. His eyes looked weary but warm. His face looked older than she remembered. It was the face of an elderly man, sunken and beginning to hollow beneath the cheekbones. But it was him, all right. Her father. And this young girl had captured something true about him. Something in his rich brown eyes that could only be described as love. How could someone with eyes like that cause so much damage? She didn't really want to answer that question. It was something she had put behind her and planned to keep behind her.

Etta's closet door had a sign that said "Don't go in." And it had a padlock on it so Julia didn't dare touch it. She just hoped there wasn't a closet full of fleas or rats filling up in there.

She went to the open window and saw Etta ducking into the old boat shed behind the house — the one her father used as a makeshift studio. She caught her breath, walked down the stairs and out to the shed. The door was locked. She knocked on the door for several minutes. Finally the child appeared in the door window and unlocked it. Then she darted back to a table in a corner, then crawled under and curled up into a little ball, holding her knees to her chest.

"Hey, Etta." Julia just stepped inside the room but didn't go toward the table. "I know you know me even though we haven't seen each other in a long time." The little ball rocked ever so slightly and the red boots made a little squeak. Julia grinned and looked at the old easels leaning against the wall. "You might not want to talk to me, but I did want to tell you that I saw the paintings in your room. You're quite a talent. I'm an art professor, so I'm a pretty good judge of that sort of thing."

Then Julia crouched down a little, and Etta made a quarter turn to face the wall, pulling her knees up even tighter to her chest.

"Did your father teach you?" No response. She waited a couple of minutes, watching the little child's curved back with its knobby, delicate-looking spine rise and fall with each long breath. She had a long golden ponytail with lumps and bumps on the top of her head, and she reached up to scratch her scalp a couple of times.

"Well, he taught me too." Julia felt her voice crack. She cleared her throat. "He was a good teacher."

Not a budge.

Suddenly a foam Nerf bullet hit the glass window of the shed, its suction cup taking hold. Then another. *The Cat in the Hat* must have been over because the shed was now under attack.

Julia stood up and addressed the easels. "So I'm here to tell you that you're going to go visit your mom at the hospital in a little while. Glenda is going to take you. And we're also going to spend the night at Skeeter and Glenda's so we can air out the house and get rid of these fleas."

No response.

She leaned down again. "Do you think you can shower, get dressed, and take your clothes for your overnight bag to the laundry room and be ready to head out in the next half hour?"

The little golden head nodded ever so slightly as three more bullets stuck to the old, thick glass windows.

"Good," Julia said. Then she turned and stepped out of the shed, shutting the door gently behind her. When she turned, Charlie had her in his sights, and he fired one straight at the center of her chest.

"Nice shot, Spider-Man," she said as she stepped toward him. "Now let's go in the house and put some real clothes on you so you can go see your mother."

"Catch me first." He licked his red lips and grinned before turning and running toward the woods. She rolled her eyes and started to chase him, the hot, thick breeze blowing her hair back, the familiar smell of a muddy low tide filling her nose and taking her back to her childhood. She found him beneath the remnants of her mother's decaying garden, which was now overgrown with wild fig vines and a few stumps of scrub palmettos. She grabbed him, picked him up, and slung him over her shoulder as he cackled and cackled.

"Spin me, spin me!" he said, and she spun him round and round until she could see stars before setting him down and challenging him to a race to the house, which he eagerly accepted.

Beyond the classroom Julia hadn't had to herd people — especially little kids — in a long time. Heath took forever in the shower, so long that Julia finally had to knock on the door and holler that it was time to get out. She handed her a tube of hydrocortisone, then instructed her to lather up her flea bites and hurry to get changed so Etta could have a turn in the bathroom.

Though Etta didn't talk or look you in the eye, she did listen pretty well. Julia told her she had five minutes, and she was in and out in four, lathered up with cortisone and all, though Julia had a strong suspicion that she didn't wash her long blond hair.

When the girls were dressed, it took Julia a minute to find Charlie, who was fairly high in an oak tree and had already gotten some sort of mud stain on his bulldozer shirt. She peeled it off of him, then ran out to the laundry room, found a gray T-shirt that looked about his size, and slid it quickly over his head.

Julia was winded and half-exhausted by the time she loaded them in the car and drove them the mile down the road to Glenda and Skeeter's. Glenda was waiting in her red, mud-encrusted US Postal Service Jeep with the steering wheel on the right side. She'd been delivering the mail on Edisto for thirty-plus years, and she looked nearly the same as she had when Julia was a child — long, full jean skirt, floral shirt, Keds tennis shoes, big orange bun on her head with a pencil stuck through it.

The children gave Glenda a hug and she gave them each a stick of Juicy Fruit gum.

"Let's go see your mama and your Aunt Dot. Then we can go to Ye Old Fashioned for a hot dog and ice cream."

"Hooray!" Charlie hollered. "Can I have a scoop of chocolate *and* mint chocolate chip?"

"Why not?" Glenda said as she lifted him up into the backseat where Heath had just laid his booster seat in the center. After Heath buckled him in, she sat down beside him, and Etta moved quietly around the other side of the Jeep to take her place in the car.

"I tell you," Glenda whispered to Julia. "You're something to come down and watch them."

Julia shrugged. "I didn't really have a choice."

"No, you didn't," Glenda said. "But I know this: your daddy is looking down right now with a thankful heart. He didn't think you'd ever come back here for any reason. And your daddy, despite his many flaws, sure loved his children."

"Well," Julia said, "I guess he only has himself to blame for that."

Glenda nodded. "You're right, Julia. You're right." She settled her eyes on Julia and bit her cracked lips. "But aren't they beautiful kids? And innocent too, though

144

they've seen their share of pain already."

"Let's go!" Charlie shouted from the middle of the backseat. Then Glenda patted Julia on the shoulder and walked toward the driver's seat. "Good luck with the cleanup."

Julia nodded and waved back to Charlie, who was waving furiously as the engine started. Heath already had her nose back in *Harry Potter and the Goblet of Fire,* and Etta had her back to them all, staring out of the opposite window. It was only after the cloud of dust settled as the Jeep started down the dirt road toward the paved one that Julia squinted and noticed that the only one looking at her now as the car turned toward a curve in the road was Etta.

CHAPTER 12
JED

Jed couldn't explain the spring in his own step. His plan had been to crash on the cot as soon as he got to the cottage, sleep until lunchtime, then get up and take a sledgehammer to the two shoe-box bedrooms in the back of the house, which he aimed to turn into one large master by the end of the month. After a day of sleep followed by manual labor, he thought he'd do what he always did at sundown on Edisto Island: wet a line on the dock, open a Coca-Cola, and pray for a flounder for supper. If he was unlucky, he'd pull something out of the freezer, eat on the picnic table watching the moon on the water, and then crash on the cot for another eight hours until it was time to head back to the hospital.

But here he had spent his morning at King's Market selecting greens, ripe tomatoes, peppers, and lemons for a meal, then wiping down the plates and glasses and votives and setting his outdoor picnic table. After that he started his stone-ground grits, which he would simmer all day, adding a little whipping cream every hour or so to make them rich and fluffy.

It was midday now, and he only needed one more item for his meal, and that was a couple of pounds of local shrimp. He changed from his scrubs into a T-shirt and shorts, slid on his old, chewed flip-flops, and, with Rascal at his side, hopped in his little whaler and set out for the bay where the shrimp trawlers would be pulling in this time of day with their fresh catch.

He loved the feel of winding down Store Creek and hanging a left onto St. Pierre and then another left onto the South Edisto River toward Bay Point. Each turn led him to a wider passageway with a stronger breeze and a broader view of the horizon where the water met the sky. Rascal loved it too. He would stand on the edge of the bow, letting the air lift his floppy black ears, barking at the porpoises and the occasional heron taking flight from a mud bank. The wildlife on this side of the island never ceased to amaze Jed, and on this short journey out to the shrimp boats, he spotted an osprey guarding her nest at the top of a dead oak tree, two groups of porpoises, schools of mullet skittering along the creek's edge, and what may very well have been an alligator tail swishing at the entrance of Fishing Creek.

Shortly after his turn toward Bay Point, he spotted a small trawler from Cottageville, covered in seagulls, and he held up his wallet as the boat approached and put its engine in neutral. Rascal barked as Jed drove toward the trawler's stern where a toothless crew member, his skin baked red from a day out at sea, spat over the side of the boat. "How much ya want?"

"Three pounds," said Jed as Rascal ran over to him for reassurance. He petted his scruff and looked up at the toothless man who was scooping shrimp into a grocery bag. "I really appreciate you stopping."

"No problem." The man nodded as he tied the bag in a knot and tossed it to Jed.

"How much do I owe you?"

The fellow looked back at the captain, who put up two fingers.

Twenty was a bargain for fresh shrimp like that. Jed handed the man thirty dollars and said, "Buy yourself some lunch." The man smiled, revealing his pink gums, as Rascal barked approvingly before taking his place back at the bow where he wagged his tail as

Jed made a U-turn, pointing them toward home.

When Jed turned back onto Store Creek, he noticed the moon waxing gibbous and hanging low above the live oak trees on the far left bank, and as he gazed at it — a large moon in broad daylight — he was blindsided by the memory of the night he took Julia for a moonlit boat ride all those years ago.

Jed was fifteen at the time and Julia was sixteen, beautiful and talented, with several sixteen- and seventeen-year-old boys from Charleston dropping by to say hello and use her dock for fishing or to tie up their boats. He knew they were there to gain her attention, and he thought he'd never have a chance. But one day after a weeklong family vs. family gin rummy marathon that left him and her duking it out for the winner's title, he got his courage up and asked her to go for a boat ride. It was a hot August evening just days before they had to head home to Atlanta before packing for their new life in Texas. The moon was low and bright. He had no intention of kissing her. He knew he didn't have the nerve, and he had never actually kissed a girl before.

But as she was stepping from the floating dock into his little aluminum boat, her toe caught on the edge and he caught her and held her tight for whole seconds until the boat stopped rocking. She had turned and looked into his eyes at that moment with the moon lighting up the creek and he had bent down, as if impelled by some force far beyond his control, and pecked her right on the lips.

She had stepped back and blushed — he could see that even in the darkness, and his throat became so tight and the fear of rejection became so strong that he immediately sat down and started fiddling with his engine as if nothing had happened, and then he turned back as she was fastening her life jacket and said, "Ready?"

"Sure," she had said. She was grinning and confident, and he knew that she knew that she held his heart in the palm of her hand at that moment. They took the boat ride and headed back, and he said good-bye and never had the joy of laying eyes on her again.

Now, as Jed parked and tied up his boat at the end of his floating dock, he wondered how in the heck Julia had been talked into coming back here to look after these kids. He wondered what in the world the story of her life was. He did notice the hefty sapphire on her left hand. How could he not look?

Well, at least he'd been able to lay eyes on her again, he thought as he headed back to the cottage to clean and boil the shrimp. And he would be able to cook for her tonight. It was as if an apparition had become flesh and blood. As if a daydream had become real life. It was just for today as he had to head back to work tomorrow and wouldn't be back out until after Julia's departure on Saturday. But he had a feeling he would enjoy the next several hours, flea bombs, furniture moving, and all. And he would store this moment up in his mind and in his heart in hopes that it might revive — if but for a few hours — the young boy soul still inside of him, the one the world had not yet frayed and starved with its constant onslaught of disease, grief, and, most acutely felt, loneliness.

Chapter 13
Julia

Cleaning the house took all day. Julia managed to find some rubber gloves, scrub brushes, Comet, and Clorox, and she started with the kitchen, then worked her way through the living room. The oven hadn't been cleaned in eons, and Julia feared if they turned it on the fire alarm would go off. Where was the fire alarm? She hadn't seen one, but it had to be somewhere.

There were palmetto bug carcasses in the bottoms of the drawers and beneath the major appliances, and even in the kitchen doused in Comet, she could feel the fleas nipping at her scalp and arms. When Julia went into Marney's room, her parents' old room, she started with the bathroom. She scrubbed the tub and toilet and sink with a kind of fury and strength she hadn't mustered in a long time. It felt good in a strange way, good to scrub away filth in someone else's home, good to see some results.

When she opened the cabinet beneath the bathroom sink, she was startled to see her dad's old Dopp kit there. The one her mother had given him many Christmases ago when Julia was a teenager. She lifted it up. It felt full inside, and when she unzipped it, she found a rusting bottle of shaving cream, a couple of plastic razors, his old square-shaped brush with the sharp bristles, and a frayed toothbrush lying next to a tube of toothpaste. She reached in and pulled out the brush. It still had strands of gray, curly hair gathered around the edges and even flecks of dandruff deep within the bristles. Without thinking, she lifted it to her nose. It smelled ever so faintly like him, musky and manly, a combination of spice and rubbing alcohol and whatever thick sweetness made up Charles Bennett. She had never known a scent quite like it; it made her feel comforted and safe.

She blinked back the tears. *Lord, have mercy. Christ, have mercy.* She zipped it up quickly and shoved it back in the cabinet. *Deal, deal, deal,* she told herself. Don't open up any old wounds. Just keep cleaning.

After scrubbing the bathroom, she headed to the bedroom, where she dusted, vacuumed, mopped, and stripped the sheets off of the old bed. She did not want to open the large cedar closet her mother had insisted they build back when they spent their summers out there, but she knew she had to in order for the flea bomb to make its way into every nook and cranny.

When Julia finally opened it, she was astonished to find all of her father's clothes hanging on one side — his suits, his jackets, his oxfords, his fatigues, his shoes all lined up in a row as if he would step back into them at any moment. She recognized most of the clothes. They were the ones he'd worn during her childhood with a few exceptions: the tan overcoat she remembered him wearing once when he came to visit her in New York shortly after graduate school, the white dinner jacket he'd purchased from Berlin's for Meg's wedding, a down vest in bright red that didn't look like anything he'd ever actually wear.

She didn't want to get too close. If she did, she might smell the fullness of his scent and that would send her over the edge. She was human, after all, and she had her limitations. She only needed to do a quick sweep of the open floor and mark the dresser Jed and Skeeter might want to lift before they set off the bomb.

She picked up all of the shoes, Marney's

and her father's, and put them on an empty shelf above the hanging clothes. She vacuumed well and also mopped the hardwood floor. Just as she was about to pull the string to shut off the old bare lightbulb in the center of the walk-in, she saw something behind an overcoat: the gilded edge of a familiar frame. She pulled back the jackets and overcoats and found a painting, one of the first she'd ever done, at age five or so, of a sunflower from her mother's garden with a beetle crawling on a petal toward the flower's center.

Tears filled her eyes before she could stop them, and she went running out of the closet and out of the bedroom door, which opened up onto the screened porch. She sat down on a rocking chair and wept like a child, barely able to catch her breath. She pulled off the rubber gloves and rubbed her eyes. She had to get out of here. She didn't know if she could stand this place another day, another minute. How had she gotten herself into this crazy mess? This was *not* her mess!

She looked down at her left finger, at the sapphire she'd meant to take off before the cleaning began. Simon had resized it and it was a little too snug now. It took a good deal of soap and cold water to get it off when she needed to.

"Good," Simon had said with a wink. "Let's keep it that way, Jules." She needed to call him or e-mail him, but there didn't seem to be any computer in the house and her phone had no bars out here. Also, she needed to call the Art Institute in Budapest. She had left the professor there a message about a family emergency that was going to delay her a few days, but she was scheduled to give a lecture on American art in the twenty-first century on Friday, and there was no way she was going to make that.

"Hey there," came a warm voice on the dock. It was Jed and he had come by boat to the house. She wiped her eyes more firmly with the back of her hand, but there must have been some Comet on it because it only made the tears worse, and she could feel her eyes puffing up.

Jed walked up to the screened door and opened it. "You all right?"

She shook her head and groaned, and he came over, sat down beside her, and gently handed her a handkerchief.

"Hey, I'm old-fashioned." He shrugged his broad shoulders. "My dad used to carry these around, and you'd be surprised how often I use them. The nurses make me swear to wash them in Clorox after I offer one to a patient. Which I do."

She took the soft linen cloth with his father's initials embroidered in the corner and wiped her swelling eyes. So many surprises in twenty-four hours — the least of which was Jed, the first boy she ever kissed, showing up on the doorstep as Marney's surgeon. The low country was a small, small place.

He looked to her and then back out at the water. "I can't believe you came to help out. You must have some serious guts."

She shook her head. "I don't know how it happened. This is like a nightmare I've been promising myself all of my adult life that I'd never have."

"Most of them are like that, aren't they? They blindside us, and we certainly wouldn't choose them."

He put his large hand gently on her back. It felt warm and comforting — a little light in the freakiness of this dream, like Charlie's birthmark or Etta's artwork.

"I'm supposed to be in Budapest on a Fulbright right now, painting and lecturing. Most of all, trying to find a 'new voice' for my art."

He nodded, stayed quiet for a long time, and just kept his hand on her back, then gently removed it and crossed his lanky arms. How nice that he didn't say anything, Julia thought. She just needed to have a meltdown without any words of advice or wisdom. He must be married to know such a thing. Curiosity overtook her, and she glanced at his left hand. No band.

She twisted the ring on her left finger, a habit she'd formed in the last few months since she'd received it.

"So what's the story on the fellow who gave you that nice rock?"

She smiled through her tears. "My fiancé." She shrugged and wiped her nose with the handkerchief. "He's an art dealer, someone I met in New York, but he's actually from London." She looked out over the marsh.

"And what does he think of you being here?"

"He thinks it's nuts." She noticed a wasp working its way up the outside screen of the porch. "And I'm sure he's right."

Jed followed her gaze toward the wasp and then to the water, which was reflecting the chips of light from the late afternoon sun.

He cleared his throat to say something, but just as he did, the dryer buzzed in the outbuilding next door and Skeeter hollered from the side yard, "Where're you, Julia? I've got the bombs."

Chapter 14
Julia

Julia left the men to move furniture and set off the foggers, and she went over the bridge to the library in Hollywood, the first little town off of the island, where she was able to e-mail Budapest and call Simon from the two bars she found in the far end of the parking lot by the Dumpster. She only got his voice mail so she texted him and he texted back. *Middle of big deal dinner mtg with Tate director. Call u when?*

Try u tomorrow, she texted back. He'd been after the Tate Museum in London for almost a year to add Hockney to their permanent collection of twentieth-century painters, and maybe that was coming together. If so, it would be enormous for Simon's career. Then, if her muse never came back, and if she was beat out of the department chair job, she could just resign, set up house anywhere they wanted in the world, and start that family she'd been wanting. Maybe Lerici, maybe Corsica. That wouldn't be the end of the world, would it? Nesting on the Mediterranean. Painting when she felt like it. Raising a child.

She spotted the tail of a raccoon that had darted from the Dumpster and into the bushes of a double-wide on cinder blocks next to the library. Then, as a woman came out of the double-wide and yelled, "Scat!" he scurried into the little creek that ran behind the trailer.

Julia could hear the plunk and then see the marsh grass parting on the other side of the bank. The sun and humidity were baking her by this point in the afternoon, but she was thankful for the little glimpse of wildlife. There one moment, gone the next. She couldn't remember the last time she had stopped and watched the natural world. Taken the time to simply observe, to take in the moment before it passed. Somehow she had forgotten that the moment was always irretrievable. She leaned against the hood of her hot rental car and allowed an old memory of her father to surface.

"No minute is quite like the one before it," he had told her when she was ten and he was teaching her how to paint the sunset. "Watch carefully. And keep watching, Julia. And then you'll be able to capture it." She had let her mind wander for a moment, daydreaming about something else — who knows — maybe a friend at school or the reddish fox she'd seen slinking along the dirt road the day before. Then when she came back to the vista, it had changed. It was too dark to capture the tops of the trees or the cloud formations above them or the last light — capturing the last light was everything to an end-of-the-day painting. She could remember blinking hard, holding the brush loosely in her hand, and then looking over to where her father had been able to get it down, at least the outline of it, and he was going to have a stunning work. "I think I missed it again," she told him, and he had turned and looked at her with those deep brown eyes he'd passed along to his son. His eyebrows had softened and he laid his brush on the easel and reached over to squeeze her knobby little shoulder. "We'll try again tomorrow."

Julia's phone buzzed, waking her from the remembering. It was her mother, who must have gotten wind of her whereabouts and had already left her four messages.

"Hi, Mama."

"Oh, Julia!" she said. "My stomach has been all in knots. Are you okay out there?"

"I'm fine." She chuckled at the truth of it. She was totally fine. "I'll be out of here within the week. It's going to be okay."

She could hear her mother holding back a cry on the other end. "Yes, it will. You'll be fine and on your way in no time. But when can I see you?"

"Maybe tomorrow or the next day? I'll call you as soon as there is a window. You know, I'm in charge of these children and I don't know exactly when I can get away."

She heard her mother swallow hard. "Well, you can bring them too, darlin'. I won't bite them, I promise. But I do want to see my daughter in the flesh from time to time, especially when she's less than fifty miles away."

That would be awfully interesting and potentially hazardous. Taking her daddy's second family into her mama's home for a visit. Of course, her mother would be the ever-gracious hostess as usual, but it would be painful for her.

Julia sighed. How was she going to figure this one out? "I'll make sure I see you before I leave, Mama. I promise."

"Okay, sweetheart." Her mother's voice seemed to rise slightly with a controlled expectation. "Just call back when you can. And let me know if you need anything."

■ ■ ■ ■

When Julia arrived back on Edisto, the house was off limits and the children were at Glenda and Skeeter's. Skeeter had a satellite he'd installed himself, which offered three hundred channels, so Charlie was glued to a television show while Skeeter played a game of crazy eights with the girls on the deck.

"How was the visit?" Julia asked Glenda, who was peeling the skin off of some hard-boiled eggs at the kitchen sink.

Glenda looked to Julia and then back down to her colander of eggs. "Marney looked *good,* and she was so glad to see those children." She nodded and cut her eyes at Julia. "Makes her almost seem human when you see her around them, you know?"

Julia shook her head. She did not know.

Glenda shrugged her shoulders and continued, "And as for Dot, she was her usual talkative self, sending you her thanks and regards, though she didn't have the best coloring . . ." Glenda chuckled as she looked out of her kitchen window. "That is, she didn't until I showed her the half a caramel cake I'd brought her." She turned

163

to Julia, winked, and leaned in. "Dot does love her sweets, you know?"

"Yes, she does." Julia could remember Dot's little crystal candy dish in her house — always full with Brach's candies and butterscotch — and how she'd let you have two or three pieces whenever you went to visit. And her freezer was full of ice cream and frozen cookies and pies. She never went anywhere empty-handed, and dessert was a must at the end of each meal.

"Good news for you, though, child." Julia hadn't been called *child* in a long, long time. She twisted her graying hair into a knot at the back of her neck and chuckled.

"What's that, Glenda?"

"Marney was finally able to get ahold of an old babysitter." Glenda raised her eyebrows and nodded toward the road. "The Lindsay child who grew up on Red House Road — Brooke?" The woman gently cracked an egg on the side of the sink and began to peel back the shell. "She's in college now up in the mountains, but she was looking for summer work, so Marney has hired her to watch the kids all the way through August while she gets her strength back. She says she can be here by Saturday."

"Great." Julia took a deep breath and

exhaled slowly. "That sounds like a terrific plan."

" 'Course, I don't know how Marney can afford a full-time sitter all summer." Glenda shook her head. "She's never been one to hold down a job, and you know . . ." Glenda turned to face Julia head-on. "She's *sold off* your daddy's paintings *one right after the next* to survive."

The thought hadn't crossed Julia's mind yet. Where were her father's paintings? She had seen a few prints on the walls but not any originals. Glenda read her mind. "They're all gone, Julia. She let them go to keep the place afloat. He didn't have much in the way of savings or life insurance. But the paintings did go up a good bit in value since he passed, and the Gibbes Museum even bought a few."

Of course, nothing surprised Julia about her father or Marney. She didn't expect Marney to be set for life, as she knew her father's law firm went under years ago. And she was half-surprised Marney hadn't sold the house. She knew Meg was chomping at the bit to get that property, and she seemed to remember there was some drama surrounding that after her father's passing. Meg had asked Julia if she could buy her out of her share — which her father had willed evenly between Meg, Marney, and Julia — but not until the last of Marney's children reached eighteen. Julia said she'd be glad to sell hers anytime. She had no plans to use it. In fact, it had been her mission in life to never return to Edisto Island. So much for that. Well, that was for Marney and Meg to sort out. She would be long gone in less than a week.

Julia bit her lip. "I'll help if she needs help . . . with the babysitter . . . I can certainly contribute." She couldn't think of a better cause to give money to at the moment.

"That's nice of ya, sweetheart," Glenda said. "Dot will pitch in, I'm sure, and we can too. This isn't your problem, heaven knows."

"I'd like to contribute, though." Julia was suddenly overcome with the desire to peel eggs, so she jumped in beside Glenda and started cracking one against the side of the sink. She used to do this with her mama all the time, and she loved to peel back the jagged edges. One egg never broke the same as the next, but they all had that beautiful, smooth oval beneath the outer skin — white and dense and exquisite to behold. She held her first cleaned egg under the faucet and then held it up to the late afternoon light.

Then she turned to Glenda. "And I'm going to do all I can to get the house in order before Marney gets back."

Glenda took the egg out of Julia's hand and handed her another that needed cracking. "Well, that's real nice of you, Julia. I imagine that place is a wreck." She leaned over to Julia and whispered, "She hasn't invited us over in years." Glenda shrugged. "Anyhow, the sitter will arrive the day before Marney will likely be released. So you're free to go by Saturday. I can fill in any gaps on the weekend and Skeeter can help too."

Julia cracked the next egg and began to peel off the shell. "Okay. I'll make my flight arrangements as soon as I can get back over the bridge."

"I've got a computer at the post office if you need to use it. We're plugged in good on that side of the island."

"Okay. Thanks." Julia reached for another as the sound of two ninjas fighting on television rose and fell.

Julia dried her hands and went over and sat down by Charlie. "How about we turn off the TV? Let's go play some tag or wet a line."

He furrowed his brow and she had to hold

back an urge to squeeze his full cheeks. "You know how to fish?"

She shrugged. "I used to."

Skeeter, with his bionic ears when it came to anything angler-related, hollered from the deck, "I've got some bait in the wet well over on the dock. And a few rods already set out there."

Charlie shook off his TV glaze. "Let's go!" he hollered as he jumped up and held out his strong little hand to help Julia up. She took it and then she followed him as he raced out to the dock and grabbed a rod.

Julia saw Etta nudge Heath out of the corner of her eye. "Life jacket," Heath called from above her hand of cards.

"Okay," Charlie said, and he lifted one from the railing and put it on. It was a little too big but would probably keep him afloat a little while if he fell in.

"Do you know how to swim?" Julia asked.

"Oh yeah," Charlie said. "I've been swimming since I was a baby."

"That's true," Skeeter called over his shoulder. "He's a fish."

Julia found the bait and put some nice-sized mullet on the end of the hooks. After a few rounds of showing Charlie how to cast, he tried it himself only to snag the back of his life jacket. Julia decided to cast for him. The tide was coming in so she wanted the line to land upstream and move its way back to the dock pilings where they tended to congregate. Charlie didn't seem to protest too much about her taking over. When she got it in the optimal spot, she handed him the rod. He held it tightly and his eyes followed the float as it bobbled and dipped in the dark, moving water.

"Just keep your eye on that bobber." She pointed out to the orange orb resting on the surface. "As soon as you see it pulled down or feel a tug, then yank back hard and you'll snag whatever's trying to get the bait."

He nodded vigorously. "All right."

She had a feeling that maybe he'd never been fishing before, which was a shock since he was the son of one of the most passionate anglers to ever live on Edisto. Then it occurred to her: he never knew Daddy. And as much as he looked like and reminded her of Charlie, he never had the chance to see him in the flesh.

"Got one!" he hollered and she helped him reel it in. It was a nasty old dogfish, but that didn't matter to Charlie. He was ecstatic and wanted to touch the fish's tail and was eager to watch it swim away after Julia knelt down on the floating dock and released the creature back into the water.

Next, Julia caught a small croaker. It was too small to keep, but she let Charlie hold it for a moment before returning it to the creek. It croaked in his suntanned hands and he giggled at the sound.

After the croaker they hit a hot streak. Julia caught a nice eating-sized spot-tail bass and then Charlie caught a beautiful flounder.

"He's got two eyes on the same side!" Charlie pointed with his thick little finger.

"Yeah." Julia looked at him as she pulled the hook out of the flounder's mouth. "Haven't you ever seen a flounder before?"

He shook his head back and forth. "Nope." She held it up for him to touch and then turned it over so he could see the smooth white eyeless underside. "He lies on one side beneath the mud. His eyes are together so he can see the baby shrimp and other sea life he eats."

"Cool." Charlie reached out to touch him. By now they had caught Skeeter's attention and he abandoned the card game and ambled down the dock with his cane.

"Haven't you ever eaten a flounder?" Skeeter said to the little boy.

Charlie crinkled his nose as he continued to rub the fish's underbelly. "Nope."

"Then you're in for a treat." Skeeter

170

clapped his hands together.

Julia leaned down to the little boy and caught his eye. "This is the fruit of the sea, Charlie. Super flaky and delicious."

The boy licked his full red lips and tilted his head. "Yeah."

Next Julia set Charlie up with another good cast and Skeeter handed her a rusty old scaler and an even rustier knife and nodded to the dock sink. "Go on and filet these so I can get them on ice and over to Jed's. I'll go get the cooler."

"I don't remember the last time I've done this," Julia said. He clucked his tongue and flapped his hand in the air as he hobbled up the dock. "Like riding a bike, gal. It doesn't leave you."

She looked down at the bucket where she'd put the flounder and the spot-tail bass. She took a deep breath, leaned down, pulled the spot-tail out first, and laid it on the wooden counter by the sink where it flopped a moment before she held it down firmly. Then she grabbed the scaler, set its metal teeth at the tail, and scraped toward the head. The scales came off in iridescent tufts, and she wiped them off with the back of her hand and into the sink, which had an opening that drained right down into the creek.

Charlie stayed focused on the bobber and out of the corner of her eye, Julia noticed Etta, who had made her way soundlessly out to the dock. The girl was pretending to help Charlie, though Julia could feel her eyes at the sink, watching Julia intently as she continued to scale the bass.

Eventually Julia got into the groove of it, and it did all come back. She made the incision behind the bass's head and then carefully eased the knife along the backbone, making her way from the head to the tail, inch by inch, flap by flap, until she had a nice-sized filet that could feed at least two. She cut off the tough part at the edge, then flipped the fish over and cut a filet off the other side.

Once all that was left was a head, a fish bone, and a tail, she tossed it over the rail into the water, reached down in the bucket for the flounder, and then turned back to Etta. "Wanna scale this one?"

The girl nodded gently. Then she walked over and picked up the scaler. She had obviously done this before as she held down the flat, round fish with her left forearm and ran the teeth of the scaler deftly along the dark side of its body with her right hand. The flounder was an even harder fish to clean because its scales were softer and smaller, but Etta did a beautiful job as she slowly, meticulously made her way from tail to head, one row at a time, as the fish's mouth opened and closed and opened again.

Julia imagined her father training Etta at a young age to clean a fish as he had Julia and Meg. It was like second nature to her, her little hands moving steadily along the body, wiping off the scales when they piled up. When she finished, she rinsed off the scaler in the sink and then handed the filet knife to Julia. She obviously had no interest in making the incision, but she stood by her big half sister, her breathing almost soundless but steady as Julia carefully cut a filet off of the dark side.

As Julia flipped the flounder to its white side, she stopped for a moment to check on Charlie, still staring at his bobber, and then to take in the scene: the wide arcs of the dark water pushing in toward the creek's end, the softness of the setting sun, the skitter of a school of mullet beneath the dock, the stillness of the late afternoon, the moon showing nearly all of its face above the live oaks beyond the opposite bank. Julia couldn't remember a more picturesque moment.

She turned to Etta, caught her large blue

eyes, and smiled. The little girl looked down at the wooden slats of the dock and grinned, and Julia had a feeling that there were few people on earth who could take in a moment — see it fully for what it was before it passed forever — quite like Etta Bennett.

"Nice work, gals," Skeeter said as he held up his little Igloo cooler, which had a layer of dried pluff mud on its bottom. "Plop those filets right in here, and I'll deliver them to our chef."

Then he said a little more softly as he looked back and forth between Julia and Etta, "He's the best cook I know. Other than your mama, of course, Julia." He glanced carefully up to the house and then back again. "But don't mention that to my Glenda, all right?"

Etta grinned and Julia chuckled. She looked down at the girl and said, "Our lips are sealed."

CHAPTER 15
JULIA

After everyone washed up and made their way out on the deck, Skeeter drove back from delivering the fish to Jed's, opened the tail door of his old Ford pickup, and said, "Pile in."

Julia looked to Glenda, who patted her arm and said, "It's okay. You hold Charlie in your lap and I'll hold Etta."

"Yes!" Charlie hollered as Heath took his hand and helped him shimmy up into the back of the pickup. He found a spot on the rusty wheel well until Julia shooed him off and pulled him into her lap on the dirty flatbed. She was glad she had worn her blue jeans, but her white linen tunic was going to need a good wash.

Everyone else piled in, even Glenda, who sat on the wheel well and held Etta's hand.

Skeeter hollered out of the driver's window, "Ready?"

"Yeah," everyone but Etta said. Then he

drove down the bumpy, gravelly driveway, hanging a right onto Peters Point, and then in less than a mile a driveway on the right had a mailbox that said "Young" on its post.

The old cottage was just as Julia had remembered. A little white wooden clapboard on brick pilings with a wraparound porch. It was surrounded by massive live oaks, their Spanish moss waving in the light evening breeze from the creek.

It was a work in process; Jed was not exaggerating. The only room that was livable was the kitchen, and he even had an air mattress in the corner by the refrigerator where he slept. But on the huge porch he had set a large picnic table with a bright red and yellow tablecloth, ivory-colored plates, silverware, wine and water glasses. Several votives ran down the center. Julia thought Jed had likely entertained more than a few beautiful women out here.

"Wow," Heath said as she walked out on the sloping porch. "This looks so . . ."

Etta whispered a word to Charlie.

"Romantic," he said, and they all giggled. So Etta could speak. Skeeter was right. But her words were rare and whispered only to her brother.

"And smells good," Heath added.

The three children were mesmerized by

the beautiful table. They stood before it, taking it all in as their eyes sparkled with the reflection of the candlelight. With their full cheeks, their red lips, and their wispy hair they looked like three cherubs in the fading sunlight, each unspeakably lovely and mysterious in their own way. And yet remarkably familiar too.

Julia breathed in the fragrance of shrimp, garlic, olive oil, and lemon. It smelled divine and also familiar, reminding her of the great feasts her mother used to prepare many a summer night out here when they had gathered a big catch in the seine or the cast net.

Julia turned to Jed, who was busy in front of a large old cast-iron skillet. "What are we having?"

"Shrimp and grits. My own recipe, inspired by your mother, actually." Then he bent down and shook Charlie's hand. "And some fresh-baked flounder and bass as well."

Charlie turned to Julia and then back to Jed. "I caught it." He thumped his thick little chest. "I caught the flounder."

"That's what I heard." Jed lifted his large hand and Charlie slapped it hard. "You take after your father, you know that?"

Charlie furrowed his brow and looked

down as if a dark cloud had suddenly passed over. Etta, taking it all in, walked over and took him by the hand and led him out to the yard where she pointed out the nearly full moon hanging like a prop in a play above the marsh.

"I didn't mean to upset the little guy." Jed went back to his skillet, and Julia couldn't help but take him in as well. He was six-five, lean but broad-shouldered. He had been tall even at fifteen, but what a man he had turned out to be. A good-looking surgeon who could cook. He must have to beat back the ladies in town.

He looked back at her and grinned. She had been caught checking him out. She felt her cheeks redden, and she turned toward the porch. "It only just occurred to me today that he never knew Dad."

Jed cleared his throat. "That's a real loss," he said as he pulled a Pyrex dish out of the oven with fresh fish filets sizzling in butter and garlic.

"I know." Julia breathed in the amazing scent. "There's enough sadness to go around for everyone, I guess."

Now they could hear Skeeter chuckling on the porch as Charlie held out his arms wide. "It was this big, Glenda! Didn't you see it?"

"No, I didn't," Glenda hooted. "I've never seen a flounder *that* big."

"Well, it was," Skeeter said, backing Charlie up. "I saw it myself." Charlie crossed his arms and nodded his head. Etta was beside him, smiling, and Heath was shaking her head behind him and mouthing to Glenda, "No way."

Glenda just beamed and held out her fleshy arms to Charlie. "I'm proud of you, child."

And he walked toward her and let her pull him up onto her soft, lumpy lap. "Thanks."

Julia felt Jed's gaze on her, and when she looked back he turned back to the skillet.

"Looks like we're ready," he said.

The meal was unbelievably good. There was a field green salad with fresh blue cheese, pecans, and large thinly sliced heirloom tomatoes from the farm by King's Market. Then the shrimp, which was cooked with white wine and olive oil, and a variety of yellow, red, and orange peppers and onions, served over creamy stone-ground grits. Also, the fish cooked with garlic, lemon, and butter and served on the side, flaky and sweet. Charlie ate every morsel of fish and went back for seconds.

For dessert Glenda brought the other half

of the caramel cake she'd baked for Aunt Dot. It had seven thin layers of crusty caramel and moist vanilla cake. Julia had feasted on many a high-brow meal over the last decade during her time in New York and her trips to London and Paris with Simon or her students. But Southern cooking like this, with fresh local ingredients — it fed her body and soul like no other. She had forgotten. She had forgotten so much, and in the midst of the mess, this was a gift. A gift she devoured heartily and with a grateful heart.

Etta never made a peep, but she ate well. Charlie spoke nonstop between big bites of flounder and bass. Heath ate like there was no tomorrow, practically licking her plate and going back for a second slice of caramel cake.

"This is good," she said. It was the nicest thing to come out of her mouth yet. And judging by all their reactions, this wasn't the kind of fare they were used to.

"You should open a rest-strunk," Charlie said to Jed.

"Restaurant," Heath corrected him.

"Best shrimp and grits *I've* ever had." Skeeter nudged Glenda. "Next to yours, of course, dear, and also Mary Ellen Bennett's."

"Who's Mary Ellen Bennett?" Charlie furrowed his brow.

Julia took a sip of her pinot grigio and patted Charlie instinctively on the back. "That's my mother."

"Oh," he said. He hadn't put all of the pieces together, but Etta certainly had. Julia felt Etta staring her down and narrowing her eyes.

"Julia's mother is the best cook I've ever known," Jed jumped in. "She's my inspiration." Just as he said "inspiration" his beeper went off.

"Excuse me," he said. Julia noticed then that he had refrained from having any of the wine he offered. Perhaps he was on call.

He stepped outside, and while they couldn't make out what he was saying, his voice sounded serious. Then he came back on the porch. "An elderly patient of mine is in trouble. We may need to open him up again. I've got to head back to town."

"Oh, I'm so sorry," Glenda said.

Julia jumped up. "We'll do the dishes. You just take off."

"Yeah." Skeeter stood and shook Jed's hand. "Thank you for this fine, fine meal, son. We want to reciprocate the next time you're out here."

"I'd enjoy that." Jed rubbed his large

hands on his blue jeans as Charlie came up and squeezed his long leg. The little boy only came up to his thigh.

Jed leaned down and squeezed Charlie's shoulders. "I'll say hi to your mama if I see her."

"Okay," he said. "And tell her about my fish."

"Will do."

Then Julia walked Jed out to his Land Rover as Glenda instructed the kids to carry their dishes to the kitchen. Rascal and Phydeaux, both wearing their new flea collars, trailed behind Jed and Julia, barking until he opened the door to let Rascal in.

He closed the door gently and turned back to her. "I wouldn't let Phydeaux back in the house if I were you. And you might want to open windows and doors first thing tomorrow and let it air out for a few hours before letting the kids in."

Julia nodded. "Okay." Then she looked up into his mahogany eyes. "Hey, I really appreciate your help today. I can't thank you enough."

He met her eyes and smiled. "My pleasure. I'm really glad I had the chance to lay eyes on you again."

She couldn't conceal her return grin so she chose Etta's method and looked down at her sandaled feet. Then she looked up, unwilling to let the moment pass. "You were my first kiss, you know that?"

"No way." He bit his lip and held it for whole seconds. "I caught you at a weak moment and was lucky. You had a slew of guys vying for your attention, as I recall." He looked over to his boat bobbing at the end of the dock beneath the moonlight as the tide poured in and then back to her. "But you were *definitely* mine." He squeezed her shoulder. "And a first kiss, well, that's something that's permanently imprinted in a boy's brain. It all came back to me today."

She chuckled. "What a surreal forty-eight hours."

"More unpredictable than Budapest, I'd be willing to wager."

"I'm sure," she said.

He held up his iPhone. "What's your number? I'll update you on Marney when I can."

She gave him her cell number and keyed in his.

Then he gave her a controlled, quick embrace before hopping in the car where Rascal was slapping the opposite window with his black tail. Jed rolled down all of the windows and the dog breathed in the last smells of Edisto as he whined at Phydeaux, who barked back.

"Hope your patient's okay."

"Thanks." He nodded as he leaned his head out of the window before backing out of the dirt driveway. "And thanks for cleaning up."

Julia stood there as he drove down the drive, watching the dust of the dirt road rise like a mysterious cloud, illuminated by his taillights. She took a deep breath. *Jed Young,* she thought. *I hadn't thought about him in years.* And then she pictured that night more than twenty-three years ago when he had helped her from the dock onto his little johnboat for an evening boat ride down the creek. She smiled at the remembering, then shook her head as if to snap out of a dream.

When she turned back she caught a glimpse of Etta darting from the yard back onto the porch and she smiled. "The little eavesdropper," she said, and she walked back to the house where everyone was clearing the plates under Glenda's direction.

After cleaning and locking up Jed's house, she settled the girls in the bunk beds at Glenda and Skeeter's and Charlie on a little cot beside the bunks. She'd have her own room in the loft where there was a nice full-sized bed with no fleas.

"Will you scratch my back?" Charlie said as he turned to face the wall and pulled up his pajama top, revealing his soft little back with its perfect downy hair lining his spine.

She took a deep breath. "Okay," she said.

Then she scratched his soft, smooth little shoulder blades gently with the tips of her fingernails as he rubbed the corner of the little blanket Etta had brought for him over his cheek. "And will you pray that prayer Aunt Dot prays about no bad dreams?"

"Sure," she said, and she noticed Etta watching as she leaned closer and whispered, "Dear God, give every one of these children — Charlie, Etta, and Heath — a good night's sleep, and we pray that they would only have happy dreams about the things that bring them joy, like . . ." She paused for a moment.

Charlie said softly, "Like catching a big, giant flounder."

She couldn't help herself from chuckling as his chest began to move slowly up and down. And behind her she could sense Etta relaxing as she fell back onto her pillow and pulled the covers up to her chin.

Charlie's warm little body radiated heat, and as Julia sat there, rubbing his back, watching it rise and fall, she was overcome with the desire to paint. And she already had three images in mind: the egg she held up to the light in Glenda's kitchen, the nearly full moon on the marsh creek, and the three children as they beheld the glistening, set picnic table.

She went to her bedroom and pulled out her sketchbook. She grabbed a sharp pencil from her bag and began to sketch each one out. By tomorrow the moments would have already dulled and faded slightly, so it was now or never if she wanted to capture them. She stayed up into the wee hours, getting the images down.

As her head hit the pillow, the last thought to cross her mind was a question: How long had it been since she had drawn scenes or human figures?

Too long, she realized. *Too, too long,* she thought as she drifted off to sleep. And she knew in her heart of hearts that she was gaining something on this detour back to Edisto. Something she wouldn't have been able to get without this trip home.

CHAPTER 16
MARY ELLEN

Mary Ellen examined the small paintings in the little makeshift studio that was really just the back half of her laundry room. Winifred Kitteridge had called her more than once over the last several weeks to arrange a time to retrieve them, leaving a message on her home phone and even stopping by the King Street store when Mary Ellen was running a package to the post office for Gene. Somehow Mary Ellen couldn't bring herself to return the call.

She had touched up the frayed corner of Charles's canvas, and she had set both paintings in a simple, handsome gilded frame, two and a half inches wide. She had weathered the gilding with a little gray paint so that it matched the murky brown-green of the scene. And so that the figures stood out — she in a wide-brimmed straw hat and sundress, Meg in a bathing suit, her hair in a ponytail. Each of them reeling in a crab at

187

the end of a rope knotted around a chicken neck.

It was time to give them back, she knew. But she was disappointed in how little she had gleaned by staring at the brushstrokes, by examining the light, the shadows, the figures in motion. Part of her wanted to rip the canvases apart and throw them in the trash can. She could tell Winifred there had been an accident. She had been knocked down by an enormous dog who had mauled the paintings. Or they had fallen out into the street just as a horse-drawn carriage full of tourists trampled over them.

Somehow she couldn't bear the idea of them hanging in a newfangled beach house as if pulled from an interior decorator's inventory and hung smartly in some small corner or in an overdone powder room where they would gather dust nine months out of the year. They were artifacts of her life, and because they were art, she expected them to eventually *tell* her something. To speak the way an antique often does through its markings, its builder's imprint, its period legs, its wood type, the nicks and cracks across its surface. Every antique had a story to tell, and if you studied it long enough, you could hear it.

She left them on her worktable and went

down to check on the chicken she was boiling in a pot. She planned to make chicken noodle soup and cream cheese biscuits for dinner. Comfort food. Ever since she'd heard about Marney's illness and Julia's trip down, she'd had a knot in her stomach, and the only thing that seemed to comfort her — even in the heat of June — was soup.

As she peeled carrots at her sink, she noticed how parched her hydrangeas looked, not to mention her potted tomato plants she was experimenting with this season. She put on her straw hat and headed out to the garden where she unwound her hose and began to water the tomatoes.

She thought she heard a knock, ever so faintly beneath the hiss of the hose. Then there was an unmistakable, "Yoo-hoooooo! Mrs. Bennett?"

She peered around the corner of her house to see Winifred Kitteridge calling from the front piazza. "Are you in the garden?" She watched as the woman came down from the piazza and headed toward the driveway, which led to the back gate.

Mary Ellen dropped the hose and raced to the opposite side of the yard where she crouched down and shimmied behind the pittosporum bushes.

She felt the brim of her hat crack, and

then she looked down at her dirty white canvas espadrilles. What in the world was she doing hiding in her garden? If Winifred found her, what a fool she would look like. She didn't care. She just didn't care. She would give the woman her paintings . . . just not quite yet. She needed a few more days with them.

Mary Ellen watched as the woman opened the picket fence and, with the nerve that only someone from off could muster, walked into the back garden.

Winifred was dressed to the nines in a taupe designer suit and nude pumps. She sported a large pair of square tortoiseshell sunglasses that seemed to cover a good half of her face and made her look more like an insect than a lady. Mary Ellen listened as she called her name before reaching down to the hose, which was still dripping.

"Are you back here?" Winifred Kitteridge said. "I need my paintings before my guests arrive this weekend. It's been over six weeks."

As Winifred Kitteridge walked across the garden, Mary Ellen crouched deeper and deeper into the pittosporum bushes. She went so far into them she feared she might fall out on the other side and land right in Nate Gallagher's garden, just behind his pink sweetheart rosebush. She was surprised Luther hadn't already sniffed her out.

Winifred came awfully close to the pittosporum bushes. She clucked her tongue. "Where is that crazy woman?" And then, after a long sixty seconds, the woman turned on her heels and walked back toward the picket fence that led to the driveway. When Mary Ellen heard the click of the gate, she exhaled.

Still, she thought it would be smartest to wait until she could hear the start of Winifred's engine, so she stayed crouched down a few more minutes, becoming suddenly aware of a strange sound. It was muffled, but she could make it out. It was the sound of a man weeping. A sound that always unnerved her.

She crouched farther down on all fours and crawled into Nate's garden where she peered through the thorny limbs of the sweetheart rosebush. And there she saw Nate, on the back steps, his whiskery face in his large speckled hands, which also held a large dog collar. The two plates on the dog collar clanged together as his shoulders shuddered, and as he rubbed his eyes before looking up at the sky and then back down.

Mary Ellen's heart thumped in her chest. She was well acquainted with despair, and she knew that Nate was grieving, and she felt for him — deeply. Something had happened to his companion. To his best friend. And when someone was despairing — even if it was your brusque Yankee neighbor — there was only one thing to do: make food and deliver it discreetly.

She shimmied out of the rosebush and crawled back through the pittosporum bushes to her garden. She stood up, wiped the black dirt off of her hands and knees, and headed to the house where she washed her hands and started putting the final touches on the chicken noodle soup before whipping up some of her famous cream cheese biscuits.

By late afternoon she walked quietly over to Nate's house with a bamboo tray containing a large container of chicken noodle soup, a mixed greens salad with goat cheese and pecans, biscuits wrapped in tinfoil, and a large piece of chocolate chess pie that Jane Anne had brought over yesterday.

She had half a mind to knock on the door, drop the tray, and run. But she didn't. She waited several minutes until she could hear him clearing his throat and unlocking the door.

He narrowed his fuzzy gray eyebrows as he opened the door. Then he looked at the tray full of food and back to her.

"How did you know?"

"A neighbor knows sometimes." She smiled tentatively.

He gave a half smile back and opened the door a little wider. "Please, come in."

Nate Gallagher's home was beautiful. She'd been in the house several times before when a large Catholic family inhabited it, but she hadn't set foot it in since his arrival a few years ago. As far as she knew, he never entertained.

It was full of antiques and stunning paintings and pottery, blue pottery, everywhere — on chest tops, on tables, hanging on walls.

"May I offer you some tea or a glass of wine?"

"Tea would be lovely. Thank you."

He gestured for her to sit in the ornate living room, then he took the tray from her and walked back to the kitchen.

She examined the parlor before he returned with two glasses of iced tea. With the exception of Luther's well-worn bed by the hearth, the room was exquisite. There was a magenta silk striped Chippendale sofa with large, fluffy pale blue silk pillows, two pale blue velvet-covered baroque-style chairs with a small baroque gilded table between them, a large Victorian-style chest and desk, a seventeenth-century mirror, and dozens of small and large paintings.

On the coffee table beside a few blue pottery pieces there were two photographs: One of Nate and what must be his children and grandchildren. It was a very large crew, almost everyone freckled and redheaded. And one of what must have been a much younger version of him in a sailor uniform next to a beautiful redheaded woman he held tightly in his arms.

He handed her the glass of tea and sat down in one of the chairs. She noticed a smudge of dirt still on her knee, rubbed it off, and took a sip of the drink. Unsweet, naturally. But still, rather refreshing.

"You're quite the collector," she said. "These are some beautiful baroque and Victorian pieces." She dabbed the linen napkin on her lips. "And I ought to know — I've been working in antiques for twenty years."

He looked around the room and shrugged. "My wife was a collector."

Mary Ellen pointed to the photo. "Is this her?"

He nodded. "Yeah. She passed away just before we moved here." He took a hearty sip of his tea and readjusted himself. "I wanted to build a log cabin in Montana and retire there, but she wanted to retire to Charleston. She loved the beach and warm weather. She loved the aesthetics and the arts. She was quite a successful potter."

"So you came here? For her?"

He wiped his brow. "I guess I did." He looked around the room. In a sense, he seemed so out of place there, this scruffy, whiskery man amid all of these beautiful pieces. But he looked quite at home. As if these were the artifacts of his life, a life that had contained love and family and hope for a long future together.

She inhaled and cocked her head. "What happened to Luther?"

The man's big blue eyes watered and he turned away. "A truck hit him. Coming right down Rutledge Avenue." He shook his head. "I shouldn't have let him off the leash, but I loved to see him roam free. I could hardly keep up with him anymore, and he needed his exercise."

"I'm so sorry, Nate." She took another sip of the tart tea as he swallowed back a tear.

He stared for a long time at the back of his hand and then turned to her. "The soup smells delicious."

She smiled and straightened up. A visitor

never wanted to stay too long, especially when someone was mourning. She moved to the edge of her seat. "Well, what's the cliché? It's good for the soul."

"Blood soup, my mother used to call it."

"Really?"

He nodded. "She was a first-generation Irish Catholic, and whenever we got sick she'd make us blood soup, which meant chicken noodle." He let out a gruff chuckle. "One time my kid brother, Emmet, looked into the pot and said, 'Where's the blood, Ma?' She batted him on the nose and said, 'It's good *for* your blood. It feeds your marrow and kills the germs. There's no blood *in* the soup, Em'."

Mary Ellen laughed. "Well, she was right. I think I read an article a few years back about some scientists who studied its effects." She shook her head. "I forget the details."

Then she put down her glass and stood. "Well, I know you are probably tired and want some time to yourself."

He stood with her. "Want to have a bowl with me? Out in the garden? There's plenty and it would be nice not to eat alone."

Mary Ellen hesitated. She came up with two valid excuses in her mind, but when she opened her mouth she couldn't seem to muster the nerve to utter them. She knew all too well what it was like to eat alone, especially when you were grieving.

"Sure," was the word that came out of her mouth. Then she turned toward Nate's kitchen. "Let me help you get it set up."

Mary Ellen had a nice early dinner with Nate on the porch where she told him about Charles and the girls and her work at the Berkowitz store, and he told her about his late wife, Patricia, and their four children, Nate, Emmett, Jeannie, and Lese, who lived all over the country: one in Manhattan, one in Orlando, one in Omaha, and one in San Francisco. He had eleven grandchildren too.

As Nate walked Mary Ellen home, she could just feel Jane Anne peering from behind her drapes across the street, and as soon as she got home, her phone was abuzz.

"Spill it," Jane Anne said after she answered the call.

"He lost his dog, Jane Anne. So I took him some soup and he asked if I would stay and have some."

Mary Ellen could hear Jane Anne sucking her teeth. "Now, come on. He's human, and he's our neighbor. I know he's not the nicest one, but we Southern ladies must be kind and charitable."

"Oh, get off your high horse now."

Mary Ellen chuckled. "All right, all right." She was suddenly overcome with a need to make a phone call.

"Let me call you back in ten," she said.

"You better. I want to know what his house was like. And what happened to that beast."

"I will," Mary Ellen said.

Then she took her Day-Timer and walked upstairs to her studio where she looked at the paintings as she dialed Winifred Kitteridge's number.

"Hello?" the woman said.

"Hello, Ms. Kitteridge. This is Mary Ellen Bennett."

"Oh, thank goodness!"

"I'm sorry I've been difficult to reach. I do apologize. But I'm happy to report that the paintings are ready, and I'm going to give you a twenty percent discount because it took me so long."

"Well." The woman cleared her throat. "That's very kind of you. When can I pick them up?"

"Anytime tomorrow or this week. They'll be in the studio in the back of the store."

"I'll be there tomorrow," Winifred Kitteridge said. "And you're pleased with how they turned out?"

Mary Ellen rubbed her hands across the old rough canvas. If she had any hope of healing and moving forward, she had to let go of this old life, even the mystery of why and how it all fell apart.

"Very pleased," she said. "Very pleased, indeed."

After she hung up she called Jane Anne and gave her the scoop about Nate and suggested they invite him out on their next Collateral Damage dinner, at which she scoffed but then said, "Well, it would certainly liven things up."

When she said good night to Jane Anne, the phone rang once more.

"Mama, it's Julia."

"Hi, darling!" she said. "How in the world is it going?"

"Well, I've got the kids with me right now, but I was calling to see if I could come over for dinner on Thursday night. Glenda and Skeeter have agreed to watch them."

Mary Ellen's heart soared and in her mind she was already planning the menu. "Wonderful, sweetheart. I'll call your sister and see if she can come."

"Sounds good, Mama. Does six work?"

"Anytime works," Mary Ellen said. "Six is perfect."

"See you then!" said her eldest daughter. "I'm looking forward to it, Mama."

Mary Ellen hung up the telephone and peered out of her laundry room/studio window over the garden. Her hose was spread out haphazardly from the afternoon's escapade and her tomatoes still needed some water.

She went downstairs, turned on the porch lights, and as the moths began to flit around the lights, she filled the potted plants until they were overflowing. Though the humidity and the city streetlamps obscured the view of the night sky, she could still make out the moon above the rooftops, waxing toward full above Savage Street and Tradd Street and the harbor itself.

She turned off the hose and carefully coiled it up before slapping the dirt off of her hand. Then she walked out to the center of her garden and gazed up, thankful that while the earth could shift beneath you, and your story could take a sharp and unexpected turn, some things could be counted on. Some things were steady and loyal and reliable.

Mary Ellen wanted what everyone wants — to be loved, to be precious, to be adored. And in that moment she felt the hand of God, looming larger than even the moon. It was resting on her cheek, tenderly, the way it had when she was a girl singing in the children's choir of her daddy's parish, St. John's Episcopal on West Macon Street in Savannah. And the hand she now felt just might be enough, she hoped, to move her out of her grief and on with the rest of her life.

CHAPTER 17
ETTA

My half sister has been here four days. She cleaned the house and got rid of the fleas. She made sure Phydeaux kept the new white collar on, and he doesn't itch behind his ears as much now. She took us all to Target yesterday and told us we each had one hundred dollars to pick out some new clothes and essentials like socks and underwear. And she asked Heath if she would like to buy a bra and picked some out for her and helped her adjust them in the dressing room while I sat with Charlie on the floor by the three-way mirror and watched him play a game my half sister has on her phone called Angry Birds.

It was hard to decide how to spend my money. I'd never had so much before. Finally, I settled on a new bathing suit with pink and yellow stripes, two pairs of madras shorts, three T-shirts, and some new underwear that had geometrical shapes on it. I had a little money left over, so my big sister said it was okay for me to get the sketchbook and pastels I wanted.

She let Heath get a pair of sunglasses that were orange in the front and hot pink on the sides and part two of the *Deathly Hallows* movie, which is the only one she hasn't ever seen. She also bought her some special face soap for her bumps and a book called *The Fellowship of the Ring* that she said she would like since all Heath has done for the last three years is read the Harry Potter series over and over.

I liked the first Harry Potter, but I stopped at the third. The Dementors with their ghastly faces and frayed black robes got me. I could see them in my sleep — floating above my bed and around the house and out over the creek — and I didn't want anything else dark like that to get into my mind.

My half sister also cleaned out the refrigerator and then took us to the Piggly Wiggly. We got chocolate milk, which was already made and mixed. It is thick and creamy. Also, we got bread and cheese and sliced ham and turkey. She cooked us spaghetti the first night we were back in the house, then the next night she baked a chicken and used the juice to make gravy, which she served over rice, and she also made a cucumber and tomato salad. Last night she made fish tacos with the trout she and Charlie caught yesterday when the tide was turning. She also put chicken necks in the old crab trap, and she says tomorrow she'll make us crab cakes, but we are all going to have to help get the meat out. That can take hours. "It's a labor of love," she says. "But it's worth it."

She doesn't want to see Mama. I can tell you that much. Heath and Charlie and I have been to see Mama again but only because Glenda took us. Mama sends messages to my half sister through Glenda. "Brooke will be here Saturday afternoon. Mama will also be released Saturday afternoon. Skeeter will go get her and bring her home."

My half sister says she will be leaving on Saturday morning. Glenda will keep us in between the time when she leaves and Brooke arrives. She has to catch a plane to a city across the Atlantic Ocean. She showed it to us on the world map hanging in Heath's room. It looks a long way away, and it has a strange name. She says the city is divided in two by the river. There is Buda on one side and Pest on the other. She's staying in Buda, which sounds like a better place to stay than somewhere spelled Pest, though she calls it "Peshcht."

I haven't spoken to my half sister, and I'm glad she hasn't asked me to. I'm not ready. It's not that I think she's an enemy, at least not a direct one. But she will be leaving soon and her heart belongs to another place. Not this one, not us. I can only speak to someone who I know is with us.

A couple of times she has taken us to the post office so she can talk to a man named Simon who has a loud voice. She has a picture of him on her phone. He gave her the big dark ring and is going to marry her. She has a wedding dress and a wedding cake her friend in New York helped her pick out. She showed us a picture of the little girl who will be in her wedding. She had pretty red hair tied back in a satin ribbon and freckles. Her face was round and pretty, and she was wearing a long, creamy dress with satin ribbons woven throughout the hem and satin ribbons falling from the puffy short sleeves. "That's Chloe, my god-daughter," my half sister said. *I'd like to be someone's goddaughter,* I thought. But I don't think I am.

Right now I'm on the dock, and I've already used up too many pages of my sketchbook, so I've decided to divide each page into fours and draw quarter-page pictures. I hear the screen door screeching and shutting behind me, and I see my half sister coming out now with her own sketchbook.

Charlie is fishing on his own now. She got him a little rod his size at Target and some fresh bait and tackle. She even asked Skeeter if she could use his boat and she took us out to a spot she said our daddy used to call the honey hole. And that our daddy used to blindfold his fishing buddies before he took them there. That made Charlie laugh and, later, daydream. She told us not to tell anyone where it is. Except maybe Skeeter or Jed in case they take us fishing after she leaves.

"Of course I know you won't, Etta." She winked at me. Even though she is not with us, she understands that I am the secret keeper. I like her for that.

"Can I join you?" She pulls a plastic chair over next to mine and flips back the pages of her sketchbook. Last night, when Julia was taking a shower, Heath and I snuck into her room and flipped through her pad to see what she has been drawing each night. There was one of my sister and brother and me at the dinner table at Jed's, there was one of an egg being held up to the light, there was one of Heath reading a book, one of Skeeter helping Charlie bait a line, one of Phydeaux walking with Charlie down the dirt road. Also, there was one of me opening the door of my dad's shed and looking back. I was wearing my white nightgown and my rain boots.

Now I nod and keep drawing. My sketch is of the afternoon sun on the creek and the marsh. I am working on the oak tree whose limbs lean out over the water, casting long shadows. They are like the fingers of a giant old man. My half sister begins to draw the tree too, but she puts it more toward the center, not to the side like me.

I put my pad down and watch her. Her hands are nimble like mine and they are strong too. I like the way she holds the pencil, close to the tip, but loose. Every now and then she rests it between her index and middle finger when she needs to stop and stare.

"The light is changing quickly," she says with her head toward the creek.

I look at her. She is concentrating. Trying to take a picture of it all with her mind before she goes back to the pad. I have a lot of pictures in my mind. Sometimes I can't help but draw them. If they are about the enemy or about the light one, I hide them. For now. Because the enemy scares me. And the light one scares the others. He is like a basin of sunlight, and some people are frightened by so much brightness.

Tonight Julia is going to Mary Ellen Bennett's house for supper. She has bought two frozen pizzas for us and made a big salad. We are going to stay at Glenda and Skeeter's while she goes to town. Honestly, I wish we were going to Mary Ellen Bennett's too. I have never met her, but I know that she is Julia's mama and that means that my father must have been married to her. Also, Julia's sister, Meg, will be there with her family. Meg is also my half sister, and I have met her before, but only once when she wanted to meet with my mama after Daddy's funeral. She made Mama cry, so I don't want to see her very much.

I want Mama to come home. I miss her, her smell, her voice when she reads us stories, her touch on my shoulder, the way she playfully tugs the end of my hair when I am drawing. But I wish Julia could stay too. I wish she could teach Mama about the cooking and the fishing and the cleaning up.

When Mama comes back we won't see

Skeeter or Glenda or Jed. Mama likes to keep to herself. I think it's because of the enemies. And I can understand that. But I will miss seeing our neighbors. I'm not so lonely when I see them. And it is nice to be around a man like Skeeter who is older and who knew my daddy.

In two days Brooke, our babysitter, will be here. Brooke is fun and makes us laugh. She can make Coca-Cola squirt through her nose, she can make her tattoo of a butterfly dance when she flexes her arm muscle, she gives Phydeaux long belly rubs, and she takes us to the beach to look for shells or to the park to shoot the basketball. Plus, she can bake brownies from a box. The brownies make the whole house smell sweet and that makes Charlie smile. He is already talking about the brownies.

My half sister has talked to Jed twice during our trips to the post office. He asked if he could come to dinner at Mary Ellen Bennett's and she said yes, then her face turned pink.

I do miss Aunt Dot, who also reads to us. She reads to us from the book about God and the basin of light. That's my favorite book. And when I read it, I feel like I am somebody's goddaughter. Glenda says Aunt

Dot will be out of the hospital in a week, and as soon as she is able, she will come and visit us.

Now Julia shows me her sketch, and I show her mine.

"Nice," she says. "I really like the shadow of the limbs on the water. You've captured the light."

I try not to grin too hard. I look down at the floorboards of the dock. I can see all the way down to the water and to the poles driven into the pluff mud and to the little white barnacles climbing up them.

"Have you ever taken art lessons, Etta?"

I shake my head no.

Then my half sister crinkles her eyebrows like she does when she is getting an idea. She shakes her head slowly as if she is nodding yes to herself. Then she looks at her watch. And then over to Charlie, who is waiting for a bite, and then to Heath, who is laying out in her bathing suit on a towel reading *The Fellowship of the Ring*.

"Well, we need to take a shower and head on over to Glenda and Skeeter's. If I don't see my mother before I leave, she will be *very* upset."

Heath stands and Charlie reels in the line. When they reach us, Charlie points to Julia's sketchbook and says, "Etta said you only draw shapes."

My half sister looks at me and winks. She knows I know stuff about her, but she doesn't seem to mind.

"I do, Charlie." She holds up the sketchbook so he can see her drawing of the tree. "But I used to draw pictures like this all of the time when I lived out here, and it feels good to do that again."

Charlie nods his head as if he is satisfied with her answer and hands her the rod, which she rests on the railing.

Heath flips her thick brown hair back. Her olive skin is getting tan now, and the bumps on her face are better. She looks like she is a little more of a woman than a girl every day. Usually she doesn't like that and hides herself. But today she looks proud. She smiles and holds back her shoulders and cocks her head. She won't say it, but I can tell she likes Julia too. She has brought some sunlight with her, and I hope it will not go when she leaves.

CHAPTER 18
JULIA

Julia changed her outfit three times. *How absurd,* she thought to herself as she put lipstick on for the first time all week, but she did it nonetheless. She had started with a yellow sundress with little red wildflowers, one she bought on a whim without even trying it on the other day when they were in Target. She had been sweating like a pig in her jeans and long-sleeve shirts, and she needed a few light things to wear around the house as the temperature climbed to the low nineties. The dress felt a little too young for her — the thin straps and the flouncy-ness of the skirt. It was like something her students might wear, so she changed. Next she put on her well-worn traveling jeans and a taupe tunic that went with everything, but she was burning up by the time she dried her hair — the air-conditioning was barely limping by in the old cottage — so she went back to the sundress and a pair of old gladiator sandals she'd stuffed in her luggage as an afterthought when she was packing for Budapest last week. She grabbed a red gauzy shawl from her bag and tied it around her shoulders. Then she pulled her hair up into a French twist and put on some drop pearl earrings her mother had given her a few Christmases ago.

After getting a pizza and salad ready, tracking down Etta in the woods, and then convincing Charlie to change out of his filthy, polyester Spider-Man costume into a clean pair of shorts and a T-shirt, Julia finally loaded the kids in the car.

She glanced at her phone as they pulled out of the dirt driveway in her little red rental car. Three messages waiting for her, two from Glenda and one from Jed, but she wouldn't be able to listen to them until she got over the bridge where she could get reception. She'd see Glenda in a moment anyhow.

They were all perspiring so she turned her little rental car's AC on full blast and they fought for a cool stream of air as she pulled out onto Peters Point Creek Road and then back down the next driveway into Glenda and Skeeter's.

As the sand and gravel crunched beneath the tires while the kids shoved one another back and forth, she noticed that the house looked awfully quiet. She had half-expected Skeeter to be out on the dock getting some lines ready for Charlie. As she pulled up to the front door, she looked back to the kids. "Let me go make sure everything is okay."

"Just keep the air on," said Heath as Etta nodded.

"Let me sit in the middle, Jewel-a!" Charlie said.

"I'll be back in just a minute." Julia left the car running and closed the door. The air was thick, thicker than syrup, and she slowly made her way up the stairs to the house.

When she knocked on the door, Glenda opened it, a little hunched over and looking rather green. She was in her nightgown and slippers. "Oh, Julia, I left you a couple of messages." She leaned on the doorway and held her gut. "That stomach bug that's been going around at the PO has hit us both over the last two hours. It's an ugly one. They say it came from the cruise ships in Charleston, but I don't know." She cleared her throat. "Anyway, I don't think we can keep the kids, and I would hate for y'all to get this. Especially you before you head out on Saturday."

Julia backed away from the door. She did

not want to be yacking on an international flight. "Okay. I hope you feel better. Let me know if you need anything from town."

"I will, child," Glenda said, then she closed the door quickly and padded away.

Julia hopped back in the car and turned to look at the children in the backseat. Both Etta and Charlie were peeking beneath the tinfoil-wrapped pizza on Heath's lap.

"Well," she said. "I'm not sure what to do."

"What's wrong?" Heath pulled the pizza away from them and gave them a stern look.

"Glenda and Skeeter are sick. They've got a bad stomach bug."

Charlie screwed up his nose. "Yuck," he said.

Etta's eyes were wide. She looked nervous and Julia wanted to put them all at ease. She exhaled and wrinkled her brow. Then she looked each of them in the eye one at a time. "How do you all feel about going to my mother's house with me?"

Heath shrugged her shoulders. "Fine by me." She held up her book. "I'll be fine."

Charlie's eyes lit up. "What food does she have? You think she'll have a cake?"

Etta looked down at her long, narrow fingers. Then she rubbed her palms on her legs.

"Etta, are you okay with that?"

She nodded slowly to her knees.

"Well, I'm not even sure if that is what will happen. I have to call my mama and ask her, but let's head on over the bridge and figure out what's next."

Julia pulled over at the Hess station in Hollywood and left the kids in the car with both the radio and the air-conditioning on. Halfway down the road she had given in to Charlie's request for a slice of pizza, and he had already smeared his white T-shirt with tomato sauce.

"Hi, darlin'." Her mother answered the phone with great zeal. Julia knew she was excited about getting the family back together for an evening at her house.

"Mama, I've got a situation here." She cleared her throat and could almost see her mother's wrinkled brow. She swallowed so hard her ears popped. "Glenda and Skeeter are sick, and I've got nowhere to take Marney's children."

Her mother paused for a long moment at the other end of the line. Julia suddenly realized this was probably asking way too much of her. Had she ever even met these children? Would seeing them break her heart? Julia cleared her throat. "Maybe I can meet you for lunch day after tomorrow —"

"Yes, of course you can bring them tonight." Her mother's voice was warbly but intent. "I have plenty of food. I'll just put all of the kids in the backyard anyway. I pulled out the old croquet set from the shed for Meg's kids. It will be fun."

"Are you sure?"

"Yes," her mother said, and Julia could feel the sincerity and the yearning in her voice. "It will be all right, sweetheart."

"Okay," Julia said. "We're on our way, then. We'll be there in a half hour or so."

Next Julia checked the messages. There was one from Jed. "Hey, Julia . . . Something's come up. I had this commitment I had completely forgotten about, and I don't think I can get out of it. I'm incredibly bummed. Really, I am. It's just something I can't miss. Please tell your mother I'm sorry. If something changes, I'll come by . . . I was really looking forward to it."

Julia exhaled. Some other commitment definitely translated into some other woman, some date or event or preexisting relationship. Of course. How ridiculous she had been. Like a teenager. Still, she had really wanted to see Jed one more time before she left and stepped back into her real life. Now she looked down at her ring and tapped her head with the heel of her hand. "It's for the best," she said to herself. "Definitely for the best."

It had been eight months since she'd seen her mother. It had been almost two years since she'd seen Meg and her nephews and niece. This would be awkward, terribly awkward because of the children, but she had no other options at this point. And she was sure they would understand that.

She got back into the car where the children were listening to the oldies station. "Shama Lama Ding Dong" from *Animal House* was playing. The kids seemed to know the words, though Etta only sang with her eyes. Julia turned up the volume and sang along with them as they headed up Highway 17 toward the Charleston Peninsula.

She remembered how much her daddy liked to play this song on the old record player, and how he would do a merry dance called the shag with her mother, step-two-three-ing, rocking back and twirling her around and around in his arms. They moved beautifully and dream-like together, her mother's sundress swaying, her father's arms gently leading. Julia could see the college kids still in them — the twenty-year-olds who met at Folly Beach at a summer dance and fell in love as they danced beneath the moonlight, the soft sand between their toes.

Sometimes he would put on the Beach Boys or the Catalinas or the Embers and teach her and Meg to dance. Up-two-three, back-two-three, rock back. They would take turns dancing with Daddy on the piazza on Savage Street and out on the dock at Edisto. And her mother would laugh and clap, and her father's eyes would twinkle beneath the stars — looking back at his wife — as he spun his daughters around. And Julia — when it was her turn to count the steps, taking her father's hands, sliding her summer-tough bare feet across the wooden slats — was certain that she belonged to the happiest family under the sun.

Two more days, she thought as she drove the children up the well-worn highway that traced the coast. *Forty-eight more hours until I'm on that plane and out of this strange Southern gothic dream.* A dream that had somehow become a part of her personal history. She had almost made it through the week without too much emotional damage, without a panic attack, and best of all without having to see Marney. And for all of these reasons, she thought as she looked in the rearview mirror to the backseat while they all sang, *"You are my shooby-dooby-doo . . . YEAH,"* she was abundantly thankful.

CHAPTER 19
MARY ELLEN

Mary Ellen scraped a little tomato seed off of her monogrammed apron. It was the pale green toile one that Meg and her family had given her last Christmas along with matching monogrammed hot mitts. She'd had yet to cook for them since then, and she wanted to be sure they saw her using their gift. It was nice to have something fresh to cook with.

She had been working for the last forty-eight hours preparing for this feast. She'd cooked a ham with a honey pineapple glaze and several tomato pies with fresh basil and Johns Island heirlooms. She'd fried three cut-up chickens from Mr. Burbage's with her special flat beer batter. She'd made red rice with sausage, deviled eggs, creamed corn, and a leafy spinach salad with strawberries and blueberries and goat cheese. She'd baked a fresh peach cobbler, which was Meg's favorite, plus a pecan pie and a batch of double fudge brownies. Also, she'd marinated some creek shrimp in olive oil and vinegar with sweet Vidalia onions to have for an appetizer because that was Julia's favorite.

Julia. Mary Ellen couldn't wait to see her. The children? Well, she would steel her nerves against whatever kind of emotional upheaval laying eyes on them might wreak. She had seen them before. Well, not the littlest one, but she had seen the others at Charles's funeral. They were just children like any other children, unaware of the past and certainly not answerable to it.

She couldn't wait to see Jed Young too. How she had loved his parents, whom she had heard through Jane Anne Thornton — a distant cousin of theirs — had both passed away in Texas over the last several years. Both from cancer after a life of working to find a cure. That didn't seem fair somehow.

They were such lovely folks, Evelyn and James. They had spent several summers on Edisto and she and Charles had looked forward to their annual visits. Evelyn couldn't cook at all, but she would bring the most wonderful Moravian sugar cakes and key lime pies that she'd buy in Aiken on her way to the coast. And she always brought several big baskets of peaches from

Georgia, which Charles used to make peach ice cream in the old churn. Evelyn was strikingly stylish in a way that was a perfect blend of new fashion and old-world elegance. She was an interior decorator and always on the hunt for antiques. Mary Ellen used to love to go to Savannah with her on Sunday afternoons to the auctions. She had bought one of her favorite pieces there, a rolltop desk she still had in the foyer. Evelyn had insisted she buy it and she had never regretted it. It was the perfect size and shape for that little nook where the stairwell turned from one angle to the other in the foyer, and she loved to set a crystal bowl of hydrangeas or camellias there whenever she was entertaining.

Mary Ellen and Evelyn had kept in touch marginally through the years, a few Christmas cards here and there, a few letters, but they eventually lost touch, like so many others after the divorce. Once she had run into Evelyn at a silver vendor's market on a buying trip to Atlanta with Gene and Jeanne. They'd had coffee at a Starbucks down the street and caught one another up on their lives and their children's lives. Evelyn had shaken her head and readjusted her Chanel scarf. "I'd heard about it, but I just can't believe it, Mary Ellen." She'd put her goldbangled hand gently on Mary Ellen's forearm in a gesture of genuine grief. "I'm so, so sorry. Y'all were one of the most loving couples and one of the most delightful families I'd ever known." She'd taken a sip of her latte and leaned back and breathed deeply. "I don't understand life sometimes." She looked out of the window onto the busy Buckhead sidewalk as if peering into her own personal view of sadness.

It was the last time Mary Ellen had seen her. And she regretted not accepting the invitation she had sent a few weeks later inviting her to join her at St. Simon's Island for a little vacation and shopping trip. Evelyn's treat.

"I'm so sorry," she had said. "I can't take off the time from work." She could have, probably, but somehow the thought of getting in the car and driving several hours unnerved her. It was one of those low points when all she could do was get up and get out of bed in the morning. She never heard from Evelyn again. And then, just a few years ago, Jane Anne brought over the clipped obituary from the *Houston Dispatch* her cousin had mailed her. "You knew her, didn't you?" Jane Anne had asked. "Brain cancer," she had said. "And now her husband has it in the pancreas."

Now Mary Ellen looked over the dining room table. Nate had helped her add the extra leaf in the center, and she and Jane Anne had set the table with her favorite silver and her more casual Blue Canton china. After that she'd pressed her linen napkins and wiped the more casual crystal glasses and set them out. Then she'd polished the silver candlesticks and the silver salt and pepper shakers and the silver bowl in the center in which she had a nice bouquet of periwinkle hydrangeas. (She'd had to buy them at the florist since the pale green ones in her garden were well past their peak.)

She stepped out onto the back piazza where she'd set a table for the kids, complete with sturdy paper plates, bowls of Goldfish, grapes, strawberries, and their own little bouquet of hydrangeas.

She'd quickly added three additional spots for the second Bennett clan, and she'd run over to Jane Anne's and borrowed a few folding chairs to add to the porch.

"Mary Ellen," Jane Anne had said. "You aren't going to have those children in your house, are you?"

"What other choice do I have?" she had said as she took the folding chairs from Jane Anne's shed. "If I want to see my daughter, I have to have them."

Jane Anne cocked her hip and planted her right fist firmly on it. "You're a better woman than me." She scoffed at the air. "Well, call me when it's all over and I'll help you clean up."

"I will," Mary Ellen called back over her shoulder.

Mary Ellen heard car doors opening and closing in her driveway. It was Meg and Preston and the three children, Preston, Cooper, and Katherine. No one disliked Marney more than Meg, so Mary Ellen had to think how to break the news to her.

"La La!" Katherine called out as Preston and Cooper banged on the door so hard the panes rattled.

"Coming!" she said, shocked by the emotional delight in her voice. "La La's coming!" And she opened the door to find her three adorable grandchildren standing before her, looking exceedingly clean and darling. The boys were in bright yellow and blue Izod shirts tucked into pressed khaki shorts and wearing navy blue belts with the South Carolina flag stitched across them.

Katherine was in a yellow and blue gingham sundress that crisscrossed in the back and was trimmed with bright blue rickrack along the edges.

Preston Sr. was dressed just like the boys, and Meg wore a pair of pedal pushers that was made of the same material as Katherine's dress along with a white linen tunic and some bright yellow espadrilles.

Preston presented a serene smile, the same one he used when he was concealing an emotion or ignoring a question he didn't feel like answering. And Meg, while lovely in a fresh and freckled, well-kept way, could hardly veil her restlessness as her shoulders tensed and her eyes darted quickly here and there. Mary Ellen used to think this unsettled look was because it was hard for Meg to return to her old home after her parents split, but she had noticed over the last few years after Charles's passing that Meg seemed to carry this restlessness everywhere: a basketball game, a holiday party, one of the children's productions, and even at church on those rare occasions when Meg invited Mary Ellen to join them. Jane Anne thought the look had to do with Meg's eyes, which she was sure had already had some work done.

"Oh, don't be ridiculous," Mary Ellen had

said. "She's only thirty-six."

Jane Anne, whose nephew was a plastic surgeon in town, said, "Please join us in the twenty-first century, Mary Ellen. They start early, honey. Very early. That way it's not so noticeable as the years go by."

Mary Ellen hugged them all as tight as she could. "Come in! Come in!" she said. Then she smiled at Meg. "I'm so glad y'all are here."

"Thanks for having us," Preston said as he leaned down to peck her cheek.

Meg handed her a bottle of chardonnay. It was nice and cold. "Glad you like the apron, Mother," she said. "It looks adorable on you."

Mary Ellen stepped back so her daughter could get a better look. "Oh, I do, darling. I needed something fresh to cook in."

Cooper came out of the kitchen brandishing a brownie. "Where are your manners?" Meg came over and snatched it out of his hand. He was the chunky one in the family, the middle one, and he'd had trouble for the first few years of elementary school until they realized he needed reading glasses. He had a sparkle in his eyes that Mary Ellen loved.

"It's okay," she said. "Julia's running a little late. They can have a bite of something before she arrives. It's fine by me."

Cooper looked to his mother and nodded triumphantly, then he slid it out of her manicured hand and took a hearty bite.

"Mama, please don't undermine my authority," she said. "We're trying to follow a certain model here. And we need you to support us."

Mary Ellen exhaled. Meg and Preston were very serious about their role as parents, and they went to many a parenting class and conference on the subject.

"Of course, Meg." Mary Ellen took the bottle of wine from her daughter's little hands. "I'm sorry, honey. I'm just so glad y'all are here."

Meg looked at Preston and rolled her eyes. "So how long until Julia will be here?"

Mary Ellen winced as she took the bottle to the butler's pantry and retrieved the corkscrew for Preston. As he went to work opening the bottle, Mary Ellen lowered her voice and said, "Well, Meg, she'll be here in about fifteen minutes, and she had a child care snag."

Meg's eyes widened and Mary Ellen could almost see her daughter's pupils expanding. Her back went as rigid as a mannequin's. "What does that mean?"

Preston seemed to be holding his breath,

and Mary Ellen turned to him and then back to Meg and then over to the kids, who had already opened the toy drawer in the living room and were trying out the light-up yo-yos from the Dollar Store as well as an old electronic Simon game.

"It means the children are coming with her, Meg."

Meg batted her eyes. "It's Margaret, Mother. *Margaret.*"

Mary Ellen could feel the burn beneath her arms and she gladly accepted the glass of wine Preston handed her.

"I'm sorry, sweetheart." And she was sorry, sorry for everything.

Meg set her chiseled jaw and turned to Preston, who was smiling that same smile again. "It'll be fine, honey," he said. "It'll be good to see Julia, and the kids can play together out in the backyard, all right?"

"You think I want our children mingling with those kids?"

The buzzer for the tomato pies buzzed and Mary Ellen gladly excused herself. She took her fresh toile mitts and pulled the pies out one by one and set them on a hand towel on the counter to cool.

She was half-angry and half-sad, but more than any of those things, she was excited to have her family together for a few hours, feasting on one of her well-prepared meals. And she prayed Meg would see it that way and make the best of it.

"Hey there." She could hear Preston calling from the foyer to the piazza. Julia had arrived! Preston opened the front door wide just as Mary Ellen made her way back to the front of the house. When she rounded the corner of the living room to the foyer, she stopped. There, standing on the threshold, was a sight that stole her breath. Julia, radiant in a pale yellow sundress with her hair up, two girls — one tall with a thick, dark mane and the other thin as a reed with blond hair and serious hazel eyes — and then a little golden, curly-haired boy with full cheeks and a little birthmark near his chin and luminous brown eyes that were her husband's, precisely. The boy looked at her and blinked, and it was as if she were staring at the old portrait of her husband at age three, though it had come to life and was wearing a smudged dinosaur T-shirt and camouflage shorts. The whole room seemed to hold its breath, even Meg's kids in the living room came and stood in the foyer to behold these strangers, bathed in the afternoon light.

"Welcome," Mary Ellen said as she stepped forward and reached out her hand to introduce herself to each of them. And then she embraced Julia, who was watching her, smiling. "Oh, I've missed you," she said as she took her in her arms and rocked her back and forth. Her grown daughter. In the flesh. Looking more alive and more youthful than she had in years.

"Me too, Mama." Julia returned her embrace heartily. "Me too."

CHAPTER 20
MARGARET

Meg (who would always feel like Meg in this house) could feel the bile rising in her throat as she watched her mother embrace Julia. She took another sip of her wine and narrowed her eyes, watching the three mismatched vagabonds in the doorway. The pitiful little ones who were daily devouring up what was rightfully hers.

And Julia, the traitor. None of the shame and loss Meg had experienced for decades now would have ever happened if it weren't for Julia bringing her slutty friend home to mooch off of her parents summer after summer.

Not unlike their father, Julia had a penchant as a child for collecting strays — stray animals, friends with oddities, any living being that was awkward or weak or ill-fitting. One spring she brought home a half-dead puppy from the Sergeant Jasper Dumpster, thin and whimpering, who defecated worms on the piazza. Her father took the pup to the vet and spent hundreds of dollars trying to get the animal well. The creature died before the end of the week, and Meg and Julia had to go without new dresses for Easter because of the unexpected expense of their futile attempts to save his miserable, withering life.

Julia had only shrugged and worn the same dress she had the year before without seeming bothered. And Meg, who had to wear Julia's hand-me-downs to begin with (except for Easter and Christmas, when she was allowed to pick out her own new dress at the children's boutique), feigned illness and stayed in her nightgown all of Easter day because she refused to go to church in the same dress, the one with the little purple Magic Marker stain in the front fold of the skirt that she'd been wearing all spring.

Now her son Preston tugged on her arm and motioned for her to bend down. He knew about these children, but he'd never met them. "Are those the ones from Granddaddy's other family?"

She looked him in the eye and nodded solemnly.

He ground his teeth, a habit he had picked up from her when she was disgusted, then blinked several times before looking back at them. Preston was the child she connected with most. He saw the world the way she did, in clear blacks and whites, and she appreciated him for that.

Her youngest, Katherine, who had not yet put the whole sad, embarrassing story of her grandparents' divorce together, came up on Meg's other side. "Who are those kids, Mama?"

"They are some children your Aunt Julia has been caring for because their mother is sick."

"Oh," she said as she stuck out her bottom lip, assessing them. "Where do they live?"

"Edisto Island," Cooper, the middle son, said as he came into the doorway, all smiles. Then he looked at his mother and tried to conceal his excitement. Cooper loved drama, and she knew he could sense the tension in the room. Meg rolled her eyes at him.

Then Julia turned to Meg and her crew who were huddled together in the corner of the foyer near the formal living room. They must have looked like models in a Vineyard Vines photo shoot that had just been rained out. Attending this dinner was a concession Meg had made to her mother, but already it was more than she bargained for.

"Meg . . . I mean . . . Margaret," she said to Meg. And she stepped over and embraced her younger sister, who hugged back as loosely as she could.

Julia always had a strange smell — part earth, part urban. Would it hurt her to put on a little perfume? Meg grimaced as she watched Julia bend down to embrace the three children who waited for their mother's nod to embrace back.

Then Julia stood and turned to Meg's husband. "Great to see you, Preston." She flashed her big smile. He was holding out his hand to shake hers, but she opened her thin arms wide and he embraced her back. While Meg complained about Julia regularly, he never had much to say back. Because of this Meg suspected that he admired Julia, making her way in Manhattan. Truth be told, he had regretted turning down a job with one of the big banks up there when he finished getting his dual business and law degree ten years earlier. He had been offered a marginally good salary with an opportunity to grow big, but they couldn't turn down the better offer from an established Charleston law firm. Plus, Meg was already expecting Preston, and she had no desire to raise a child in a cold, crowded city where the only person she knew was her strange artist sister.

Mary Ellen was still trying to coax the limpish children over the threshold. Meg watched as Julia turned back to them and motioned for them to come over. They made their way tentatively toward the living room where Julia introduced them to Preston, Cooper, and Katherine.

"I know who you are. You're my granddad's children," Cooper said. He was the first to reach out his hand and shake theirs. "I guess that technically, you're my aunts and uncle."

The younger girl, the waifish one, glanced nervously up toward her older sister and then to Julia. And the little boy, the spitting image of Meg's father, just cocked his head in confusion as if Cooper had just said, "I know who you are. You're Martians from another galaxy."

The eldest girl shrugged and tried to conceal her blush. She appeared to be her mother's daughter. Attractive in an exotic way with a tough outer shell. She'd probably slit your throat if you handed her a knife. She had a book in her hands, *The Fellowship of the Ring.* Meg had no appreciation for fantasy novels and had discouraged her children from reading them. They were, in her opinion, a waste of time. Why not read a biography or at least a historical novel?

"I guess you're right, Cooper," Julia said, as the hostess of this dreadful event, their mother, popped over and said, "I've got juice boxes and treats out on the porch. I set out the old croquet set too, and the mini-trampoline and some crayons and paper . . ."

"C'mon, let's go!" Cooper said to the new children, and they followed him, with Katherine trailing a few strides behind, out to the backyard, though the waifish one looked back a few times at Julia, who nodded encouragingly.

Preston rolled his eyes at Meg and she gave him a little push toward the backyard. "Go on," she said. "I bet you're the only one who knows the croquet rules, so you can teach everyone." Preston turned and walked toward the back door slowly with a serious face. His father tousled his head on the way and then turned to Julia. "Can I pour you a glass of wine?"

"A little one," she said. She set her red leather bag down and readjusted her loose French twist.

"So when is Jed coming?" Their mother beamed. She was looking back and forth between Meg and Julia as if this was the

238

happiest day of her life.

"Oh, Mama, he had to cancel." Julia reached over and patted her mother's forearm tenderly. "I'm sorry. He had something else he'd forgotten about."

"Well, that's okay," Mary Ellen said, flapping her hands in the air like a wren. "I'll track him down and have him again another time." She leaned in toward her girls. "I sure would love to see the grown-up version of him. Jane Anne says he's quite the surgeon and professor at MUSC. And I was so sorry to hear about his parents. They were both young. In their early seventies or maybe younger than that."

Julia smiled back and forth between Meg and her mother. Then she turned to Meg as Preston handed her a glass of wine. "Your children are just beautiful, Margaret. And they've grown up so much. I think the last time I saw Katherine she had just learned to walk and still had that full baby face."

Meg softened slightly. Her children were her pride and joy. She had worked hard to raise them well — reading all of the books by the experts, taking all of the parenting classes at school and at church, comparing notes with the mothers she admired most. She was serious about discipline, about setting goals, about order in the house, about academics, and about good manners. She was vigilant about the company they kept and made sure they were not exposed to any bad influences. This was of the utmost importance.

Preston, who was in fourth grade, had suffered a few issues with reading and this had led to some outbursts on his part at home and at school. He had a temper; that was true. But with enough clear order and established authority and consequences, they seemed to have it under control. Cooper, on the other hand (who was only in second grade but smart as a whip), liked to stir the pot, and he wasn't afraid to disagree with her. She found this exasperating, and she worried he'd be rebellious as he grew up. For this reason she came down harder on him than anyone, but she couldn't quite get rid of whatever it was in him that made him unafraid to present an opposing perspective. And whatever it was in him that made him drawn to people outside of their carefully selected circle. As for Katherine, she was easy enough, a little in her own world, but pliable and teachable. All was well with her.

"Thank you," she said. "They are a lot of work, but I enjoy it."

Julia looked down at her engagement ring

and Meg asked to examine it. "I hope it's not too late for me," her big sister said.

It probably wasn't too late, Meg thought. But the risks did go up substantially every year, and Julia would be forty before her wedding date. There was a strong chance she'd have to go the in vitro route. Or maybe adopt, a topic that made Meg nervous but likely appealed to Julia.

"We're looking forward to meeting your fiancé." Preston nodded and smiled at Julia. "Mary Ellen tells us he is a quintessential British chap and one hundred percent charming."

"Oh yes." Mary Ellen clapped her hands. "I met him last year. He just adores Julia, I can tell you that."

Julia grinned and turned to Meg. "Well, I know you all can't make it to the wedding, but maybe you could come to New York sometime this spring with the kids and you could all stay at Simon's. He's got a large corner condo with lots of windows on the Upper West Side. And he has a guest bedroom and a pull-out couch in the den. I'll be moving in with him after the wedding."

Meg furrowed her brow. That was the last trip she ever wanted to make. "Oh yes, we'd love to." She put on a pretend smile and turned toward Preston. "Wouldn't we?"

Preston shifted his weight and brought his fist to his mouth as he cleared his throat. She knew he knew her fake face, and he was probably deciding how enthusiastically he should respond. Knowing him, he would like to visit.

"Well, I'm sure Bess will miss you, Julia," Mary Ellen piped in. Then she motioned for everyone to take a seat in the living room.

"Oh no," Julia said as she sat down on the end of the Chippendale sofa. "I'm going to keep the old spot for a painting studio so I'll still see them a good bit."

"Perfect," Mary Ellen said as Preston took his place in their father's old leather wingback reading chair and Meg took a spot on the leather ottoman at his feet. How many times had she sat there as her father read her the funny papers or asked her about her day at school? The smell of the leather and the cracked surface of it brought back too many emotions, so she stood and took a seat on the other end of the sofa a good two feet away from Julia.

Mary Ellen took a seat on the gilded Victorian chair with the pale green silk upholstery before standing again, picking up the crystal bowl of pickled shrimp and silver skewers, and passing the bowl around.

They chatted briefly about the wedding plans and Meg's children's interests and Preston's family and then about the week and about Aunt Dot's recovery and about Julia's Fulbright and her upcoming trip to Budapest. No one mentioned Marney and that was fine by Meg. The cancer could devour her for all Meg cared. She knew some of the folks who were all into grace at her church wouldn't think it was very Christian to think that way, but some desires she would not compromise. Didn't justice matter? Didn't certain actions reap certain consequences? She sure hoped so. If not, what was the point?

The voices of children in the yard rose and fell. More than once Preston had to go out and settle a dispute over the rules of croquet and whose turn it was. After the small talk, the conversation came to a lull, and Meg admired her new manicure as their mother excused herself to put the final touches on the buffet.

When it was time to eat, the children came in with their paper plates and went through the abundant buffet line Mary Ellen had set out in the pantry. Marney's kids had wide eyes as if they'd never seen so much food, and they helped themselves to huge portions of fried chicken and macaroni and cheese and brownies.

The adults ate at the dining room table where Meg and her family of origin had hosted every Thanksgiving, Christmas, and Easter dinner. Her father almost always invited an odd assortment of family, friends, and neighbors to share in the feast. Aunt Dot was usually present, and old Mr. Vincent, who had such a bad case of palsy it took him several tries to bring his fork to his mouth. And for years they had the Wentworth family down the street because Mr. Wentworth's wife had been hospitalized for some sort of mental illness. Mary Ellen always said, "The more the merrier." And she cooked for days preparing for a holiday gathering. Meg never felt comfortable around the strangers at her table. They were loud, they ate too much, they didn't always smell good or have decent manners, and more often than not, they ate the last slice of pie or the heart of the cobbler before it ever made its way to her.

After dessert the kids raced outside to play croquet again. Meg could hear her eldest son's voice. Preston was frustrated, and when she turned to check on them, she watched him yank the club out of young Charlie's hand. Meg shook her head and watched her husband, who looked up from his cobbler as the voices rose again. He wrinkled his brow, but then he shrugged and took another hearty bite of dessert as things settled back down.

Their mother was asking them about all of their old friends and catching them up on the news of the neighborhood. "Mr. Gallagher giving you any more trouble?" Preston asked.

"Quite the contrary." Mary Ellen looked toward his house and smiled. Meg could tell she was carefully weighing her words. When she went to open her mouth to continue, there was a loud knocking noise and then there was a horrifying shriek from the backyard.

Meg thought it was Katherine and she ran out through the back porch to the garden, half-expecting one of the vagabond children to be assaulting her daughter. The little boy, Charlie, had a stream of blood running down his face, and he was shrieking and shrieking and running in circles as the little waifish girl chased him.

"Preston hit him," Cooper was shouting, pointing to Preston, who was scowling and saying, "No, I didn't." He looked to his mother and pointed at the little waifish girl. "She did it. She hit him."

Meg's husband was right on her heels. "That's not true," Cooper said. He pointed to his brother. "He hauled off and hit him with the mallet, Dad."

"You're a liar, Cooper," Preston said.

"Oh no!" Julia came running out and called back to her mother, "Please bring a towel, Mama. Charlie's bleeding!"

Julia darted over and scooped Charlie up from his circle-running and immediately applied pressure with the linen napkin she had carried out from the table. After a moment, she peeled back the cloth and they all glimpsed the gash. Julia winced and Meg watched her turn to her mother. "He needs a stitch or glue or whatever they do nowadays."

"No!" Charlie screamed a terrified scream. "I don't want to see the doctor!"

Julia rubbed her cheek against his and whispered, "Charlie, it will be okay. It won't be bad. I promise." She turned to Meg. "Where should I take him?"

"Roper, I guess." Meg straightened up. "Their ER is a lot faster than MUSC's."

Meg's husband was still trying to get to the bottom of what had happened. If Preston had done it, if he had done it on purpose, there needed to be a serious consequence.

Katherine hadn't seen it, and the eldest daughter had been reading her book on the porch, so she wasn't a witness. Cooper was biased toward anyone other than Preston and so Meg turned to the waifish little child.

Meg grabbed her by the arm. "What happened? I need to know what happened," she said.

She looked the child firmly in the eye and could not hold back her distress. "I want you to tell me what happened. Now." Then she tightened her grip as firmly as she would one of her own. She ground her back teeth. "Tell me."

"Meg, let go of her!" Julia screamed as she stood up with Charlie in her arms and walked over. Heath was out in the garden by now, and she pulled Etta away from Meg and toward Julia, who had two trails of blood now running down her forearm and her fresh-looking — albeit cheap-looking — yellow sundress.

"I need to know, Julia." Meg pressed down on the wrinkles at the bottom of her linen tunic and addressed her sister firmly. She nodded toward Charlie. "He's okay. He just needs a stitch. I need to know who is responsible. Get this girl to speak up."

"No," Julia said and Etta hid behind her. "She *can't.*"

Meg rolled her eyes. She had seen the child whisper something in her brother's ear earlier that afternoon. "Don't be ridiculous, Julia. I saw her talking to her brother a little while ago."

"Yes, she does." Julia's voice was a combination of sadness and anger. "But she doesn't speak to anyone else. And I'm not going to make her."

Julia turned to Heath. "Will you grab my pocketbook and keys in the foyer? We've got to get to the hospital."

"Oh, I'm so sorry." Mary Ellen was patting Julia on the back as she carried Charlie toward the car. Meg followed too and watched as Julia put him in the middle of the backseat where the car seat was. Then Julia instructed Heath to sit on one side and asked her to keep applying mild pressure on the bloodied linen napkin on his forehead. Next she helped Etta in on the other side. The girl snapped herself into her seat and immediately started rubbing her brother's arm.

"I'm just so sorry," Mary Ellen said.

Julia quickly hugged her mother and turned to Meg, who narrowed her eyes and muttered, "As soon as the little boy talks, you need to call me."

Julia nodded solemnly, then jumped in the

driver's seat. Meg turned back to the garden as the crunch of Julia's tires moving quickly over the driveway stones reverberated in her ears and chest.

"He did it, Mom." Cooper pointed to Preston as she walked back over to her children.

"I didn't," Preston muttered angrily. "The dumb girl did it."

Meg felt her temples pulse. She had a familiar taste in her mouth. The taste of bitterness and shame. Preston Sr. looked to her. He was holding Katherine, who was crying from all of the excitement. Meg was the expert on discipline in the house, and while he attended the parenting classes and read some of the books, he always seemed to defer to her.

"Well, you're both going to be punished." She put her hands on her hips and looked back and forth at her two sons. "No television for two weeks. And no dessert."

"Ah, c'mon, Mom!" Cooper put his palms up in a gesture of innocence. "That's ridiculous."

Preston just ground his teeth and steadily pounded the croquet club on the soft, carefully pruned grass of her mother's garden.

"Want to make it three?" Meg said to Cooper. She could see his cheeks reddening and his eyes filling with tears. He shook his head as though he couldn't stand her.

"Don't try me, son," she said, then turned to her mother, who was wringing her hands by the pittosporum bushes . . . as clueless as always, Meg thought, as to how and why things had all gone so suddenly wrong.

"We have to go, Mother," she said.

CHAPTER 21
JED

Jed strode briskly down Savage Street. It was dark, but he thought he saw Julia's rental car parked on the street so he pulled into the first available spot and headed toward Mary Ellen Bennett's house.

Maybe they'd still be having dessert. He'd gotten out of the set-up date as quickly as possible. It was something his colleagues, Dana and Rick Strozier, had arranged weeks ago with Dana's first cousin, Stephanie, who owned her own wedding-planning business in Charleston. It kind of gave Jed the hives just to think about dating a wedding planner, but Dana and Rick had been talking her up for months. One night not too long ago — after they all finished a six-hour operation involving the removal of three separate portions of a man's large intestine — Dana pressed him again about it, and he said, "What do I have to lose?"

They'd met at the bar at Husk for a drink.

A drink to him meant just a drink, but she'd ordered several appetizers and more than one blackberries-in-champagne cocktail. She was nice enough. Attractive in that sort of carefully made-up and put-together way. She had a bridesmaid luncheon and a rehearsal dinner to plan the next day, so he thought it would all go very quickly, but she wanted to talk on and on about her life, the local celebrity weddings she'd coordinated, and her adventures traveling the world after business school. He was relieved when she got a call from her current bridezilla who was having a meltdown over a dress malfunction at a nearby hotel.

She rolled her eyes as she put down her phone. "I better go see about her."

"No problem," he said. "Best of luck with the weddings."

She'd jutted out her lower lip, which looked as though it had been surgically augmented. Had she wanted him to talk her into staying longer? He just wasn't up to it.

Then she'd shrugged her shoulders. "Okay. But I'm going to tell Dana you didn't even spring for dinner."

He'd laughed cautiously. Then he quickly paid the bill, walked her to her car, and darted over to the old Bennett home in hopes of seeing Julia.

As he walked toward the open privacy door of the single house, he heard voices and the clamoring of dishes. He stepped up onto the piazza and peered through the front door that was open.

Through the foyer he could see the half-cleared dining room with the candles still glowing. His second cousin, Jane Anne Thornton, peered around from the butler pantry.

"Jed!" she cackled. She was a tiny little spitfire of a woman, in her midseventies by now, and she had on a hot-pink apron and her signature gold charm bracelet that was as big as she was and clamored loudly wherever she went.

She called over her shoulder, "Come see who's come to call, Mary Ellen!"

"Oh my," said the voice in the other room. "I'm not sure I can take any more excitement."

The elegant woman was wiping her hands on a kitchen towel as she rounded the corner. Her eyes widened with surprise. "Are you Jed?"

"Yes, ma'am." He couldn't contain his big grin or his delight over the amazing smells coming from the kitchen.

He embraced her and then his cousin. "I'm sorry I'm so late." He looked back and forth from the dining room to the living room. "I was hoping that y'all might be eating dessert. I really wanted to see Julia . . . and you too."

Mary Ellen put down the towel on the butler's pantry counter and dusted off her hands. "Well, I'm so sorry you missed everyone. It all broke up very quickly after little Charlie got hurt."

"Little Charlie was here? What happened?"

"I don't know for sure." Mary Ellen said this in the direction of Jane Anne. Jed had the feeling that they had talked about it since all of the other guests had left.

"Julia brought the kids because Glenda and Skeeter were both ill. They were playing outside after dinner with Meg's children."

"Margaret," Jane Anne corrected her.

She chuckled. "Yes, Margaret. Anyway, Little Charlie got hit in the head with a croquet mallet and the blame was flying every which way —"

Jane Anne cocked her hip and pointed at Jed. "But we know who did it."

"Is he all right?" Jed pictured little Charlie's face. He hated the idea of him in pain.

"Well, yes," Mary Ellen said. "Julia just called to say they were on the way home from the ER. It was a pretty long gash, but not real deep, thankfully. Julia said they just put some of that skin glue on it, and it really wasn't too bad at all."

Jed exhaled. "Wow. I did really miss it, didn't I?"

"Well, you must sit down and have some dinner or at least some dessert if you've already eaten."

"I haven't eaten," Jane Anne said. "And Mary Ellen was going to make me and our other neighbor a big plate."

"I'm here," a burly voice called from the piazza. "And I'm hungry."

"Well, come on in, Nate," Mary Ellen said.

A gruff gentleman rounded the corner. "My mouth has been watering all day from the smells coming from this kitchen."

Mary Ellen beamed with pride. "Jed, this is my next-door neighbor, Nate Gallagher."

"Pleasure to meet you." Jed put out his hand.

Nate returned the handshake. "So this must be the surgeon."

"Yes," Jane Anne said. "He's just getting here too, and we will be offended if he doesn't join us, won't we, Nate?"

"Most certainly," the man said as he winked at each of the ladies. "Plus, it would be a terrible mistake" — he pointed to Mary

Ellen — "to miss one of this lady's meals. She might very well be the best cook in Charleston."

"Oh, I don't doubt it." Jed smiled and turned to the hostess. "I remember your meals on Edisto with great fondness."

Mary Ellen blushed and swatted away the compliment with the back of her hand.

"In fact, I've become a bit of a cook myself." Jed turned to her. "I've taken a few classes at the Maverick Kitchen and Alice's." He shook his head. "But I've never been able to replicate your shrimp and grits or your deviled eggs, and I've never found anyone else who could do it either, not even the best restaurants in town."

Mary Ellen laughed a delightful laugh as Jane Anne pulled out the chair at an unused place setting at the end of the table. "Have a seat, then," she said. "You are in for a treat."

As excited as Jed was to eat, he felt a longing in his heart as he stepped toward the table. His desire to see Julia was palpable, and he had to find a way to see her again before she left.

"May I make a phone call real quick? I'm so sorry. I just want to catch Julia before she goes over the bridge and out of cell service."

"Well, of course," Mary Ellen said. He could tell she was trying not to meet Jane Anne's eyes, which were already twinkling, probably with all sorts of notions. "We're in no hurry."

"No hurry at all," Jane Anne said. "We've got all night. Go on in the living room and call that beautiful girl."

"Jane Anne," Mary Ellen admonished.

"Well, she *is* beautiful." The lady shrugged her shoulders and walked toward the kitchen as if she owned the place. "Finish cleaning this crystal with us, Nate, and then we'll warm up some plates."

Jed smiled as the two ladies moved toward the kitchen with the gruff man following behind them, then he stepped into the stately living room, sat down on the Chippendale sofa, and hit Julia's number in his contacts.

"Hey," the warm voice said from the other end of the line.

"Hey there," he said. "I'm glad I caught you." His voice cracked as if he were fourteen again. He cleared his throat. "I heard you had quite the evening."

"Boy, word travels fast around the hospital, doesn't it?"

He smiled. "Actually, I'm at your mother's house right now. I was hoping to catch you all for dessert. She filled me in on the whole thing. How's the little guy doing?"

"Well, after we promised him a full day of fishing tomorrow and a candy bar from the gas station on the way home, he was hunky dory. There was a lot of blood at first, but thankfully it wasn't too bad and they just sprayed some of that glue on. He seems right as rain now. He's gobbling up his Kit Kat and slurping down a can of Sprite."

"Ah, to be the age when candy was the cure-all."

"It would be nice, wouldn't it?" she said.

"Hey, I'm really sorry I missed you tonight." He couldn't hold back. He was too tired and old to play any games.

"Don't be," she said. "You wouldn't have wanted to partake of that particular gathering. My sister is like a stone, and I'm pretty sure she can't stand me. You could cut the tension in the air with a knife."

"Hmm," he said. "Well, I'm glad you got to see your mother and your nephews and niece."

"Me too," she said. "I won't be seeing them for a while so I'm glad it worked out." She answered a question from one of the children in the backseat, then she said, "So how was your *appointment*?"

His cheeks reddened. She was onto him.

"Nothing special. Kind of relieved it's over."

"Okay," she said. "Well, I hope it wasn't too painful."

"Listen," he said, "I want to cook for you one more time before you leave. I think I can switch some things around at work. Will you let me come out and make you all dinner on Friday? As kind of a farewell?"

She paused for a moment. "Yeah. That would be nice. Our crab trap is full if you want to use those. I was thinking of making some crab cakes in the next day or so."

"That's one of my specialties," he said. "I'll be out there midafternoon day after tomorrow, and I can probably have dinner ready at six or so. I'll pick y'all up by boat."

"Sounds nice," she said. "Oh, and don't leave my mother's without getting some food. She cooked enough for an army."

"I won't," he said. "She and Jane Anne are making me a plate as we speak."

"Good," she said.

"Tell the kids hi for me, and tell Charlie I'll take a good look at him when I get out there."

"I will," she said.

He swallowed hard. "And let me know if you need anything between now and Friday, okay?"

"Okay," she said. "Good night, Jed."

"Good night, Julia."

"Hmm-hm." Jane Anne was standing in the doorway with her hands on her hips. "Dinner is served," she said. "But you may need a moment to wash that blush off of your face." She winked at him.

He stood and looked around the living room for a moment. There were photos of Julia and Meg everywhere — Christmases, summers sailing, out on the dock at Edisto. There was even one of Mr. Bennett with his arms around his two daughters. Julia was about eleven and Meg was eight. They were standing in front of a huge catch of fish — five flounder and half a dozen trout.

Then Jed turned to walk toward the dining room where the amazing smells were coming from and saw heaven on a plate — fried chicken, honey ham, tomato pie, deviled eggs, spinach salad.

"Now save room for dessert!" Mary Ellen said as they all took their places.

"And go slow," Jane Anne said. "We want to hear about everything going on in your life."

"Yes, ma'ams," he said to them. Being in their presence made him miss his own mother. He nodded at Nate, who seemed to have the same sentiment in his eyes. One that said, "We're lucky men tonight, aren't we?"

Jed couldn't have been happier to sit and chat with this band of senior Savage Street neighbors, and he did so until it was nearly midnight, sampling every dessert, sipping delicious sweet tea and then decaf coffee.

When he walked out to his car, as full and satisfied as he'd ever been, he looked up to the moon that was waning ever so slightly and uttered the first prayer he'd said in a long, long time.

"Thank you."

Chapter 22
Margaret

Meg curled herself up on the upholstered porch swing on her back deck, tucking her legs beneath her white eyelet nightgown. She had wept all the way over the Ravenel Bridge, all the way down Mathis Ferry Road, and all the way to the back of their Mount Pleasant subdivision where her three-story white clapboard home sat at the end of a cul-de-sac that overlooked the inmost fingertip of Molasses Creek.

Preston had dealt with the children without even asking: the bathing, the story reading, the teeth brushing, the vocabulary quizzing, the prayers. And now, as the last of the bedroom lights on the third floor was turned out, she balled herself up even tighter as he made his way out and took a seat beside her.

"You all right, honey?" He reached over and rubbed her knobby knees.

"No." She looked out toward the marsh.

Something was rustling in the tall grass. A squirrel or a possum or a raccoon. Its marble eyes flashed for a moment and then there was a *kerplunk* sound and the parting of the water as it crossed the narrow waterway to the opposite bank.

Preston yawned, untucked his golf shirt, and ran his fingers through his hair. She knew he'd had a deposition that morning and a Charlestowne Prep board meeting that afternoon. No doubt he was exhausted.

"C'mon now," he said. "It was a difficult night, but it's not the end of the world."

Difficult didn't begin to describe it. And neither did bad, tough, or challenging. Meg felt *exposed.* As if someone had ripped the mask off of her face for a moment, revealing the spindly little sister who didn't have any natural eye or artistic talent. The child who had no scholarships or awards or specific career aspirations. The kid sister whose own kid probably assaulted one of the little vagabonds, sending him to the emergency room. And all of this after she had bragged and bragged about how exceptional her children were, about how superior her mothering was. About how her life's work was yielding the sweetest of fruit.

Preston leaned over to massage her neck, but she stiffened. He fell back into the cushions, rocking the swing slightly. Then he watched the moon above the live oak trees as it cast its soft light on the creek. The beauty of the night made Meg all the more miserable, and she sucked her teeth as she held back the tears.

"What can I do to make you feel better?"

She gripped the swing's chain and cleared her throat. Then she swung her head toward him. "You can stop acting like Julia is the bee's knees." She scoffed and narrowed her eyes. "Just because she went off to New York and made a living painting bizarre, pointless images in tacky colors."

Preston gave her a side-angled glance. "The bee's knees?" He chuckled. "Honey, I know you've got some wounds from your childhood, but —"

"Don't go there." She held up her small, manicured hand. "Don't lecture me about my childhood when yours was downright idyllic."

He rolled his eyes. "Not this again."

Her throat tightened and she swallowed hard. "You've had everything, Preston. And you've always had it: two normal parents who stayed together, every material thing imaginable, an exceptional education, a well-paying job your father's friends hired you to do."

Preston shook his head and a little burst of air escaped his lips. "Okay, you win, Margaret. Your life was harder than mine. Your dad was a little crazy and your mom was a little clueless." He shook his head and met her gaze straight on. "But even so, you were loved. And that's a lot more than a lot of people can claim. You can't deny *that.*"

They both sat stone still for several minutes, and Meg became suddenly aware of the crickets chirping. *Loved, loved, loved,* she thought she heard in their repetitive calling, backing Preston up like a unanimous and unyielding jury.

Eventually her husband stood and stretched and looked back at her. "I'm no shrink, babe. But you and I both know that you can't hold on to this forever. Whatever it is that ties you in a knot about your family." He leaned down and stared at her until she looked up. "It's going to eat you up, Margaret. And it has the potential to devour our marriage and our kids too."

She turned away from his gaze. There was a gentle breeze that lifted the Spanish moss on the live oaks up and back down again, and it rustled the stiff, long fronds of the palmettos. She heard Preston sigh. Then he stepped away, calling back over his shoulder, "I'm going to check the evening news and the baseball scores, all right?"

Meg sat still as a statue, looking away as he walked back to the door. She heard the doorknob click and then the light come on in the den and then the muffled sound of the television. She looked back at her house and spotted the blue glow of her computer on the kitchen table. She hadn't posted anything on Facebook today. And she wondered, for a moment, what it would be like if people actually posted what was going on in their lives, what was ripping their hearts apart, what was turning them to stone. Perhaps she would write in her status box, *Wounds from my family of origin may destroy my marriage and the lives of my children.* Perhaps she would post the image that she had yet to shake after all of these years: driving out to the Edisto house to surprise her father one summer afternoon when she was seventeen. Finding her father embracing her sister's friend on the porch, a little too long, a little too close. Then meeting the girl's enormous blue eyes as she turned and stared Meg down. Meg was no fool. She knew just what those eyes were saying as her father backed away and hurried out to greet his daughter: *Isn't this too bad for you, kid sister? Isn't this too, too bad for you and your sweet little family?*

266

Meg kept the secret from Preston and her friends for as long as she could. She went off to Wofford College that next month and displayed the silver-framed Christmas picture of her family in her dorm room as if they were one happy unit. She pledged Tri-Delt after a long rush season, she studied history and English literature, she joined the community service organization and volunteered at the local soup kitchen, and she met Preston at the University of South Carolina on the weekends for football games and fraternity parties.

She managed to keep the secret under wraps her entire freshman year, though her father had already moved all of his belongings out of the Savage Street house by Christmas, leaving her mother needy and wringing her hands. By Easter her mother informed her that he had filed for divorce.

During this time, Meg learned how to put on a mask, and she busied herself with building friendships, heading up sorority committees, putting enough work into her academic life to get above-average grades, procuring a fine wardrobe, and exercising constantly so that she looked fantastic at all of the socials she attended on Preston's arm.

It wasn't until the news of Marney's pregnancy her senior year that she had to come clean. Her father was living with a woman half his age, and they were starting a second family.

Meg could remember her father showing up outside of her dorm room one October afternoon. He had driven the three hours to Wofford to break the news to her, sitting on her bed with his bushy, unkempt eyebrows furrowed in a look of concern.

"Marney's expecting, and we're getting married," he had said. "I'm sorry, Meg." He reached across the room to her, and she stepped back. "I didn't plan for it to turn out this way," he continued, his thick, tanned arm outstretched, his hands seeking her approval.

"You're a selfish oaf." She had stepped back and stared down on him in disgust. "An idiotic narcissist. And I can't believe I got stuck with you for a father."

He had dropped his arm and exhaled heavily. When she wouldn't return his gaze, he looked up at the ceiling of her dorm room, his brown eyes filling with water. "You're right, Meg." Then he looked back to her and their eyes met. "Everything you've said about me is true."

"Leave," she'd said, and he'd shaken his head before standing and shuffling to the door. Before she swung it open, she leaned against it and faced him. "You better provide for me until I get married, Dad. It's the least you can do."

He had nodded. "Of course I will."

Marney had lost that first baby, and for a few years Meg thought maybe that would be the end of it all. That they would split and he would come back to her mother. But when the woman announced her second pregnancy the same month Preston proposed to Meg, she knew that would never happen. And she would have to face her family shame at her own wedding when Marney showed up at the ceremony, bursting at the seams with her father's child in her womb, as the old ladies clucked and the bridesmaids whispered and giggled.

Now Meg listened to the crickets whose incessant calls were filling the night: *Loved. Loved. Loved.* And she realized how very worn out she was. How exhausting it was to wear her masks, to build her reputation, to prove to the world day in and day out that even though her parents were fools, she was not. She was a responsible, morally upstanding citizen. She could be counted on. She was worthy of admiration. She would not shame her husband or falter in any way. She had the blessed life, and she would not squander it.

Or would she?

Now Preston was snoring so loudly in the den that she could hear him outside. It was a familiar sound, a comforting sound, and she felt sad that her pain was wearing him down. But how could she help herself?

She uncurled her legs, turned off the porch light, and walked up the stairs to the den where she shook his knee until he roused, cut off the remote, and followed her to bed.

As she checked on each of her children before she tucked herself in beside her husband, pulling her clean white sheets beneath her chin, she replayed the horrid events of the evening in her mind, and then she replayed Preston's charge: *"You were loved. You were loved. You were loved."*

It's funny what the adult brain pulls up from childhood. There are certain seemingly insignificant moments that are forever seared in the memory. Perhaps children are interpreting the events correctly, but usually they can't understand the full context. She had read once that children were the best recorders and the worst interpreters, and she supposed that was true.

Meg often recalled the first time she and her father went sailing down Store Creek in the 420 he had bought for her the Christmas after she won the Junior Sailing Award at the Yacht Club. She was ten years old, and she had beaten out Preston Rutledge, who had won the last two years, as well as Tricia Simons, who had won the annual Junior Regatta that July.

Her dad had been a great sailor in his youth too, winning several awards and even sailing on the College of Charleston team, and he was delighted that she enjoyed the sport. Together, they had tied the sails and put the boat in the water, and he took his place by the jib sail and followed her directions as they drifted out into the creek, tacking left and then right into the wind as it carried them toward St. Pierre Creek.

"You make a great skipper," he had said after she yelled, "Tack!" and let out the main sheet, then ducked beneath the boom. He popped back up once the main sheet was steady again and he watched her until she met his proud gaze.

"You make a good crew member," she had responded as she held tight to the tiller extension and steered them to the right of a motorboat.

After the passing boat's wake faded, he reached over and patted her back. "We make a good team, you and me."

"We do," she had beamed back at him as

the wind pushed them out into the waterway. She couldn't stop smiling as she held
tight to the tiller and mainsheet, calling out
the next instruction. To have her father's attention, to have him proud of her ac-
complishments, her skill, her independence.
That was her true desire. To feel his love, to
know that he wanted to build her up and to
be a part of something she was good at,
something they both loved — it was pure
joy.

My dad and I make a good crew, she had
thought as they made their way out to the
bay, tacking left then right, the warm air
filling the sails. She believed this. It was her
truth. And she held it like a prized posses-
sion close to her heart until that day seven
years later when he disproved it right before
her teenage eyes, exposed it for the lie that
he must have always quietly known that it
was.

Chapter 23
Etta

The oldest brother did it. Preston. Not that you had any doubt, but just in case you had a shadow of one. Charlie kept jumping in front of him in the game, hitting the heavy, colored balls through the wired domes without waiting for everyone else.

"Just let him play around," the other brother, the younger one who smiled at me, had said. It was what I would have said too.

When Charlie hit one of Preston's balls, one of the blue ones, while Preston was looking the other way, his face puffed with anger once he turned back and realized what had happened. Then he jumped right in front of my brother and said, "My turn!" With that, he swung the club back hard and clocked Charlie right on his forehead, a little left of the center, so hard I could hear the knock of club on bone. It was no accident.

"What are you *doing*?" the younger brother hollered to Preston as I ran to Charlie, who had fallen on his rump and was stunned into silence himself, the way one is just after a bee sting or a fall from a swing that leaves you winded.

"It's okay," I whispered to him. But this was before he had fully inhaled or let down his hand from his forehead to see the blood. It scared me, both the blood and his silence, and he saw the fear in my eyes and that's when he drew in one large breath and shrieked a horrible shriek, then stood up and started running around in circles.

The grown-ups showed up quick after that, and Julia protected me from an enemy as she held my brother in her arms and stopped the blood from coming so fast. Heath and I followed her directions on the way to the hospital, and we took turns holding a bloody napkin on Charlie's forehead in the emergency room as Julia filled out the papers on a clipboard and insisted that the doctor see us as quickly as possible.

Two nights have passed and Charlie seems fine now as we sit on the little spit of land that shows up in the center of our creek at low tide. We are all in our bathing suits and life jackets swimming around and throwing chicken necks into the murky water where almost always one or two blue crabs is on the other end nibbling as we carefully pull them out. Jed will be here soon to collect all of the crabs. He's making us supper tonight.

Tomorrow Julia leaves, and I feel uneasy about her leaving. She spent the last two days recleaning the house, washing the sheets and clothes and towels, cleaning out and restocking the refrigerator, and running the vacuum cleaner. She changed Phydeaux's collar and still has not let him back inside, though Charlie snuck him onto the porch a few times. She also made us pick up our rooms and clean out our drawers and refold all of our clothes. Julia helped Charlie with this, but Heath and I were on our own. Heath hemmed and hawed about it at first, but by the end of the day yesterday we all felt better. Our rooms haven't been this clean since one of the enemies came by to inspect a few years ago. It feels good to put things in order.

Last night Heath came into my room to see how I was coming along. "Let's try and keep it this way," she said.

I nodded, and she walked up to me and rubbed my back. We are both eager to see Mama again. And we are excited to see Brooke too. But we are both going to miss Julia. She is part of our family, after all, even though she does not like my mama and would do anything in the world to avoid her.

Yesterday Julia called her old art teacher and told her about me, and she left a note with a check and the woman's number and e-mail address. She wants me to have some private lessons at the local arts school if Mama says it's okay. She also wants me to send her a copy of my work after I have the lessons because she wants to see my progress.

"Do you think you will be Etta's art teacher one day?" Charlie asked last night as we played go fish on the porch after supper.

Heath looked up from her hand to correct him. "Art professor."

"Maybe," Julia said and winked at me.

I looked down at my hand of cards and smiled.

Now as I throw my chicken neck out into the dark water, I can't help but think of Mary Ellen Bennett's house and how beautiful it was, like a scene in a book or a movie. Everything was fancy and neat and there were a lot of paintings framed in gold and a lot of photographs of Julia and her sister when they were younger. There was even one with Daddy in it. He had his arms around his daughters, and he looked very happy and very proud and very strong. His hair wasn't all the way white like it was when I knew him, and his middle wasn't quite so wide.

And then there was the garden where the awful croquet game took place. The garden was a lot like how I picture *The Secret Garden* because there were stone walls on two sides and walls of thick green bushes on the other two. There weren't roses in the garden the way there are in the story, but the scent of roses was strong in the air. I peeked through the bushes and found some next door, several bushes in a kind of maze of seashells and bricks.

My dad's first family in his first home must have been a lot different than my family. They must have had a clean, ordered life with good health and good food and perhaps no enemies. I guess I am a little jealous of Julia. She had Daddy all the way until she grew up. And she didn't have to see him go. I wonder why.

I guess the sunlight man knows the answer. Or maybe even Aunt Dot.

"Are you feeling okay, Etta?" Julia says to me now. She walks over and puts the back of her hand on my forehead. "You look awfully pale."

Come to think of it my stomach does feel like it's twisting itself up, but I think it's because some sand got in the peanut butter and banana sandwiches we brought to the island for lunch.

Julia hands me a bottle of water. "Drink some of this. We're going to pack up and head home in a little while."

Just as she says this, we see a boat coming around the bend in the creek. The man driving it has on shades and a T-shirt and a bathing suit that's navy blue with white tropical flowers on it so I hardly know who he is at first. Then I see that it's Jed in his little Boston Whaler.

"Hey there!" Julia waves to him.

"How's it going?" he says as he circles back and throws his anchor.

Julia rubs my back. "Okay," she says, looking at me. "I think."

"Okay?" Charlie hollers at Julia as if she's just made the understatement of the century. "It's going *great,* Jed!" He tries to lift up the bucket to show him our catch. He can't do it so Heath goes over to help him. We must have caught at least twelve blue crabs plus there are a lot more in the trap by the dock. I can hear the little creatures clacking their claws together as Jed anchors the boat and hops out where he momentarily loses a flip-flop in the pluff mud.

"Impressive, little man." Jed finds his shoe, slides his large foot in it, and walks over to the bucket to take a look inside. He raises his eyebrows. "Extremely impressive."

Then he bends down with his hands on his knees, takes off his sunglasses, and lets them fall so that the rope he has tied around his neck catches them. "Let me take a look at that head of yours."

Julia leaves my side for a moment and stands by Jed, who begins to examine Charlie's forehead, looks up at her, and then back to Charlie again.

Jed looks at Julia as if he could eat her up, but he tries to hide it. Julia's cheeks are turning a little pink so she lowers her sun hat and takes on a more serious, teacherly look.

Now Jed puts both of his thumbs on Charlie's forehead, concentrating now, and turns his chin up toward the light. It looks a whole lot better than it did two days ago. The swelling has gone down and Julia has had him dunk it in the salty water of the creek twice a day and let the sun dry it. She says that's what she had to do once when she cut her shin real bad on an oyster bed as a kid at Edisto, and it worked.

Jed looks Charlie in the eye, puts his

hands on his little shoulders, and smiles. "Doesn't look bad at all." He turns to Julia now. "I don't even think it's going to leave a mark."

Charlie smiles back and puffs up his suntanned chest. I can tell he feels good being around a fellow man, a big man, a man who knows how to examine gashes and how to predict how they will heal and how to cut diseases out of people. He shakes his head and then runs over to grab another chicken neck. "Want to try?"

"Sure," Jed says. "I haven't done this since I was a kid."

Jed ties the rope to the neck and then to a stick and tosses it out in the water. A few minutes later he is reeling it in, and he obviously forgot how to pick a blue crab up because he goes right for the back and gets pinched pretty bad on that tender little flap of skin between his thumb and forefinger.

"Son of a — !" he hollers and shakes his hand until the creature lets go.

"Let me show you how to do it," Charlie says, and he strides after the large blue crab, grabs him by his last set of hind legs so that his pinchers are facing out, holds it up to Jed, and then drops it in the bucket.

Everyone laughs, especially Julia.

"All right," Jed says. "You're showing me

up today, big man. Let me have another go at it."

"Go ahead." Charlie beams, and then he and Jed stand side by side, reeling in one crab after the next as my stomach really starts to cramp.

"You don't feel good, do you?" Julia walks back over to me. I hold my stomach and shake my head.

Jed notices what's going on. "Let me give y'all a ride back to the dock."

"That would be great," Julia says. Then we gather up our towels and cooler and bucket and nets and hooks pretty quickly, and Jed goes over to the boat and holds out his hand and helps us all in one by one before driving us quickly back to our dock.

On the way back, I can't hold it any longer and lean over the side of the boat and lose my lunch.

"Ew!" Charlie hollers. Then he leans toward me. "Whatever you do, don't get it on the crabs, Etta!"

"Shut up, Charlie," Heath says. "I don't feel so good either," she tells Julia.

"Uh-oh." Julia turns to Jed, who is sucking on his wound between his forefinger and thumb.

"Might be that Norovirus that's going around — the one Skeeter and Glenda had."

"Oh dear." Julia holds back my hair with one hand and rubs my back with the other. By the time we get to the dock, Heath is losing her lunch too as Charlie covers the bucket of crabs with a towel and rests his body over it.

Jed stays outside with Charlie, and they hose off the boat as Julia gets us both inside and takes us to the two different bathrooms. She pulls back my hair into a ponytail and tells me it's okay as I lean over the toilet, feeling a little bad about messing it up after she's just scrubbed it clean. After I don't think there is any more to come, Julia helps me to my bed and then she helps Heath to her bed too.

I hear her as she goes outside and asks Jed if he will go to the store to get some ginger ale and saltine crackers and Pepto-Bismol.

"Can I come?" Charlie asks, jumping up and down.

"Sure, sport. Then you can help me clean the crabs."

"I don't think we're going to be able to do dinner. Glenda said this was a pretty violent twenty-four-hour bug."

"No problem," Jed said. "Maybe I can bring some over to you after Charlie and I rustle it up."

"Okay," she said, and within the half hour I can hear Jed's voice again.

"Another one down, Julia," he calls from the screen door. Julia comes running out, picks up Charlie, and races him to the bathroom. Now I can hear Heath snoring in the next room as I curl myself up into a ball under my sheets and hope that the fist squeezing my belly will decide to release it soon.

"I'll check in a little later," I hear Jed say.

"Okay," Julia says. "Thanks for helping." And in a few minutes his Rover is pulling out of the dirt driveway and Julia is delivering little cups of ginger ale to each of us.

CHAPTER 24
JULIA

Julia couldn't remember when she'd washed and folded so many sheets and towels. Maybe the summer she and Marney were hired to clean the condos at Fairfield Resort on the island's sound. Julia wanted to buy her own car, and Marney always needed extra cash. Their nightly tips at Dockside weren't cutting it so they took the extra day job and cleaned houses Saturday through Tuesday of every week.

Julia looked down at her hands, raw from all of the hand washing and the cleaning with Clorox and Comet. The poor kids. The bug hit them all at once, and it seemed pretty violent. Thankfully, Julia felt fine, but she made sure she washed her hands every time she came into contact with one of them. She did not want to be yacking on an international flight tomorrow.

She had her bags packed. She was ready to go. She hummed John Denver's "Leaving on a Jet Plane" as she picked up Charlie's tinker toys on the screened porch and put them in a basket by the rocking chairs. It was the first song she'd ever learned when she took a few guitar lessons back in college. She was a terrible musician.

Despite the trip to the ER and the illness and the flea infestation, the week had actually flown by. And there had been moments, if she admitted it to herself, that were sweeter than any she'd had in a long time, partly because they were a surprise and partly because they reminded her of some of the happier times of her childhood. Catching that first fish with Charlie was one, seeing Jed for the first time in more than twenty years was another, buying the kids some new clothes and sketching the surroundings were two more.

All in all, she would come out of this fairly unscathed. It hadn't been as hard on her heart as she imagined it would be. Maybe that was because she never actually had to see Marney. Maybe it was because the kids and the cleaning kept her too busy to think. Maybe it was because folks like Skeeter and Glenda and Jed and even her mother seemed to be supporting her in some unspoken way. The one person she'd yet to see or speak to was Aunt Dot. All reports were that she was recovering steadily with her new hip, but Julia was shocked that she hadn't called to check in. Maybe Aunt Dot would make it to the wedding in December. Maybe they could have a long chat then about the bizarre eight days Julia spent on Edisto Island looking after her half sisters and half brother, facing the thing she dreaded most — not necessarily full on, but not cowering away either. And how — all things considered — it hadn't been nearly as bad as she imagined.

Well, tomorrow she would be on her way to Budapest and Simon would meet her there. Through a series of e-mails, they had decided to cancel the Istanbul trip. They'd wait and go back for their honeymoon. However, he would take the time to help her get settled in Budapest before heading back to the States to meet with Hockney and begin the preparations for the Tate Gallery exhibit.

Now Julia could hear a little puttering out on the creek. She watched as a boat tied up to the floating dock, and she walked out to see Jed pulling the bow rope tight.

"Hey." He swung his leg over the bow, putting one foot onto the dock, and in the darkness his outline looked almost exactly as it had that night that they'd taken a boat ride back when they were teenagers — tall, thin, broad-shouldered. "How's everyone doing?"

"They're all asleep." She smiled. "And I'm all packed but utterly disgusting."

"Well," he said. "Why don't you go wash up and I'll set up a little dinner for us out here."

She felt her stomach grumble. She was hungry, which she hoped was a sign the bug was not going to get her.

"All right," she said, and she raced back to the house and to the upstairs bathroom where she quickly showered, threw on a pair of jeans and a crumpled white tank top from the top of her bag, and slipped on her old leather sandals. She checked on the kids, who each felt cool to the touch and were sleeping deeply, and slipped quietly through the screened door and back out into the balmy June night.

As she walked toward the dock, framed by the shadows of the live oak trees, the Spanish moss swaying in the thick breeze, she admired the moonlight on the water. And then she admired Jed, bent over a well-dressed card table, lighting a few votives. He smoothed out the tablecloth, stood, and turned to her. "Dinner is served."

As she stepped onto the dock, she stopped

for a moment and savored the smell of pluff mud and burning wax and fresh seafood. She couldn't help but grin as he pulled two of the plastic chairs toward the table and held one out for her like a maître d' at a fine restaurant.

"Thank you, sir." She took her seat and let him push it in.

On the table was a serving plate with a tower of crab cakes, a bowl of rémoulade sauce, another with fresh corn and butter bean succotash, and another with an arugula and grape tomato salad. And there was also an old iron skillet with homemade corn bread sliced in large triangles.

"Wow." She leaned forward and admired the bounty that filled the makeshift dining room table as he made a plate for her and then for him and poured them both a glass of white wine in some plastic tumblers before sitting down across from her.

He raised his plastic cup. "From pestilence to disease, you have survived the week."

She chuckled and met his glass with hers and they both took a sip. Then she raised hers again. "To the chef," she said.

"No, no, no," he said, pushing away her compliment. "To Edisto Island, which provided the fare and the inspiration, some of it anyway."

She nodded and looked back to the old cottage that was lit up with lamps and seemed just as it was when she was a kid. *To an old home,* she thought to herself, but she didn't speak the words. Instead, she touched tumblers with Jed a second time. Then he said a short blessing and they began to eat.

The meal was delectable. The crab was fresh, and he'd barely put any bread crumbs with it so that the texture and flavor came clearly through. So sweet and rich.

She watched him as he dished up the corn bread and offered her some butter. He seemed to take great pleasure in preparing and serving a meal.

"So." She cocked her head, and his eyes, glistening from the votives, met hers.

"Besides becoming a surgeon and a five-star cook, what else have you been up to the last quarter of a century?"

He looked out over the creek, scratched his head, and then turned back to face her full-on. "Honestly, Julia," he said, "I've been up to the usual plus a little of the awful — school, college, med school, a short-lived marriage, divorce, work and more work, burying my parents, work and more work . . ."

He took a bite of his corn bread and met

her eyes again. "But I think very little about me has changed since that summer twenty-three years ago."

"Really?" She smiled.

He nodded as his eyes moved back and forth as if he were reading his own story for the first time. "Maybe that's why I bought that old cottage at the auction. I guess there's a part of me that's always wanted to re-create my time here as a kid and return home to it. You know what I mean?"

"Those were good times, weren't they?"

He shrugged his large shoulders. "Yeah, they were. I guess I was never happier than those summers I spent out here, fishing and swimming, puttering around in the johnboat, getting stuck on pluff mud banks, playing endless poker games." He cleared his throat and looked up from his plate. "Daydreaming about a bright and beautiful sixteen-year-old girl . . ." He cleared his throat and leaned back. "Hoping I might somehow be able to catch her attention."

Julia swallowed hard. Her cheeks were warm, and she didn't know how to respond. Was this just the longings of a young man in a grown man's body? Didn't we all idealize our childhoods, our first crushes, our first kisses? Didn't we set them on too high of a pedestal?

As if he read her mind, he shook his head and leaned toward her. "Boyhood fantasies." He went back to his crab cakes and took a hearty bite. "Hard to shake, I guess."

He cocked his head and smiled at her. "But what about you? What have you been up to for the last quarter of a century?"

She looked down at the flickering candle and then up to him. What had she been up to? Heartbreak, therapy, baring her teeth in order to survive, learning how to seal off certain sections of her heart and her history and burying them deep, deep below her consciousness.

She rested her chin on her hand and watched him waiting for her to give him an honest answer, an answer that would require a lot of vulnerability. Was she up for that?

"Well, I'd like to say I've been building this wonderful career and life, but that wouldn't be the truth." She looked back to her old house and then to him.

He sat back as if he had all the time in the world. "What is the truth?" he said.

She took a deep breath and put down her fork. "I guess the truth is I've been trying to get past the pain of my dad leaving our family." She looked out to the glistening water and then up to the gibbous moon, now waning. "You know, Marney was my best friend from college."

He nodded. "I'd heard that."

"Well, I was devastated when I realized what was going on between her and my father. It broke my heart, and it broke my heart to watch my mother's life shatter, and my sister's too."

Jed swallowed hard and kept his eyes right on her. "I can't imagine, Julia. I can't imagine a worse betrayal."

"Well, you know I was really close to my dad. And I blame him mostly. I mean, Marney was young too, although she may have been the one to make the first advance." Julia shook her head. "She was a lonely kid, and she loved our family like everyone else." She turned to meet Jed's tender gaze. "And maybe she didn't really care what happened as long as she found a permanent place in it . . . I don't know."

Julia took a sip of her wine and twisted her wet hair up into a knot. "I just ran away, really. And I didn't look back. I refused to." He smiled at her as she pulled a slice of corn bread from the skillet. "I was pretty good at running away and starting a new life . . . though I've had some eruptions, mainly in the form of panic attacks and bouts of depression, which haunt me from time to time."

Jed nodded solemnly. He breathed in the air slowly and leaned forward. "Did you ever find any resolution with your father . . . before he passed away?"

"No, I can't say that I did." Now she felt the sting in her eyes and she blinked back the tears. "I would love to say that we had this moment of reconciliation or forgiveness or something. But we didn't. We just didn't."

She patted her eyes with the paper napkin, and he handed her his.

"I'm sorry, Julia."

She swallowed hard and felt her ears popping. She hadn't meant to open all the way up. She couldn't remember the last time she'd been so honest with anyone.

Julia looked back at the house and down at her half-eaten plate. She was tired, very tired. And tomorrow would be a long day.

"I guess I better head on back and get some rest, Jed."

He nodded. "Okay." And then he reached out his large, warm hand and put it firmly on top of hers. "Thank you."

She blinked back the sniffles and smiled at him through her watery eyes. "I should be thanking you," she said. "You've come to my rescue and filled my stomach more than once this week."

He moved forward as if to say more, but

she was too weary to hear it and too afraid of what it might be.

She stood quickly as the plastic chair scraped against the wood of the dock. Then she stepped back and looked into his eyes. "It's been great to see you, and I wish you the best with the cottage and your work and whatever else is in store for you." She thought of his "appointment" the other night. And she imagined that one day the right woman would come along and love him well, and he would be happy.

She held out her hand for a handshake. Something businesslike and curt. She couldn't help herself. She had to protect her heart.

He stood up and peered down at her and returned the handshake with a warm, firm grip. Then he started to load up his cooler with the leftover food as she blew out the candles and folded the tablecloth.

After everything had been loaded back up in his boat, he stepped back on the dock, and before she realized what was happening, he embraced her and she embraced him back, tightly, this tall, broad-shouldered man who had reappeared on the craziest, most Southern gothic dysfunctional week of her life and taken her breath away.

Then he let go as quickly as he had held

tight, and she had the urge to step forward toward him, but she stopped herself.

He stared at her for several seconds as the incoming tide pushed into the creek, and then he turned, stepped back in his boat, and started the engine. She untied the rope and tossed it over his bow, and then she watched him turn and putter down the creek toward his dock. He looked back only once to wave and then continued down the waterway, the moon and stars lighting his path.

Julia felt a fullness, a fullness from a remarkable meal and even more so from the honest conversation with an old, safe friend. But there was something more beyond the fullness. There was a longing, a longing from the warmth between them and from the sudden embrace and from the kiss years ago that somehow bound them together.

She shivered as his boat rounded the bend and the sound of his outboard motor faded away. She needed to shake this longing quickly because it felt a good deal more complicated than mere friendship. And because she sensed that the feeling was mutual.

She breathed in the balmy Edisto air for what was likely the last time in a long, long time. It was thick and dense and salty just like she'd remembered it from all of those summers ago. And it seemed both strange and true that nostalgia and longing and love and loss could coexist in the same space in the same moment in the same . . . deep . . . breath.

CHAPTER 25
JULIA

It was Skeeter who woke Julia up the next morning, banging steadily on the screened porch. "Anyone home?" She had forgotten to set her alarm, and they had all overslept. It was ten a.m., and her flight from Charleston to Atlanta left at noon.

Now Julia bolted out of bed and let Skeeter in. He was supposed to keep the kids until Brooke, the babysitter, arrived midafternoon. Then he and Glenda would go to town and pick up Marney, who was set to be released, and deliver her home.

"Go, go, go," Skeeter said. "Glad I kept knocking."

"Me too," she said, then raced back up the stairs and threw on her jeans and T-shirt and the brown leather jacket she always flew in. Charlie arrived on the threshold of her bedroom door as she zipped up her suitcase. He was groggy-eyed and she could hear his stomach growling.

"How are you feeling, buddy?"

"Okay," he said. "I want some chocco milk."

She uprighted her suitcase, double-checked that her passport was in the side pocket of her purse, and turned back to him. "Charlie, you know I'm leaving this morning, right?"

He nodded. "And Brooke's coming," he said. Then his eyes widened with excitement. "And then later, Mama."

"That's right," she said. "And right now Skeeter's downstairs, and he'll help look after y'all." She crossed her arms. "But I don't think your stomach is ready for milk. I'm going to leave out some plain toast and some applesauce and water for you. If that goes down all right, then you can try something with a little more flavor for lunch, okay?"

He nodded, and before she realized what was happening, he ran toward her and hugged her legs so hard she nearly toppled over her suitcase.

She caught herself and then bent down and looked into his big brown eyes with their impossibly long, dark lashes. They were the eyes of her father and the eyes of a little cherub.

"I'm going to miss you," she said, shocked

by the lump in her throat.

He nodded solemnly. "When will you come back?"

"I don't know," she said. "It may be awhile. But I hope you'll go to the library and e-mail me sometime. I want to see some pictures of all of the big fish you're catching."

He grinned and nodded. "I will," he said.

She looked up to find Heath standing at the door as well.

"You're running late." The girl shifted her weight and rested her long, tall, nearly grown-up body against the door frame.

"Yeah," Julia said. "We overslept and I have to go. I left you . . ."

"I heard," Heath said. "We'll be all right."

Julia held out her arms and Heath walked into them. Julia rocked her back and forth and felt the child's body soften and embrace her back.

"I'll order you the rest of the Tolkien trilogy this week and have it mailed to the PO box."

"Okay," Heath said. She stopped for a moment, stepped back, and looked into Julia's eyes. "Thank you." And Julia could tell that her thank-you was for more than the books. She pecked the girl's beautiful forehead, then grabbed her bags and walked toward the top of the stairs. She peered in Etta's room, but the bed was empty and the child was nowhere to be seen.

Charlie and Heath followed Julia downstairs.

"Where's Etta?" She looked on the porch, then in the kitchen, then in the den.

"She just went out the door," Skeeter said.

Julia stood outside and called her. She looked at her watch and ran to the shed. No sign of her. Then she checked the dock where the tide was pouring in. No sign of her there either. When Julia came back out in the yard to scan the woods, Skeeter opened the screened door and called out, "You better go on. You can't be delayed another day, Julia."

She turned back to Skeeter, Heath, and Charlie, who were all on the porch watching her. "Will you tell her good-bye for me?"

"We will," Charlie said.

Julia scanned the property one more time, picked up her bags, and piled them in the car. Charlie chased her a little ways, barefoot and in his pajamas, as she drove down the dirt driveway. Then he stopped and held his stomach, his hunger likely getting the better of him. Julia waved and he waved back and then turned toward the house. As Julia drove on down the tree-lined road, she kept looking back and forth between the live oaks and scrub pines and palmettos, hoping to catch a glimpse of the little girl in the white nightgown and the red rain boots, but Etta was nowhere to be found. It was probably just the way Etta wanted it.

Julia made it to the Charleston airport in the nick of time. She turned in her rental car and raced to the terminal and onto the flight that would carry her to Atlanta where she would catch her international flight. As the plane took off, she peered out of the window at the waterways and rivers and salt marsh creeks like enormous snakes winding their way out to sea. The sunlight was almost blinding and the creeks themselves looked like little rivers of gold reflecting the light on their moving surfaces. The thought occurred to Julia that it might not be so easy to put this visit out of her mind, to tuck it away like she had her childhood and seal it closed like so many places in her heart.

As the travelers around her pulled out their iPads and laptops and began clicking away, she knew she had to move on. She had to shake this reconnection with her old home, with her half sisters and brother. And with her old teenage crush. She had a lot of work ahead: two months of painting and lecturing in a foreign city, planning a wedding, moving to a new place, preparing for a department chair bid. This was no time to get confused or emotional. No time at all.

She opened her own laptop and started responding to e-mails. She'd send them during her wait in the international terminal in Atlanta, but she could get a jump on responding right now. Simon's was the first she read. He had already arrived in Budapest for their weekend together before he had to return to the States. He would meet her at the airport and help her get set up in her flat. He couldn't wait to see her and give her a tour of the city. He had spent a semester there in college, and he would give her a personal tour of his favorite spots.

Then she continued on with the e-mails from work and Bess and others: Yes to the departmental meeting in mid-September, no to the lemon-flavored wedding cake by Kerry Vincent, and yes to the winter white one with raspberry sauce by Mark Joseph. No to the roses and yes to the calla lilies and lilies of the valley for the bridal bouquets. No to the veal and yes to the beef tenderloin. No to the imported shrimp and yes to the Maine lobster. Yes to sitting on the president's advisory committee at Hunter College and no to the college's tenure committee. And thank you to her friend and former student Rachel Muldoon, who'd been looking after her rooftop plants. "Eat all of the tomatoes and lemons, please," she wrote.

As the plane descended she sat back and snapped her laptop closed. Her head spun and she wished she could have had just a few more hours on the old dock, watching the tide move in and out. Once she was on the ground and checked into the international terminal, she got a croissant and a big cup of coffee. She reached for her laptop but instead pulled out her sketchbook. *Just a few more minutes of drawing,* she thought. Then back to work. As she flipped open the book to the next blank page, she found an image that was not hers tucked inside. It was a charcoal sketch of Julia sketching on the dock with Charlie fishing in the background and Heath on the rope swing reading a book.

"Good-bye," it read at the bottom and it was signed, "Etta."

Julia didn't know how long she sat there staring at the image, replaying the week in her mind as her heart raced. She hoped they were all feeling better, she hoped the babysitter arrived on time, she hoped the house would stay clean, she hoped Marney was rid of the cancer, she hoped the children would grow up well and strong and make their way in the world and find joy and be blessed.

She sat this way, trance-like, for a long time, not sending her e-mails, not going over the lecture she would have to give next week. Suddenly she realized what the voice on the intercom was saying, "Boarding Air France, flight 337 to Paris, with continued service to Budapest."

She shoved the sketchbook back into her carry-on bag, quickly stood, and looked around. Everyone at her gate was already in line at the entrance ramp. She had meant to finish her coffee, she had meant to go to the bathroom, she had meant to send her e-mails.

She felt for her boarding pass and raced over to the gate door and got in line behind all of the other passengers. The flight looked full. She'd be lucky if there was any room left in the overhead bins for her carry-on bag.

A little boy was sleeping on his father's shoulder a few passengers ahead. His father was gently patting his back, and the child looked up for a moment and seized eyes with Julia before laying his head back down.

Julia had the urge to run over and kiss his round cheeks and ask to hold him. This must be her clock ticking or some sort of premenopausal outburst. She shook her head and readjusted her posture.

Get a grip, she told herself. And then the mantra that worked even better than that one. *Lord, have mercy.*

CHAPTER 26
JULIA

Simon was standing just outside of the customs checkpoint staring at his iPhone when Julia rolled her bags out. He looked up suddenly as she moved toward him and shook his head, half-concealing a grin. Then he slid his phone in his jacket pocket and walked down the corridor toward her, his grin growing wider by the moment. She stopped and they embraced. Simon. Her fiancé. The handsome salt-and-pepper, leather jacket, British chap she was going to start a family with, spend the rest of her life with. She longed to breathe in the scent of him, but when she inhaled all she could smell was cigarette smoke and stale coffee and gasoline and airport air, and the combination turned her stomach a little.

She pulled back and he lifted up her chin. "You okay, love? You look a little green."

"I think so." She nodded. "I just need some fresh air."

"Come on, my little magnolia blossom," he said with a chuckle, then he took her bags and led her toward the taxi queue at the far end of the airport by the baggage claim area. "You're going to love this city, Julia." He was gesturing with his free arm. "It's one of my favorites. I've got a reservation for dinner tonight at the castle quarter on the very top of the west bank. We'll have a fantastic view of the city and the Danube. Oh, and tomorrow we can go to one of the thermal baths or the spa. You don't have to check in at the university until Monday, right?"

"Right." She was concentrating on the front door, but her eyes kept glazing over. She really did need some fresh air.

"Well, we'll have a romantic weekend then," he continued. "And you can tell me all about your trip to the backwoods." She took a deep breath. She hated to say it, but she just wanted him to be quiet for a moment. He grinned down at her and winked. "You're crazy, you know that? Absolutely crazy." He shook his head and she blinked and tried to steady herself. Her hands felt clammy and the airport seemed unusually warm. "But charitable," he continued. "I suppose I can't fault you for that."

■ ■ ■ ■

Julia peeled off her jacket when they got in the cab. Simon was busy pointing out the sites as they bumped along the crowded streets — the State Opera House, Mathias Church, Heroes Square flanked by the Fine Arts Museum and the Mucsarnok Art Gallery. As they crossed over the picturesque Chain Bridge, which spanned the Danube River linking Pest to Buda, she saw stars and felt like she might faint. So she rolled down her window and took long, deep breaths as he pointed out the promenade and the massive Parliament Building, which even in her green and fuzzy state she had to admit was truly grand with its Gothic Revival spires, symmetrical façade, and enormous central dome, its mighty image reflected in the river.

She was staying at the foot of the Buda Hills in the green belt of Budapest at the Congress Center where the Hungarian University of Fine Arts had a few studio apartments for visiting faculty and Fulbright scholars. The inside of the Center looked promisingly modern with mirrored walls and a well-suited doorman, ornate cap and gold-trimmed jacket and all, but the heat hit her immediately as the doorman confessed, "The air condishun is under restoration." He pulled his cell phone out of his pressed black pants and nodded. "To be fix afternoon."

Julia felt so tired she thought she might collapse right there. She thought she had slept pretty well on the flight, but she seemed weary to the bone in addition to feeling queasier by the moment. Simon and the doorman divided her bags and settled her in her room on the eighth floor where she was shocked to have a view of the river and the Parliament building. Then the men went around attempting to open the windows, most of which seemed sealed or stuck closed. They managed to get one open near the futon and she plunked down there and closed her eyes.

"I'm going to let you rest, all right?" Simon said. "I've got an appointment with another art dealer in Pest who has a well-heeled client, a parliament member, who wants to commission Hockney for a piece. I'll be back at seven to pick you up for dinner. Call me in the meantime if you need anything, love."

She fanned herself and nodded. He pecked her on the cheek and left, and she fell into a fitful sleep that must have incorporated the honking cars below and the foreign city — new to her — into her dreams. She woke in a cold sweat and could only remember bits and pieces of her imaginings: walking across a bridge, chasing a man who grew smaller by the moment. She thought it might be Jed or Simon, but when he turned around she saw it was her father back in his prime without the gray or the shuffle or the potbelly, and she stopped in her tracks as he stared at her, the cars and taxis flying by them, the river spinning below them. She could remember two feelings. One of which was to run into his arms. The other of which was to run away, head in the opposite direction back to the bank. She had wanted him to give her some indication of which he'd prefer, but just as he started to move his arms as if to open them, a car came up behind him honking and barreling in his direction, and she opened her eyes.

She sat up in bed. The sun was setting. Simon would arrive in less than two hours — she had managed a long rest and seemed to feel a little better as the apartment cooled down. She unpacked her bags, putting her clothes in drawers, setting up her laptop, her few files, her camera. There were two boxes in the closet, which she had ordered.

They had a few small canvases and paints and brushes.

After a shower and a debate over what to wear — she decided on a gray linen sundress and a gauzy, pale green wrap — she put on a little lipstick and was not surprised to hear him, right on time, rapping on her door.

She stood up from the vanity, feeling a little dizzy, caught her breath, and opened the door.

He was freshly shaved and in a new tweed jacket and polished cognac loafers he must have bought over the last few weeks, smelling like some sort of expensive European cologne.

She made a step toward him and before she realized it, she was sick, and she lost her airport dinner — with immense violence — all over his new shoes.

"That's romantic." He stepped back as she leaned against the open door and wiped her mouth with the back of her hand.

"I'm sorry," she said as he scooted back in the apartment and went to wipe off his loafers. "There was this stomach bug going around Edisto, and I must have gotten it."

She felt her stomach flip-flop again, and she raced toward the bathroom, shoving him out of the way.

"So I'm guessing dinner at the castle is canceled?"

She coughed and pulled herself up from the green tiled floor. "I'm sorry, Simon. This is probably going to last twenty-four hours."

He grimaced and nodded solemnly. "All right, then. What can I get you? Want me to track down some ginger ale or tonic water?"

She felt so awful she lay right down on the floor. "Why don't you go have a nice meal? I hate for you to spoil the reservation. Just bring me home some bread and some sort of soft drink afterward."

"All right," he said. "I will."

He squatted down and squeezed her shoulder. "Call me if you need anything."

"I will," she said. And after a few more trips to the bathroom, she drifted into a very deep sleep, so deep that she didn't stir when he came back and left three sodas and a baguette in the little studio kitchen.

The weekend did not turn out to be romantic at all. After Julia recovered, Simon went down with the bug, and he left for the airport looking very green on Monday afternoon.

"Call you when I get to New York," he said.

"Good luck on the flight."

He embraced her hard. "I love you," he said.

It wasn't something he said very often, and she noticed that he was staring at her with a great intensity that could have been caused by the sickness or perhaps something more. He lifted up her left hand and held the sapphire to the sunlight.

"Five more months and it will be official."

She smiled and nodded, feeling strangely separate and distant — from him, from the wedding, from New York, from everything.

"You're okay, aren't you, Julia? Nothing has changed, right?"

She nodded firmly as the taxi honked from the sidewalk. "Yeah, I am." She swallowed hard and felt her ears pop. She hoped she was all right.

He embraced her again and turned toward the cab. "Paint like crazy," he said. "I can't wait to see what you come up with."

She crossed her arms and smiled at him as the driver clicked the door shut. Then she turned and walked back into the building. She had a lecture on postmodern American art at the university in three hours, and she needed to go over her notes.

CHAPTER 27
JED

It had been three weeks since Julia left. Jed had looked her up on the Internet, studied her paintings, even bid on one at an online auction, but he lost. The painting was of a triangle within an octagon within a heptagon. He didn't particularly like it nor could he afford it, but he longed for her so much that he wanted something he could hold on to. Something she had made, something that could teach him more about the woman she had become.

"You've got to give it up," Rick Strozier told him as they scrubbed up for surgery. "She'll be married in a few months, man. It's time to move on."

Jed exhaled. "You're right."

As if Rick could read his mind, he said, "Let me know if you decide to sell your Edisto place. Dana's been riding me about getting some digs out there for a while, and we just inherited a little money from her uncle we need to invest."

Jed hadn't been able to muster the strength to go out to the Edisto cottage the last few Saturdays, much to Rascal's disappointment. He just felt too tired to knock down a wall with a sledgehammer after a long work week. And he didn't want to remember the last few times he'd had out there and the light Julia's presence had brought back into his heart.

"I just might sell." Jed glanced at his friend before turning off the faucet. "I don't need an extra place to keep up with. And there's a lot of work still to be done out there."

Rick grinned and nodded. Then he punched Jed's arm. "That's what contractors and building crews are for."

Jed raised his right eyebrow. "Not if you're a purist."

"Never claimed to be." Rick dried off his arms with a disposable towel. And then, "Hey, did I mention that Stephanie's been asking about you?"

Jed rolled his eyes.

"Don't you want to give it another try? Maybe come over to our condo for dinner one evening. Dana makes a mean shrimp creole."

Jed tried not to wince. He had partaken of

Dana's creole before, and it was nothing to write home about. It was bland, overcooked, and he didn't think she even used local shrimp.

"Not yet," he said. "Maybe in a month or two."

"You're pitiful, you know that?" Rick scoffed. "The girl you kissed when you were fifteen comes back into town for a week, and you can't get her out of your mind."

They both tied their masks around their necks and walked toward the X-ray room where they were to view the lung images one more time before heading to the operating room. The patient was a man Jed's age, with four young children, and he'd never smoked, but he had a bad case of cancer in both lungs, and the surgery was going to be major.

The surgery took six hours and the patient seemed stable. Jed went out to the waiting room where the man's wife was tapping her foot nervously as she read from a book. Her youngest child, a boy with dark curly hair, was asleep in her lap.

When she looked up at him, he smiled reassuringly. She straightened her back, which roused the little boy who sat up and rubbed his eyes with his thick little hands.

"How did it go?" she said.

"It was major and the next few days will be critical. But it couldn't have gone better, and he is resting now."

Back home in his apartment overlooking Colonial Lake, Jed put a leash on Rascal and went for a long run along the battery as the sun set. There seemed to be little boys everywhere, on bicycles, climbing the cannons at White Point Gardens, vying for a spot at the water fountain at Hazel Parker Playground.

Jed couldn't help but think of Charlie and the girls. It seemed crazy, but he wanted to be a part of their lives. Who would take them fishing? Who would teach them how to drive a boat? Who would throw the football with them?

He always thought he'd have a large family like the man he operated on today. It was how he had imagined his grown-up life — pushing a stroller, throwing a football, baiting a hook, attending a piano recital or a spelling bee.

As he watched the sun dip behind the Ashley River on his jog back to his apartment, he decided to call Skeeter. When he got home, it was the first thing he did.

"Hey, boy," the old man said when he picked up the phone after several rings.

"Glenda and I were just saying we hadn't seen you out here in a while."

"Yeah," Jed said as he filled Rascal's bowl with water and set it out on the deck. "Work has been crazy, but I think I can get out there this weekend. I was wondering if you and I might take Charlie fishing at the honey hole. And the girls too."

"You don't have to ask me twice," Skeeter said. "Your boat ready?"

"Ready as ever."

"Then I'll call up the sitter and tell her we'll be there first thing Saturday morning."

"That sounds great," Jed said. "I'll see you then, Skeeter."

"You bring the drinks, and I'll have the live bait."

"Got it," Jed said as he hung up the phone, walked out to the deck, and plopped down in a chair beside Rascal, who came over for a long head scratch.

After rustling up a little dinner, sautéed okra and tomatoes over orzo, he checked his e-mail only to find a recommendation from the fine arts site where he had bid on Julia's painting.

"We've recently acquired another Julia Bennett," the note read. He clicked on it and was delighted to find the image of three lumpy, ripe heirloom tomatoes on a kitchen windowsill. And just beyond the window-panes, the live oaks framing the dock and the marsh. He tried to catch his breath. Now this was the Julia he could connect with. The Julia who saw the beauty of the natural world the way he did. The year on the painting said 1990. She would have been seventeen then, and he sixteen.

He glanced at the price, then put in a competitive bid. This was a Bennett paint-ing he loved, and he would not regret put-ting down some serious money to own it.

CHAPTER 28
JULIA

The next several weeks rolled by quickly, and Julia felt more herself with each day that passed. Aunt Dot had called to thank her for keeping the children and to tell her she was up and moving about with her new hip. Her mother had called several times to check in and to remind her that her old college roommate, Estelle Macomson, had a daughter who lived just outside of Budapest and here was her e-mail address. Simon called every other day, often with some exciting piece of news about Hockney sales, and Jed e-mailed once to say how much he had enjoyed seeing her and how he hoped her time in Budapest was fruitful and to please call him if and when she found herself back in the South Carolina lowcountry.

Julia never did hear a word from Marney. No thank you, no update on the kids or her health. She assumed that no news was good news, and she really had no desire to talk with Marney. But she would have loved to have heard something from the children whom she thought about and dreamed about regularly.

Budapest was one of Europe's most vibrant and beautiful cities, with a storied history that involved everyone from the Celts to the Romans to the Magyars to the Mongols, and of course, the Ottomans. The people were truly a stunning and exotic blend of all of the cultures and conquerors that made their way through Central Europe over the last two thousand years or so. Many had smooth, tawny skin, chiseled jaws, large, slightly curved eyes with dark brows, blond or reddish-orange hair. Nearly everyone seemed confident and busy, well on their way to somewhere or someone.

But to what and to whom? That's what Julia wanted to know as she sat and observed the pedestrians at the little portable easel she'd set up each morning in different parts of the city before heading to the university. At first she focused on the vistas with pedestrians making up a hazy portion of the foreground or background of places like the Chain Bridge, Parliament, the Jewish synagogue, the Old Castle. But she was quickly bored by the vistas that had surely been painted thousands and thousands of times by artists with a much deeper connection to them. So she turned to what she was most naturally captivated by: the people and the mystery of their lives. She couldn't help staring at them constantly: an elderly man shuffling down the street with his two baguettes, one under each arm; a teenage girl, her tattooed hand in the back of her boyfriend's pants pocket, the boyfriend's triple lip rings catching the morning light; a middle-aged woman with graying hair and a settled face that was more beautiful, more youthful than she dared to imagine and how her expression turned from one of weariness to delight when she crossed an acquaintance on the promenade.

Julia looked into their faces as they approached, sometimes staring at them for whole minutes at a time before they felt her gaze and looked up. She would try to look away in time so they didn't feel as though they were being stalked by some obtuse American, here today and gone tomorrow, though in many ways that's exactly who she was. If she stared long enough, she could imprint the image on her mind and she would quickly turn and paint the subject as she imagined who the person was, imagined the dramatic arcs of their life, imagined their deepest longings or regrets. In that way she felt connected to them. No one could walk this planet without experiencing pain.

At first she found that painting the pedestrians helped quell the mysterious longing in her heart, but as the weeks passed, it almost made it worse, and she found that the more she watched others, the lonelier she felt. The loneliness was useful when it came to the art; it helped sharpen and define it. So she fed on it, the way she remembered Hemingway fed on hunger during his time in Paris when he couldn't afford lunch, and she hoped against hope that she could create something fresh to ship home to New York. Some new way of defining who she was and how she saw the world.

One Saturday afternoon she was sitting on the edge of the Chain Bridge beneath the lion, just watching for that right person to trigger her imagination and fill her blank canvas, when her phone buzzed in her jacket pocket. It was a text with the name Jed Young on it, and it contained a photo. She clicked to open it and found an image of Charlie holding up an enormous spot-tail bass with a grin the size of Texas. And Skeeter was in the background, his old shirt splattered with pluff mud, clapping. *Mornin' trip to the honey hole,* the text read.

She smiled at the image of the proud little boy and then at the letters that made up the name just below the image. Jed Young. She took a photo of her view from the Chain Bridge, including the edge of her easel, the lion, the Danube, and the Parliament building. *Congrats to Charlie from Budapest,* she wrote. And then, *Thank you for taking him, J.*

The text did not go through. She tried it several times, but it didn't work. She had half a mind to fold up the easel, run to the top of Castle Hill where she was sure to have service, and call him. Maybe he was calling her right now, yearning to hear her voice the way she was his.

Her engagement ring was catching the afternoon light, and she blinked several times. *I have to shake this,* she said to herself. *This is crazy.* She deleted her response and went back to her easel and set out her paints. She was getting married in a few short months and whatever nostalgia or romance or whatever it was she had felt for Jed during her week at Edisto, she had to stamp it out. Ignore it. Seal it up.

She went back to her observing and was delighted to have the chance to take a long look at two young girls on either side of an older woman who must be their grandmother. They were making faces at one another as the woman pulled them along the bridge. One of them, the younger one, looked right into Julia's eyes for whole seconds at a time. The look was a blend of boldness and pride. As if to say, *Of course I am a worthy subject.* Julia smiled at her and winked. The girl smiled back and nodded once. *What a gift,* Julia thought, and then she turned away and dipped her brush into the acrylic paint.

CHAPTER 29
MARY ELLEN

Nate and Mary Ellen were driving up to Moncks Corner in his thirty-year-old Mercedes convertible to visit a woman named Charlene who raised Australian terriers.

"Well." Nate gave a side-angled glance to Mary Ellen as they veered from Highway 17 onto I-26, the wind whipping her hairdo out of place. "This lady tells me their life span is twelve to sixteen years, so I figure this pet may very well outlive me."

Mary Ellen chuckled as she tied an old silk scarf around her head. She'd come to enjoy Nate's company over the last several months as he invited himself over to dinner with her and Jane Anne, or invited himself along with the Collateral Damage gang to the symphony or to try a new restaurant on upper King Street or even out to the Woodlands for high tea.

He was a good deal more well-mannered and interesting than Mary Ellen expected him to be, and he seemed to genuinely enjoy the company of ladies his age, though sometimes he got a little quiet at the end of the evenings and excused himself. Mary Ellen suspected he was missing his wife or missing Luther, and she never pried or pressed him on the matter.

"You'll help me pick one out now, right, Mary Ellen?" He reached across the seat and patted her forearm gently with his speckled, weathered hands. "You've got a good eye and a good heart."

"Oh, stop," she said. She hadn't owned a dog in decades and had no interest in such a labor of love. Her old and independent cat, Bad Girl, was all the pet she'd ever want this side of heaven.

"I mean it." Nate squeezed her arm ever so slightly as the wind whipped his gray hair and his jowls back. "I trust your judgment."

Mary Ellen looked out of the windshield as the setting slowly changed from urban to suburban to rural. Julia's wedding was a few months away, and the thought had crossed her mind to invite Nate to come along with her. Just as a friend. A platonic escort. A neighborly companion. It would be so nice to have someone to accompany her.

"Why not?" Jane Anne had said when Mary Ellen brought it up on a walk around

Colonial Lake last week. "Why the heck not, Mary Ellen?"

But she didn't think she could muster the nerve. She just didn't.

They pulled off the interstate and followed Highway 52 until they turned onto Cypress Gardens Road where they wound their way through remnants of an old rice plantation, catching glimpses of the swamp where cypress trees and knee stumps rose up out of the murky green water as if history itself had been preserved and pickled in the submersion. (Mary Ellen half-expected to see the Swamp Fox peer around one of the trees with his musket in hand, on the lookout for unsuspecting redcoats.)

Nate had his eyes on the winding road and turned abruptly by a crooked mailbox that read "Jeter." Mary Ellen hung on tight as they bumped over the deep mud holes in the unkempt dirt lane before pulling up to a double-wide trailer on the river where there were three dog pens, one with an English setter, one with a couple of hounds, and one with a small litter of yellow Labradors.

A large woman in a faded tropical print muumuu alighted on the steps and cocked her head. "Here to see the terriers?"

"Yes." Nate nodded and stepped forward

to shake the woman's hand as Mary Ellen made her way out of his car, straightening out her tweed skirt and pressing down on her hair after untying her scarf.

"I'm Nate Gallagher, Ms. Charlene, and this is my friend, Mary Ellen Bennett."

The woman cocked her hip and put her fleshy fist on it. "You two are a sight." She looked down her nose at Nate's antique car, its underbelly caked in orange mud, and rolled her eyes. Then she turned and pointed her head in the direction of her den. "We keep the terriers inside with the poodles."

Nate turned to Mary Ellen, who couldn't mask the look of trepidation as her pumps sank into the soggy dirt of the front yard. He winked and put out his elbow for her to take. "Come on, Ms. South of Broad," he said. "Don't you enjoy an adventure every now and again?"

Mary Ellen took his elbow and walked up the cinder-block steps and into the house where numerous brown and apricot poodles were running in circles on the shag carpet floor. The house was surprisingly clean and fresh-smelling, so Mary Ellen wasn't too concerned when the woman urged them through the den and down the hallway to where the four terriers were in a blue plastic swimming pool in a sewing room curled up one beside the other.

The woman picked up the largest one — about the size of a half-carton of eggs — and held him up for Nate to see. The rich brown puppy with pointed ears stretched for a moment, then rolled over and curled himself up into another C.

"They're awfully relaxed." Charlene wiped her nose with the top of her free forearm. "All of them. Very well adjusted." Then she handed the pup to Nate before snorting down at the plastic pool. "Go on, Ms. Bennett. Pick up the one you like. I'll give y'all a deal on two."

Mary Ellen, in an effort to be polite, bent down and reached her hands toward the litter. She felt instantly drawn to the smallest one in the center and pulled him up and nestled him on her chest. He was so soft and warm, and she could feel his little heart beating beneath her manicured fingers.

A puppy. She couldn't possibly take on a puppy at this stage in life. She'd have to leave him when she went to work, and she'd have to get up early and walk him, and she'd have to pick up his droppings all along the sidewalk, not to mention her pristine garden, stooping over with a plastic bag.

Nate stepped closer to Mary Ellen and lifted up the one he was holding in his hand.

The little pup slept soundly as Nate moved his head from side to side and pulled on his pointed ears. Mary Ellen held hers up next to his, and hers half-opened his eyes for a moment, licked her hand with his warm tongue, and nuzzled against the sloop between her forefinger and thumb.

"He's had his shots?" Nate turned to the woman in the muumuu.

"Yes, sir," she said. "My cousin works at the vet in Goose Creek, and she gives us a good deal on all of that. Every one of these terriers is ready to go."

Mary Ellen bent to put the puppy back down in the pool so she could get a good look at Nate's, but when she did her little pup put his paws up on the side and started to whimper.

"He likes you, Ms. Bennett," the woman said.

Mary Ellen took Nate's pup from him to inspect. "Well, I'm really not up for raising a dog at this point in life."

"Humph." The large woman sucked her teeth. She was probably the same age as Mary Ellen.

Mary Ellen smiled her best Southern belle smile. "I'm just here to help Mr. Gallagher."

Nate smiled her way and said, "Do you approve?"

She rubbed the scruff of the little puppy and nodded and Nate pulled out his wallet. "We'll take him," he said as the little pup in the pool continued to whimper.

On the drive home, the terrier in a seat-belted cardboard crate in the backseat, Nate slid an old Buddy Holly CD into his stereo, spread his fingers on the wheel, and they both tapped their fingers along to "Peggy Sue" and "Crying Waiting Hoping" and "Everyday" as they drove down the inter-state back to Charleston.

"That's it," Nate said as he pulled into the driveway.

"What?" she said.

He turned and nodded toward the back-seat where two little black eyes peered out from the holes. "I'm going to name him Buddy."

She took off her sunglasses and grinned. Music had a way of taking her back to an entirely different place as if shaving decades off of her life, and she felt transported to her long-ago twenties.

"Good choice," she said. "I always pre-ferred Buddy to Elvis."

"Oh," he scoffed. "No question about it. No question at all."

Mary Ellen got out of the car with a spring

in her step. It had been nice to get off of the peninsula, and it had felt wonderful to hear Buddy Holly again. She really ought to get one of those iPods everyone seemed to have now. She could load all of her old favorite songs on there and dance around her house and remember the days when her whole life was ahead of her, the days when her daddy told her that God had a future with her name on it and that it was full of hope.

"Well, I'm sure I'll see you soon, neighbor," she said as she turned and headed home, thinking of the music and the little puppy, swinging her purse from side to side. She wondered for a moment if she should drive back out to Moncks Corner and get the little fellow or if she should be so brazen as to ask Nate to accompany her to a wedding several states away.

She shook her head and untied her scarf as she muttered to herself, "Simmer down, old woman. Simmer down."

"Mary Ellen," Nate called. He had taken the pup out of the crate and was letting the little fellow lick his jowls.

She turned around on the sidewalk and cocked her head as Nate ambled toward her, cuddling his new pup. His eyes didn't look near so bulbous as they had when she'd knocked on his door to inform him of her shattered window a few months back. His face didn't look near so whiskery.

"I've been meaning to ask you something?" He narrowed his white brow and a softness came over his eyes.

"What's that?" she said.

"Well . . ." He looked up at the sky and shifted his weight to the other side. Then he nuzzled the pup beneath his neck and looked back to her. "My kids and grandkids are coming for Thanksgiving at the end of the month. Most of them, anyway. And I've got reservations for us at the Charleston Place Hotel restaurant." He put the puppy on his chest and looked into her wide eyes. "Anyway, I was wondering if you'd like to come along. You know, sort of be my date."

She chuckled a little nervously and patted down her windblown hair. She needed to make an appointment at Stella Nova for her weekly hairdo. He was looking right at her with his pale blue eyes, waiting for her response as she measured her smile.

"On one condition," she said.

He cleared his throat. "What's that?"

The words came out before she had time to weigh them. "That you take me back up to Moncks Corner to get that puppy this week."

He laughed and nodded toward the car.

"Let's go right now."

She clutched her purse and nodded. "All right."

Then Mary Ellen walked briskly back to Nate's driveway and hopped back in the passenger seat as he put little Buddy back in his crate and turned on the CD player again. "That'll Be the Day" came on as they drove back down Savage Street and sang out loud all the way down Ashley Avenue toward the highway. Mary Ellen felt like a kid again as the fall breeze lifted her hair beneath her scarf while she belted out the first stanza:

Well, that'll be the day, when you say
   good-bye

Nate must have felt it too as he watched her at the stoplight and smiled. When she turned to meet his gaze, he turned back to the road and shook his head.

Mary Ellen inhaled deeply. She was on her way to get an Australian terrier that would most likely outlive her; she was going to Thanksgiving dinner with Nate Gallagher's Irish, Yankee family; and by the end of the week she knew she would work up the nerve to ask her neighbor to her daughter's wedding.

CHAPTER 30
JULIA

The last month of summer went by quickly. Julia concluded her lecture series at the university, shipped her paintings home, and packed her bags for New York. By the time she was back in Manhattan, she was too busy to stop and think and long for anyone or anywhere. Bess had meetings for her with the wedding planner and the caterer and the floral designer. She'd have to pick out a simple band at Tiffany's to go with her engagement ring. She had to get her syllabi in order for her full load this semester, revise her curriculum vitae, and submit a letter to the dean of the School of Fine Arts at Hunter expressing her interest in the department chair position upon Max's retirement at the end of the year.

Simon was in London working with the Tate and Hockney, but he was due back in a few weeks to help plan some of the final arrangements for the wedding. They had finished making the guest list, and the invitations were ready and waiting to be picked up at the stationery shop on the corner of East 89th and Lexington.

It was a Thursday in early October when Julia picked them up and brought them into Bess's office on the second floor of the brownstone. They addressed them together, with Chloe carefully putting the modern art "Forever" stamp in the top corner of each one. The image was one of William H. Johnson's, and it featured a bright angular bouquet of flowers on a table and looked like a postmodernist's tribute to Picasso and van Gogh.

Chloe was more excited about the wedding than anyone. She had lost her two front teeth and she had broken her arm at day camp in the Hamptons over the summer, which she worried would somehow hamper her role in the wedding. But her arm was nearly mended by now, and she had the littlest buds pushing through her gums. It was her great Christmas wish, like so many seven-year-olds, that she would have her two front teeth by the time of the big event. Julia assured her that nothing short of a full body cast could keep her from her star role in the wedding.

The invitations went out on a Friday in

late October and the majority of the responses came back before the end of the month. Julia's mother would take the train up with her new neighbor friend, and Aunt Dot would come if she was feeling up to it. Meg and her family were unable to attend due to previous holiday commitments, but she sent an extravagant present, a crystal ice bucket and eight crystal highball glasses from a high-end gift shop on King Street, even though the insert in the invitation had requested donations be made to 92nd Street Y's "fine arts for inner-city kids" program in lieu of gifts. Between Simon and Julia, they had more than enough to outfit an apartment.

Time moved on, and it moved on fast. Julia stepped back into her New York life like an old and familiar coat worn in just the right spots — teaching all day, visiting the latest galleries on the weekend, painting on her deck on weekend mornings until the chill drove her inside. She had submitted some slides of her "Faces of Budapest" paintings to a few of the premier private galleries around the country and was hoping one of them might be interested in putting together an exhibit with a focus on Central Europe. She was eagerly awaiting their responses.

Simon came back into town like a whirl-wind in early November, carting her around to meet interested buyers, taking her to furniture stores where they could select a few new pieces to make his apartment more theirs than his, taking her to her doctor's appointment where the obstetrician encour-aged them to start trying for that baby as soon as the ink was dry on the marriage certificate.

Hockney arrived later that week with his third wife in tow, a very young woman from Lithuania who wanted to dine at the Four Seasons beneath the twinkling chain cur-tains because she'd read about them in an American magazine. It would be an impor-tant dinner meeting with Pierre Levasseur, who was the assistant curator at the Mu-seum of Modern Art. Levasseur had taken a recent interest in Hockney after the press release about the Tate exhibit. If Simon could land Hockney an exhibit at the MOMA, they both would have reached a kind of milestone in their careers far beyond their wildest imaginings. Simon was relieved to have procured a dinner reservation at the Four Seasons on such late notice, but he insisted that they be put at a table in the far corner. (The last time they had eaten there nearly two years ago, they'd sat right beside

Brad Pitt and his entourage, and Simon was completely put out by how loud they were and how many things they sent back to the chef because it had this or that ingredient they didn't like.)

The night of the dinner, Julia felt fine. But when they were all seated at their corner table with a view of the whole room, swaying silver curtains and all, she saw a man out of the corner of her eye who bore a striking resemblance to Jack Ball, the photographer friend she had lost at the World Trade Center. He kept staring at her from across the way, and by the time the entrées arrived, her heart was pounding so furiously she knew a panic attack was inevitable.

It had been so long since she'd had one. What was wrong with her? Was she hallucinating? When the man came over to introduce himself, she stood up as if drawn by some other force and yelped with fear, at which Simon quickly arose and came to her side. She realized as she stared at the man that it wasn't Jack. He was much shorter and his nose had a crook in it that was different from her friend's. The man was, in fact, a British journalist who particularly admired Hockney, and he couldn't help but be so bold as to introduce himself. Simon quickly excused himself and escorted her to the ladies' room, where she stood in the hallway trembling.

"What's got into you, Julia?" he whispered in a frustrating hush as he ran his fingers through his spiky salt-and-pepper hair. Three deep worry lines were spreading across his forehead, and she noticed a thick vein throbbing along the side of his neck. "This is one of the biggest dinners of our lives."

"I don't know," she said as she bit her thumbnail. "I'm sorry."

"Get ahold of yourself." He motioned toward the bathroom. "Splash some water on your face, powder your nose, and then come on back to the table."

"All right," she said, and she raced into the beautiful bathroom with its green velvet walls and little crystal chandeliers.

She popped the emergency Ativan she now carried in her purse, and she continued through the dinner breathing out of her mouth, nodding, smiling, and saying very little. Simon was irritated, she could tell, but he walked her up to the brownstone, with Hockney and his wife in the cab, still eager to hit the late-night scene. He rubbed her cheek with his thumb. "Get some rest. I'll call you tomorrow."

She looked into his eyes. He did earnestly

love her. She could see that, and she didn't really even know why.

"I hope I didn't mess up the evening."

He pecked her forehead. "Of course you didn't. You were the most beautiful woman in the room, and I was the envy of every man."

She shook her head as Hockney called, "Let's go, Simon! You two have the rest of your lives to smooch, and my bride wants a nitrotini at Bar 89."

Julia met with her therapist the following week for the first time in several months. She told her all about the summer — her week at Edisto, the months in Budapest, her anxiety about the wedding.

"You think I just have the garden-variety jitters?" she asked.

"Probably," her therapist said. "But I'm stunned that you went to Edisto to keep those children." She clicked her pen against her pad. "And I'm even more stunned about how much genuine fun it sounds like you had."

Julia planted her face in her hands. "I know," she said. "It was the most fun I've had in a long time. Isn't that insane?"

One November afternoon, when the first

snowflakes started falling, Julia took a break from grading papers to watch them flutter down in front of her office window. The first snow brought with it a hush that fell over the city for several months like a heavily weighted cloak, and it brought a kind of quiet, sleepy peace she always enjoyed. Just as she imagined her pulse slowing like a bear preparing for hibernation, her phone rang.

"Oh, Juuul-yah." It was Aunt Dot. Immediately, Julia could tell by the tone of her voice it was bad news and she thought of the children and prayed they were all right.

"It's back," the woman's warbly voice bellowed. "Marney's cancer. It's in her brain, and it's not good."

Julia blinked hard and continued to stare out of the window. Her office faced the inside of the building and she had a view of other offices on all sides and an old, rusted furnace no one had bothered to dispose of.

"What's the prognosis?" she said as the snow began to coat windowsills and the surface of the old furnace.

"We're looking at all of the options, but it's the worst kind. They call it glioblastoma multiforme," Dot said. "My neighbor Arthur Chutney had it a few years ago and he was gone in less than three months."

Julia blinked slowly. It was more than she could take in. And then the three round faces popped into her mind. "How are the children?"

Aunt Dot clucked. "They don't really understand, and she hasn't told them much."

Julia saw Etta in her mind's eye — her green, knowing eyes. And then the words surfaced. "What should I do?"

"I don't know, honey. I really don't know. I know your big day is approaching and I don't want to put too much on you."

"I do have a lot right now." Julia exhaled deeply as Etta's image faded. "Thank you, Aunt Dot. Thank you for letting me know."

"I guess all any of us can do is pray, Julia. Our times are in his hands."

"I will," Julia said, nodding firmly. "I will pray every day. Please keep me updated when you can."

"Of course, sweetheart."

The days clicked slowly by as the snow fell and turned to a gray slush, and Julia thought of Marney. She looked up glioblastoma multiforme on the computer and the outlook was bleak. Life expectancy was typically less than a year.

She almost called the home phone at Edisto more than once as the cold, dark evenings ticked by. Then she found herself swept up in the preparation of the department meeting where she was elected, almost unanimously, chair of the visual arts department. Now the dean needed a five-year plan to show to the provost in a few weeks before the next budget was decided on and Max gladly turned it over to her. "All yours now, Julia."

"Oh boy." She took a deep breath, brewed a large pot of coffee, and got to work preparing the plan.

A month went by, and she heard nothing more. Two weeks before the wedding, Marney called her, sounding very frail at the other end of the line. "I need to speak to you, Julia. Can you come home? I just need one meeting with you."

CHAPTER 31
JED

Jed took the elevator up to Rick and Dana's condominium. He had gotten roped into a dinner with Stephanie, the wedding planner, and he feared Dana's mealy shrimp creole was on the menu, so he brought a little side dish to add to the mix, an avocado and crabmeat salad sprinkled with a lemon vinaigrette dressing, and his new favorite dessert to make, a buttermilk pie.

Dr. Maria Tamsberg, the head of oncology, was also going to be there, as was her husband, Boris Zelenko. Boris was a cellist and professor of music at the College of Charleston, and Jed enjoyed his company because he always had something interesting to share about music or about food or about the state of politics in the Ukraine.

Jed knocked on the door, and Rick and Dana's daughter answered. She must have been about seven and she had a book in her hand and glasses on.

346

"Hey there." Jed repositioned his pie and salad and put out his hand. "I'm Jed."

The little girl grinned largely. "You're my cousin's date."

"I guess you could say that." He nodded.

The little girl tucked the book beneath her arm and put out her opposite hand. "I'm Eliza."

"Well, it's very nice to meet you, Eliza." He shook her delicate hand and she motioned for him to follow her.

"Jed!" Dana said as he ducked beneath the brass chandelier in the foyer. "Welcome."

Jed was relieved to see what looked like a hired chef in the kitchen preparing the meal.

"Hi, Dana." He handed her the salad and the pie. "I brought a few things to add."

"Wonderful!" She took his bowl and pie plate and put them on the kitchen counter. Then she led him through the den and out to the large deck where they had a beautiful view of the Ashley River. Sailboats and motorboats were coming and going, racing home before the sunset.

Maria and Boris stood to greet him, and Rick asked him if he'd like red or white wine.

He was thankful that Stephanie had not yet arrived. It would be nice to catch up with his colleagues for a moment.

Maria took an oyster on the half shell from the appetizer tray and turned to him. "You have a place out at Edisto, right?"

"Not if I can help it," Rick said as he uncorked a bottle of pinot noir.

"Yeah." Jed rubbed his hands across his jeans and leaned toward Maria as he said quietly, "I've been meaning to ask you how Marney Bennett is doing. She's my neighbor out there and I know her family."

Maria winced as if in pain. "Glioblastoma multiforme."

Jed shook his head and his heart began to pound. "Where?"

Maria pointed to her forehead.

Jed exhaled slowly. They all knew the prognosis for ninety percent of all glioblastoma multiforme cases, and it was decidedly grim. He thought of Charlie, Etta, and Heath, and he thought of Julia. What would this mean for everyone?

Just as he leaned in to ask more, Dana popped her head through the sliding glass door and clapped her hands. "Look who's here, Jed."

Everyone stood as Stephanie stepped onto the deck. She was all dolled up in a short, strapless zebra-print dress, a made-up face, candy-red dangly earrings, and red patent leather platform heels. While he guessed this was the latest look, it seemed a little over the top.

"Hey there!" Stephanie leaned toward him for a cheek kiss.

He leaned forward and pecked at the air beside her, then he discreetly wiped her lipstick off of his cheekbone. He still yearned for Julia Bennett. Had hung her tomatoes painting above the fireplace in his bedroom. It was the first thing he saw when he woke up every morning. And yet he knew he needed to move on.

The evening was relatively pleasant. The chef, Hector, served a brightly colored and delectable meal — salmon and beef satay, an assortment of roasted root vegetables, a citrus and tomato salad, and a creamy asparagus risotto.

Stephanie seemed to dominate the evening with stories about weddings. She had just helped coordinate one in Charleston for a teenybopper star on the Disney Channel, and she'd had to hire guards to keep the screaming adolescents away from the rehearsal dinner at McCrady's and the ceremony at St. John's Cathedral on Broad Street.

Boris had a good run too, and Jed enjoyed

hearing about his childhood in L'viv and how he ended up at the Moscow Conservatory before meeting Maria during a trip to the States where he served as a visiting artist at Cornell University while she was in medical school there. They had met in the cafeteria one afternoon, each vying for the last stuffed cabbage in the food line. They ended up splitting it, and the rest was history.

Toward the end of the night, Eliza came out from her room and settled herself in Rick's lap, folding up her gangly arms and legs like an accordion. Rick rested his head on his daughter's dark mahogany crown as everyone devoured Jed's pie. Jed watched as Eliza showed her father a little cut on her finger. Rick examined it lovingly and with concern before pecking it and pulling her closer. The child brought out a whole different side of Jed's tough-man colleague, and it was good to see.

Jed envied Rick and Dana. They were the same age he was, at the same point in their careers, but they seemed to have everything Jed thought he would have by now: a strong marriage, an adorable child, a dynamic home, a full life.

His patient, the forty-year-old man with the four children, had recovered beautifully, and Jed had enjoyed checking on him each day before his release, because the man seemed full of something Jed wanted and because he was always flanked by several children at his bedside who were funny and loud and boisterous and by a wife who took it all in stride. What Jed wouldn't give now for a life like that.

Now Stephanie, who seemed to have partaken rather heartily of the libations, reached over and took his hand. Then she leaned over and whispered, "Walk me to my car?"

He tried not to wince. "All right."

Stephanie wiped a dollop of pie from her mouth, stood, and announced she had to be going. She had a meeting with a caterer at seven a.m. the next day.

Jed thanked Rick and Dana and bid farewell to Boris, Maria, Hector, and little Eliza, then followed Stephanie out of the condominium.

She took his hand in the elevator, and he was relieved when it stopped on the next floor down and a group of elderly women piled in.

When they arrived at the garage, he walked her to her car and was thankful when his phone buzzed just as her BMW lights blinked when she unlocked the car.

He wasn't on call, but any diversion was a good one.

The message was from Jane Anne, his second cousin and Mary Ellen Bennett's neighbor. *Call immediately,* it read.

He looked up from his phone as Stephanie gazed at him, flipping her thick, dark hair behind her shoulders. The smell of her spicy perfume nearly turned his stomach.

"Want to get a night cap?"

Jed knew he shouldn't let her drive in this condition, but he had no desire to get a night cap. He took a step back. "Listen, Stephanie. Let me drive you home. I think you've had a bit much, and I wouldn't feel right about letting you get behind the wheel."

She clapped her long, brightly painted nails on his arm before he could finish. "Okay!" She examined the garage. "Where's your car?" Then she winked as she locked hers back up. "Maybe you can bring me back to get mine in the morning."

He lifted his phone. "I don't think so. I've got a little emergency on my hands."

She rolled her eyes dramatically. "Great," she muttered.

They walked to his old Land Rover, which was caked in Rascal hair and a Rascal smell that was not to Stephanie's liking. The woman couldn't get out of the car fast enough when Jed pulled up to her place on upper King Street. She beat at her little dress as the black dog hair fell off of it on the sidewalk.

"This is a Roberto Cavalli."

"Sorry," he said as he walked her up the stairs to her front door.

"Me too." Her tone was sarcastic as she swung around on the threshold, her long, dark hair swatting him in the face. She put her hands on her curvy hips. "What a disappointment you are, Jed Young." She glared up at him, and he shrugged his shoulders and put his hands in his jeans like a sheepish schoolboy.

"Sorry again," he said. Then she closed the door in his face, and he could hear her mumbling to herself as her heels clapped on the kitchen floor.

"Good-bye," he said as he turned and strode quickly back to his car.

Once he closed the door, he grinned at the dog hair and then dialed Jane Anne's number.

"Jed," the lady said. "You know about Marney?"

"I just heard," he said.

"Well, I don't mean to get in the middle of your business, but I thought you'd like to

353

know that Marney has summoned Julia home for a chat."

"And she's coming?"

"Tomorrow, I believe," she said.

"Thank you for letting me know, Jane Anne."

The lady cleared her throat, reminding him of a schoolmarm. "And you're going to call her, right?"

He chuckled. Jane Anne was more Southern belle busybody than schoolmarm, and he appreciated her for that. "You bet I am, cousin."

"Good boy," she said. "Good night!"

Jed started his car and drove back to his apartment on Rutledge Avenue. He let Rascal out, and they raced together over to the Horse Lot where he threw the ball for him over and over beneath the buzz of the streetlamps.

Marney was dying. Julia was coming home to speak with her. Jed hoped for one chance to talk with her — to look her in the eye, to see if there was any inkling of mutual longing, if there was any way he could stop her from marrying next month.

He chased Rascal back and forth across the grassy field over and over until they both finally collapsed in the center and wrestled one another beneath the clear November sky as the stars, millions of miles away and already burned out, still glimmered.

CHAPTER 32
JULIA

Julia nearly finished her budget proposal for the dean. She bought a ticket online and left for Charleston the next day. She would just be in and out because she had to put the final touches on the proposal and give an exam the following morning.

Her mother picked her up at the airport and delivered her directly to Aunt Dot's where Marney and the children had been staying because of Marney's need to be near the cancer center.

The children were waiting for her on the porch of Aunt Dot's old home on the corner of Broad and Legare Street. Charlie and Heath ran out to greet her when her car pulled up, as Etta slowly made her way down the steps. She embraced them all hard and pulled back to get a good look at them. They had changed so much over the last six months. Heath looked at least two inches taller, and she had chopped off her hair in a stylish bob that made her look older. Etta's hair was longer, and she was filling out just slightly. She was taking everything in as usual, recording it in that imaginative brain of hers where Julia expected it to show up in an image that spoke louder than words in the coming days and weeks. Charlie seemed bigger too. He had lost some of the baby fat in his cheeks, but there was still enough to want to kiss them over and over again, which Julia couldn't help but do as he grinned and said, "Jewelllla. You came back."

Aunt Dot looked much older. She had a walker and a tremble in her hands that made her look particularly fragile. But she had the warm smile that Julia had always remembered so fondly and a kind of inner strength unlike many people Julia knew.

As Julia watched her hobble out of the front door onto the piazza, she recalled the summer she was eight, when she and Meg stayed for two weeks with Aunt Dot while her parents took a vacation to France. How Aunt Dot would give them coffee with a lot of cream and sugar with breakfast each morning and tell them stories about when she and their daddy were little. They would play endless games of go fish and gin rummy and concentration, and at night Aunt Dot would read to them from her Bible — wild stories about a man in a lions' den and another in the belly of an enormous fish. She would snap the book closed when she was finished and look them both in the eye. "You are loved by God who made you. He came to earth and gave his life because he loves you. Do you understand how precious that makes you?"

Julia remembered how her heart swelled when she heard those words each night as a young girl. They were like life to her or like sunlight, something even more powerful than art, and they remained etched in her heart even to this day.

After a lot of chattering from the children (except Etta, who only spoke with her eyes and let out one guarded smile), Aunt Dot nodded toward the upstairs. "She's waiting on you, sweetheart."

Julia nodded solemnly and headed up the old stairwell, its wall still covered in old black-and-white photographs and thick wallpaper with pink rose bouquets from the early '60s. The wallpaper was browning and curling slightly where the seams met. Julia resisted the urge to press it down.

Julia knocked lightly and then slowly pushed open the door of the guest bedroom. It made a slow whine and she stepped in.

Marney was sitting on a chair in front of the window overlooking Broad Street. She was draped in a yellow patch of afternoon sunlight, dust particles spinning in the wide beam in a way that made the whole scene seem ethereal.

But the closer Julia stepped, the more she realized how thin Marney was, how weak. Her face was nearly skeletal, and beneath the afghan Julia could see how knobby her knees and how reedy her legs were. Her hair had continued to thin, and it had grayed a lot since the last time Julia had seen her on her doorstep that evening last March. The smell of the room was an eerie combination of mustiness and medicine.

"Hi, Julia," Marney said as she licked her dry lips. She slowly took a sip of water from a glass with a bendable straw on the side table and motioned for her to come in. Julia stepped back and closed the door until it made a quiet click, then walked over to the end of the unmade bed where she smoothed out a section and took a seat on the very edge.

"Thank you for coming." Marney looked out of the window at the clear blue November sky, so crisp compared to the humid haze of June, then back to Julia.

Marney's eyes were still those enormous

azure discs, and though they had dulled some, they still struck you with their fierceness and their hunger.

Julia nodded. She couldn't seem to find the right words for this strange, sad moment so she just uttered, "I'm sorry."

Marney cleared her throat. "This is it." She coughed into her hand and Julia noticed how loose the skin on her forearms was. She remembered the full-bodied Marney of their youth — so curvy and solid, so fully fleshed out. Marney had always been physically stronger than Julia. She was the only one on the waitstaff at Dockside Restaurant who could carry an entire tray of eight entrées on her shoulder. She was the gal the frat boys always picked first at the intramural football games at Georgia.

Now Julia looked back into the blue eyes and Marney opened her mouth slowly. "I'll be gone soon."

"Don't say that." Julia repositioned herself on the bed and the old mattress groaned. "You're going to fight this."

Marney shook her head no. It took effort for her to speak, and Julia wanted to give her room and time. As much as she loathed Marney, this was a moment in which she just needed to simply be still and listen.

Marney breathed slowly, the afghan rising

and falling. She kept her mouth half-open and it reminded Julia of a small, dark cave.

"It's not my place to ask." Marney's voice was like dry gravel, but she pushed on. "But I have to . . ." She coughed again, this time without bothering to lift her bony hand to her mouth. ". . . for the sake of Heath and Etta . . . and Charlie."

Julia's heart began to pound rapidly. She suddenly felt frightened of this scene and had an urge to bolt to the door. *Ask what?* she thought. Was this some sort of Marney trick she was about to pull off even in her drastic and sickly state? She would be one to go down swinging, and Julia wouldn't put anything past her.

Lord, have mercy, Julia thought to herself. She gripped the edge of the bed and braced for whatever the blow might be. *Christ, have mercy.*

"When I pass . . ." Marney sucked her teeth and looked out of the window as a horn erupted somewhere down the busy street. Her eyes were glassy and bulbous from that side angle and the sunlight seemed to shine right through them. Now she turned back to Julia. "Will you take them?"

Julia's throat felt dry now, and her heart was knocking around like a wild animal in the cage of her chest. The room smelled even more antiseptic than before. And she thought there was the slightest hint of mildew too. How could she answer such a request?

She stood immediately and saw a few stars. The air in the room seemed to grow thicker by the moment, and she felt like she had to escape or she'd be trapped there forever. As if glioblastoma mulitforme was an infectious disease. As if death itself was communicable. And maybe it was.

Julia had so much she wanted to say to Marney, but how could she now? In this state? Julia made a fist as if to shake off the dizziness and all of the selfishness Marney possessed, as if to beat back the thick, stifling air. Yes, the children were precious and she cared for them, but she couldn't possibly commit to raising them, to re-arranging her entire life for them. It wasn't fair. And she probably wasn't the best one to rear them anyway.

After their years at Edisto, Manhattan would be a complete culture shock. They would be miserable. Simon would be miserable. Life, as she had built it so carefully, so steadfastly through the years, would cease.

"How could I . . . ," she whispered, sitting back down. "How could I possibly?" Julia was surprised by the tightening of her throat and the tears that suddenly filled her eyes. She had trouble holding them back, and she had trouble catching her breath.

Marney nodded her head. She closed her eyes and did not speak as whole minutes passed. Had she fallen asleep? How many people had she sat in this room and asked the same thing of, Julia now wondered.

"What else am I supposed to do?" Marney's voice was bitter and her eyes were still closed, though they seemed to move back and forth beneath the thin lids. Julia sensed Marney's agony and anger at her situation. She felt for her, but she couldn't take this on.

"There has to be someone else or some other way. You have to get better."

Marney opened her eyes quickly and gazed directly into Julia's. "You're the one," she said. "You have to take them." She gripped both arms of the chair with her thin, jaundiced hands. "For your father."

Julia stood quickly. "I need some air," she said. She wiped her eyes with the heels of her hands. She couldn't stop to talk to the kids, to let them see her in this condition. She crept down the stairs and out through the kitchen onto the back porch where she ran through the garden and then out onto the sidewalk. Then she bolted up Broad

Street to Colonial Lake. She circled the lake again and again as the tears streamed down her face.

Finally, she collapsed on a bench. Then she pulled out her phone from her jacket pocket. It had been buzzing every few minutes since she walked into Aunt Dot's house, but she hadn't bothered to look at it.

Her eyes widened as she saw Jed's name. He had sent her a text. *Call me before you leave town.* How did he know she was here? She thought of dialing Simon and telling him about the meeting with Marney, but she knew it would only upset him. He had little patience for her old life. Besides, his nerves were already on edge this week as he was preparing for a meeting with the MOMA board.

Before she even realized what she was doing, she dialed up Jed.

"Where are you?" he said.

"Sitting on a bench at Colonial Lake."

"I'll be there in ten." She heard the phone click, and she slumped down on the bench and rested her head. She could hear the late afternoon joggers and bike riders and strollers rolling by her. A child's voice said, "Is that woman asleep, Mama?"

Jed's well-worn Land Rover pulled up moments later. Rascal was barking in the back-

364

seat, wiping his nose all over the back windows. Jed cracked each window for his dog, then jumped out of the car in his pale blue scrubs and running shoes and dashed over to her. She stood and jumped into his arms, and he embraced her hard for whole minutes.

She held him tighter than she'd ever held anyone or anything, breathing in his smell and the warmth of his broad chest, and she wept, hardly able to catch her breath, for so long that the sun had nearly set and the sky had become a pinkish-purple, streaked with low-lying clouds.

He rubbed her back as she wept. His hand seemed as wide as her entire torso, and she felt so very protected — if but for a moment — within his arms. When she finally looked up, he smiled down and said, "How about some tea?"

She nodded and got into his car, Rascal leaping into her lap and licking her face. She rubbed the dog's soft scruff and buried her face in his sleek black fur.

They went to Kudu, a coffeehouse on Vanderhorst, where Jed ordered two chai lattes and found a spot for them in the back corner by an antelope mount.

"So tell me what's going on," he said as he set down the steaming, frothy cups and took a seat opposite her at the table.

"Marney wants me to take the children," she leaned in and said quietly, "if she doesn't make it."

He took a slow sip from his mug and gazed at her. What a handsome man he was. Tall, dark, brown-eyed, broad-shouldered, youthful. But more than that, he was caring. He had a way of exuding warmth and compassion and concern, and he was sending that all her way as he stared into her eyes.

"It doesn't look good for her, Julia," he said. "I've known several cases, and she's right to prepare for what is likely the inevitable."

Julia balled her hands into two tight fists. Then she gripped the edge of the table and leaned into him. "What am I supposed to do, Jed? Call up my fiancé and say, 'Hey, Simon, we're going to adopt three kids. My half sisters and half brother. And move them in with us. Hope that's not too much of a curveball for you, love'?"

Jed nodded empathetically. He didn't speak, and she was grateful.

"Marney completely changed my life as I knew it once already." Julia could feel her temples pulse. There was a large container of bitterness sealed off somewhere in her, and she felt as though someone was peeling off its lid. "Should I let her do that to me again?"

She pursed her lips and looked out the café window where college kids zoomed by on bikes and skateboards and their own two feet. She noticed a man outside of an Italian restaurant speaking his native tongue into a cell phone. Then she thought of the children. Heath, Charlie, Etta. She probably sounded like the cruelest woman in the world. Like the wicked half sister from some modern-day fairy tale. It wasn't their fault. None of this. But were they her responsibility? For the next twenty or so years? Is that what was best for anyone?

She felt Jed watching her. It was as if he were willing to wait forever while she worked this through in her mind. He took a sip of his tea and sat back in his chair. She noticed for the first time that he was in need of a shave. He must have been in a long surgery today, and here he was sitting with her — just sitting.

"What do you think will happen to the children?" she said to him. It seemed like a silly question to ask of someone who was not a part of her family. But she needed to get to the end of these questions like a blind woman feeling her way around an unfamiliar room.

"I don't know." He shook his head. "What about your aunt?"

Julia shook her head. "She looked awfully fragile today. She's in her late seventies. She's older than my dad. I don't see how she could do it."

He nodded. "What about your sister?"

Julia swallowed hard. "She loathes those children . . . She's more bitter than anyone. I can't imagine her taking them. In fact, she'd probably love to see them thrown into the foster care system."

Those words, *foster care system*. When they came out of Julia's mouth, she felt sick to her stomach, and the tears came back. "I don't know what to do, Jed."

He reached over and put his large hands on top of hers and rubbed them gently. He looked at her until she met his deep brown eyes. "You'll figure it out, Julia. You will."

She blew into her napkin so hard he couldn't help but chuckle a little, and she did too.

"Lovely, huh?" she said. Then she looked at her cell phone. "I've got to get to the airport. My flight leaves in an hour and a half."

He cleared his throat and readjusted his

posture. She could tell he wanted to say something, and she looked up, wiped her eyes, and gave him her full attention.

"If you decide to take care of the children . . . and I'm not saying you should . . . I'm just saying if Marney passes and you feel . . ." He leaned in closer.

She shook her head and the lump in her throat continued to grow.

He reached over and squeezed her hand. "I will help," he said. "If it comes to that, I will do whatever I can to help you."

She exhaled, taking in the sincerity in his eyes. How could he commit to something like that? To helping raise three children? He could up and move or fall in love and start his own family tomorrow, for all he knew. Anything could happen.

And yet, somewhere inside of her, in the little eight-year-old-girl part of her who still believed in simple kindness and straight-forward love, she thought, *He means it. He really means it.*

"I appreciate you saying so," she said. "I really do. But I don't know how you or I or anyone could agree to something like that. There are too many turns the future could take."

"Maybe," he said as he rubbed his thumb across her hand again. "But sometimes the

future is straight and clear, like the South
Edisto River on a still summer day. And all
you have to do is steer in as straight a line
as you know how."

She looked at him, at his warm, dark eyes.
"You're either an idealist or a fool."

He nodded and raised his eyebrows. "I've
been called both." He cleared his throat and
took the last sip of his tea. "I've also been
called a romantic."

She chuckled as she wiped her eyes. What
a day. What a crazy, crazy day. She squeezed
his hand back. "Do you think you could
take me by to say good-bye to the children
and then on to the airport?"

"I'd love to," he said.

She made a quick whirlwind of farewells to
the kids, Aunt Dot, and even her mother as
she dropped by the antique shop where she
worked and embraced her.

"What happened with Marney?" Her
mother looked up from her bifocals as she
stood over a gilded statue in the back of the
shop, her new little puppy curled up on a
pillow at her feet.

"I'll call you tomorrow and tell you,
okay?"

Julia's mother nodded and hugged her
again. Then Jed dropped her off at the

Charleston Airport. She raced through the ticket counter and then to the checkpoint and caught the last flight of the day back to New York.

CHAPTER 33
ETTA

Some things you just can't stop. Like the leaves from turning red in November. Like their loosening from the tree limbs. Like their flutter down to the ground where they turn brown and dry. Or their crunch under your bare feet when you walk through the old garden.

It's Mama's forty-first birthday. Aunt Dot is making her favorite dish, beef stew, and her favorite dessert, coconut cake. The cake had to set for two days in the refrigerator, and it's been all I can do to keep Charlie away from it.

Charlie is restless and so am I. We've been at Aunt Dot's for six weeks now, and we miss roaming the woods at Edisto and dipping our lines in the creek. Aunt Dot doesn't move as fast as she used to because of her hips and the walker she has to lean on, and we don't get to go to the park or for walks or bike rides as often as we'd like.

We do, however, go out in the old garden behind her house where there is one good climbing-size magnolia tree whose trunk stretches beyond her rooftop and several azalea and camellia bushes that are good for hiding behind or napping beneath.

Heath is allowed to take us for short walks as long as Charlie holds her hand and we watch for cars pulling out of driveways and we don't talk to strangers, which I have no intention of doing. We are also allowed to go to Colonial Lake and to Moultrie Playground before dusk, and we can go to Mr. Burbage's to buy a piece of candy or a Gatorade.

We can even walk to the coast guard station in the afternoon and watch the junior sailing class, dozens of little one-man boats near the seawall tacking this way and that, their bright sails flapping in the wind like a rabble of butterflies. The kids in the boats don't look much older than me or Heath, but they do seem to have a lot more freedom than us, driving their vessels wherever the wind blows.

"I'm going to sail a boat one day." Charlie points to a redheaded boy who is grasping the tiller with one hand and some sort of rope connected to the sail with the other.

Heath tousles his hair, and I reach for his

chunky hand. If we didn't have Charlie to look after, we would be bored and lonely and, worst of all, purposeless.

Julia visited for a few hours last week, and she left the same day. She came to talk to Mama, who is sick and quiet and resting in Aunt Dot's guest room with several quilts across her long, bony legs. I saw Julia run down the stairs and out the back door, wiping her nose and her green eyes with the backs of her hands. Whatever Mama said or did must have upset her. Maybe that is why she never wanted to see her when she visited us last summer. Whatever Mama said or did is a secret that even I don't know.

Now as I sit in the top of the magnolia tree in Aunt Dot's garden, sketching the rooftops and St. Michael's steeple, I ignore Charlie's begging me to get down and play hide and go seek.

"Ask Heath," I finally whisper. He scoffs and walks back to the house where I hear the old screen door to the kitchen screech, then slap behind him.

I look over to one of the upstairs windows where I can see Mama resting in an old lounge chair. Her eyes are closed and she looks still. So still you would never know there is an invasion going on in her brain. A tumor growing larger by the moment, destroying the gray matter that helps her think and remember and be herself.

I hear the screech of the back door again. "Etta?" Heath has her hands on her hips and is staring up the tree. I joggle the limb a little so she knows I'm here.

"You need to set the table. I'm going to help get Mama down the stairs."

I turn and grab hold of the knobby trunk of the great tree and climb down it limb by inner limb like a leafy ladder.

Mama can't make it down the stairs so Heath carries up a card table, and I set it up in the upstairs hallway. Charlie pulls a few chairs and stools from the bedrooms until everyone has a place.

Aunt Dot slowly carries up steaming bowls of beef stew as Mama leans on Heath and makes her way out of the bedroom door before settling herself in the ladder-back chair from Aunt Dot's vanity.

Charlie burns his mouth on the stew right away and then he drops his spoon on the hardwood floor. I take it to the bathroom sink, wash it out, and give it back to him, and Aunt Dot tells him to drink his milk and blow on the stew before he takes another bite.

Mama tries hard to keep her head up, but it looks like it weighs one hundred pounds, and she drops it to the side from time to time. Aunt Dot brings the stew to Mama's lips and she slurps a little and smiles. "Mmm," she says. Then she looks to me and winks, and I know she is still in there somewhere, ducking up out of the trenches as if to say, *It's not over yet.*

After supper Heath carries up the cake and we sing "Happy Birthday. Happy Birthday, dear Mama." Then we are all quiet as Aunt Dot cuts into the cake and serves it up. She gives Charlie an extra-large piece and she cuts Mama's up into little bites and lifts it on a fork to her mouth. Mama chokes a little on the coconut bits and Aunt Dot lifts the water with the straw up to her mouth and she slurps and nods.

The cake is good. Sweet and fluffy and whip-creamy. I remember, back when I was five, when Daddy and I tried to make the same cake for Mama on her birthday. It turned out lopsided and gooey because we didn't know it needed to set a few days in the refrigerator. But Mama acted like it was the greatest thing she had ever tasted. She ate two large slimey slices just to convince us as the top layer slid slowly off of the bottom layer onto the table on the screened porch at the creek house.

"We did good, Etta baby." Daddy squeezed my shoulder and I rested back into his thick, soft chest.

"Yes, you did." Mama smiled, then she reached over and put the top layer back on the bottom as we all chuckled.

After a few more bites of cake, Mama says she needs to lie down and Heath helps her back to the bed while Aunt Dot and I clear the table and Charlie eats a second slice before putting on his pajamas. Once the Crock-Pot is soaking in sudsy water and the dishwasher is turned on, churn-churn-churning all of the food off of the china plates, I sneak back out to the darkened garden and climb the tree so I can see the steeple at night, its soft light glowing from the upper balcony above the bells and the clock tower.

Aunt Dot says she's been to the top of the tall, tall steeple a few times, and the view of the city and the harbor is like no other. And once, when the enormous brass bells rang out while she was up there, she could feel the steeple swaying ever so slightly from side to side.

What are the odds of a child losing two parents before they turn ten? What is the probability? What is the explanation? Even in the novels I read, a child doesn't lose two parents, except in *The Secret Garden* and *The Boxcar Children,* of course. But Mary Lennox's parents were never good to her when they were alive so the loss doesn't seem so bad, and it doesn't take long for the boxcar children to find their grandfather, who is loving and kind and willing to take care of them forever and ever.

Now I can see Aunt Dot take her place by Charlie's bed in the twin bedroom next to Mama's. Aunt Dot's got the little devotional book out with the yellow, smudged pages. It's called *More Little Visits with God* and she used to read it to her son many years ago. There are stories about trusting God and looking forward to heaven, and when she reads them my heart slows down and I imagine the basin of light filling a dark, cold room with warmth.

I'm scared. I'll admit it. I don't know what will happen to us. It's a secret I am not allowed to know.

Now I zip my fleece up and lean back against the trunk of the tree and stare at the steeple against the indigo sky. I rub my arms across the large knobby limbs as a cold breeze rustles the waxy green leaves. What other choice do I have but to wait?

CHAPTER 34
JULIA

Julia gave her last exam, put the final touches on the five-year plan and budget for the visual arts department, and turned it into the dean. It had been snowing lightly for almost twenty-four hours, and with a few hours to kill before she met Bess and Chloe for an afternoon fitting of the wedding gown at the boutique on Madison and 57th, she decided to take a cab down to the corner of 42nd Street and Fifth Avenue and walk her way up Fifth so she could peer into the Christmas windows of the department stores — Bergdorf, Macy's, Henri Bendel, Saks. She used to do this every Christmas when she first moved to New York as a postgraduate with barely two pennies to rub together, and she felt like both the luckiest woman and the loneliest as she passed the faces of strangers, their arms laden with bags that they carried home to families and tucked beneath beautiful Christmas trees.

All those years ago she used to always stop into St. Patrick's Cathedral. Despite the tourists and the business of the city at Christmas, there was always a precious, hushed silence once you stepped inside the cathedral. There, she'd stop and exhale and find an empty pew in the back and get down on bended knee. She could be still for a moment, and that was precious to her.

She had spent many lonely years in her early twenties on bended knee around the holidays asking God why: *Why did my father betray me? Why did my best friend betray me? Will my mother ever get over it? Will Meg? Will I?* She never received an audible answer, but she did always feel a kind of heat, even though the stone floors of the cathedral couldn't have been colder. A kind of heat that started in her solar plexus and worked its way up to her heart and her mind.

She hadn't asked those questions in several years, and when she walked into St. Patrick's this day, she lit four candles: one for Heath, one for Etta, one for Charlie, and one for Marney. Then she found a pew in the back, walked to its very end by one of the inner stone columns, and kneeled down.

"I pray for Marney to be well," she uttered. "To make a miraculous recovery. And if not, I pray for someone, the right person, to raise the children. I pray for their hearts not to give in to despair. I pray for them to have hope and hang on and survive and find faith."

"Please, please, please," she said, though she wasn't exactly sure, in her heart of hearts, what her *please* was most for. There was so much she yearned for and so much she was afraid of. And it was all so interwoven into a tangled heap of love and loss.

As she prayed she pictured that smooth surface that Jed had talked about, and she imagined herself on the bow of her father's old johnboat, moving out over the slack tide toward the honey hole on a bright summer morning as the ibises gathered on a marsh mound, as two porpoises broke the water with their silver fins. The future as a straight line? It hardly felt like that. When she looked back on the bow of the boat, she saw her father driving. He was looking over at the ibises, taking the scene in with a great inhale.

Watch, she could hear him say as he leaned over her shoulder and examined her canvas. *The scene passes quickly, and if you're not careful, you'll miss it.*

■ ■ ■ ■

And then on the hard pew on the stone-cold floor, she dozed off and woke when the pew in front of her creaked as a row of tourists — schoolchildren from China it looked like — filed in.

Julia checked her phone. She was five minutes late for her fitting. She raced out of the cathedral and hailed a cab, and when she walked into the boutique, Chloe and Bess were sipping tea and smiling at her.

She wiped the haze from her eyes. "Sorry I'm late. I somehow fell asleep in St. Patrick's."

The designer's assistant, a woman named Siri, gave her an odd look. "Well, you're the last fitting of the day, so go ahead into the dressing room and then come out and step on the pedestal for a final look."

"All right." She looked at Bess and gave her an *I'm sorry* look.

Bess shrugged her shoulders and whispered, "She's just being a snob. That's part of her job."

Julia stepped into the large dressing room with its crystal sconces and thick, creamy wallpaper with large gold bees. She peeled off her work clothes — brown corduroy suit, knee-high well-scuffed boots, burgundy scarf. Her eye makeup had smeared at the edges of her eyes, highlighting her crow's feet, and she noticed a blemish she was getting on the side of her forehead.

Lovely bride, she thought. Aging and yet somehow still pimply.

The assistant knocked on the door and came in to fasten the silk-covered buttons on her candlelight-colored gown. It was strapless and pure silk with a straight skirt and a small train bustled on the back with silk-covered buttons.

The assistant helped put the long silk gloves on and gave her her arm as they walked out into the center of the fitting room where both Chloe and Bess gasped in wonder.

"You look beautiful." Chloe smiled, exposing the little upside-down peak in her top gum where her two front baby teeth had once protruded like little pearls in the center of a perfect strand. She leapt up and walked around and around Julia, taking it all in. Bess put down her tea and walked behind Julia so as to catch her eye in the mirror.

"It's stunning," she said, and she patted her waist gently. "You look like a twenty-year-old bride."

"Yeah, right," Julia uttered as she wiped

her eye with the tip of her silk glove, leaving a smudge of mascara on one of the fingertips. "Though I suppose the big pimple on my forehead does add a certain child-bride effect."

The assistant clucked at the smudge on the silk glove, removed it, and put on another. Then she set to work pulling at the waist and hips to make sure there didn't need to be another tuck between now and two Saturdays from now when Julia would tie the knot.

"It's perfect." Bess spoke to Julia, but her message was directed to the assistant. "I wouldn't change a thing."

"Yes, yes," said Siri. "Just let me make sure."

Chloe grabbed Julia's gloved hand and stood on the pedestal beside her. "Are you the happiest lady in the world?"

Julia squeezed the precious child's hand and met her eyes in the mirror. Happy? Astonished, perhaps. Astonished that she was finally getting married, finally pinning Simon down, finally about to start that family she'd been longing for the last several years.

But happy? When was the last time she could say she was really happy? Filled with joy? She knew the answer instantly, but she didn't dare speak it or even think it too hard. If she let her mind go there, she might fall apart at the seams. *Get a grip. Press on. Don't look back.* These were her life mottos and had been for decades. She couldn't abandon them now.

"I am," she said to Chloe, who cocked her head and stared into her eyes as if she wanted to believe her more than anything as Bess fussed with Siri about leaving the dress be.

"Good." The child squeezed Julia's hand hard and gave her a serious look in the mirror. "I want you to be," she said.

CHAPTER 35
JULIA

Four days before the wedding, Aunt Dot called. Simon's sons had just flown into town and they were all having lunch at Nobu when Julia stepped into the ladies' room to hear her aunt better.

"We're moving Marney to hospice this afternoon," she said. "They think it will be a matter of days, not weeks."

Julia felt as if she'd gotten a kick in the stomach. "I'm so sorry, Aunt Dot." Then they both wept into the phone before Julia worked up the nerve to ask, "How are the children?"

Aunt Dot spoke through her warbly voice as she tried to hold back her weeping. "I've tried to tell them, Julia. Tried to prepare them. But you never really know if they understand what's happening." She paused and talked in a more hushed tone. "I know Heath knows what death means, and I suppose Etta does too, but of course she won't say a word to let me know how she's doing. Charlie really doesn't understand any of it, naturally. He won't understand what's happened for a long time."

Julia held her breath for as long as she could, then asked, "Have there been any arrangements made for the kids?"

Aunt Dot paused. "No," she said solemnly. "No, there haven't. They'll stay with me until I have my second hip operation in February . . . I'm praying to the Lord for strength and provision to take care of them, but I just don't know some days if I have the strength. They aren't even in school, you know, Julia, and I certainly don't think I can homeschool them the way Marney was . . ."

Julia could hear a clattering in the background. Then she thought she heard Charlie's muffled voice. Aunt Dot held her hand over the phone, then came back rather breathless. "I've got to go, honey." The elderly woman cleared her throat and spoke directly. "But do come down if there's anything else you want to say . . . to Marney. She's still awake, but I don't think she will be for long. I know it's your wedding week, but I can't stop what's happening here. It's a freight train barreling toward us. All we can do is brace ourselves."

Anything else to say to Marney? What did Aunt Dot mean?

"Okay," she said. "I'll call you back tonight to check in and talk to the kids."

"All right, dear. The Lord be with you." Aunt Dot had already started speaking to someone else in the background before she hung up the receiver. There was a whine and then a click and then silence.

Julia walked back out to the table where Simon's sons were toasting his success at landing the MOMA exhibit. He was planning a ski trip to Switzerland in February, and he wanted them to join him and Julia over their winter school breaks to celebrate.

Julia watched Simon beaming as he held up his champagne glass. He was a man who had everything he needed, and she was a woman who was growing more distraught by the moment. She had filled him in on Marney's condition and grave prognosis, but she hadn't told him about her outrageous request a few weeks ago. There just was never a right time. And while she knew it was an impossibility, she didn't want him to tell her so.

"Who was that?" Simon asked as she took her place and a waiter came by to hand her a fresh linen napkin.

"My aunt." She picked up a champagne

glass and watched the bubbles rising from the blackberries that had been plopped in the bottom of the glass.

Simon's clink against hers startled her, and she spilled a little on the linen tablecloth. "What's up with Aunt Dot?"

She cleared her throat and put down the glass. "They're moving Marney to hospice."

He took another sip and raised his eyebrows. "A sad end, Julia. I'm sorry to hear that."

She nodded and looked into the bright faces of his children, who were completely lost by the conversation and growing more uninterested by the moment. Then the plates of yellowtail sashimi and whitefish with dried miso arrived, and the boys put their heads down and delved in as if they hadn't eaten in weeks, loading their sushi with wasabi until their eyes watered and their noses burned and ran.

Julia couldn't eat. She excused herself, and Simon walked her to the curb to catch a cab home.

"Are you all right?" he said, pressing gently on the small of her back. "I don't want anything to ruin this week for you."

"I'm distressed," she said. "Distressed for Marney and the children. It's unspeakably tragic."

"Yes." He lifted his hand as a taxi did a U-turn and bumped up on the curb beside them. He turned to look her in the eye and squeezed her shoulders. "But it's not your tragedy, Julia. You've lived through your tragedy and so have I. This is our time for happiness."

He kissed her sweetly on the lips and opened the door for her. Once she was settled inside, he ducked his head in. "I'll call you in a few hours after I take the boys over to MOMA."

"Okay." She closed the door and waved to him. "I'll be home."

"It's heartbreaking," Bess said, and she reached out her hand to squeeze Julia's. Bess and Julia had been friends since grade school so she knew every part of Julia's story. And Julia had told her about the recent visit to Charleston, about Marney's request.

"Do you think I should go and say good-bye to her?"

"I don't know." Bess wrung her hands. "It is four days until your wedding. Isn't your mother arriving tomorrow?"

Julia nodded her head. "Yes." She looked out at the neighboring apartment building and up to the gray December sky.

"But," Bess continued, "you have to face whatever is going on inside of you, Julia. Something has changed since this summer. I can see that. If that involves seeing Marney before she passes, then do it. You'll regret it if you don't."

Julia twisted her hair into a knot and rubbed her hands together quickly as if she were on a lift chair in the Alps without gloves. She felt cold, completely cold to the bone, even though she could hear the heat pouring into the room and she knew the thermostat read seventy degrees. "Do I have the most dysfunctional life or what?"

"No, you don't." Bess let out a chuckle. "It's certainly dysfunctional, but it's not the *most* dysfunctional. I can assure you of that. And what can you do? You have to play the cards you're dealt. You can't turn them back in because you don't like them."

Julia chuckled back and then stretched. "I really just want to take a nap. I feel exhausted."

"Okay. I'll leave you alone," Bess said. She stood and hugged her friend and then headed back down the elevator to the second floor. Julia crawled beneath her comforter and took a long rest, ignoring her cell phone as it quacked, ignoring her e-mail as its bell sounded from her computer.

It was dark outside and the clock read five p.m. when she woke up and walked over to the drawer in her kitchen where she kept a stack of photographs. She pulled out the one from when Charlie was a baby, the one with Heath and Etta proudly flanking his side, their heads tilted in toward the infant who was poking his pink lips out as he gargled.

Before she knew what she was doing, she packed an overnight bag, put on her overcoat, and hailed a cab for the airport where she purchased a direct flight on Delta to Charleston. She'd be there in less than three hours.

She boarded the plane and took a seat by the darkened window. Staring at the lumps of dirty snow piled up on the sides of the runway, she pulled out her phone to call Aunt Dot.

"I'm on my way," she said. "I do need to speak with Marney."

Aunt Dot let out a long sigh. "Oh good," she said. "I had hoped against hope that you would come."

"What's the address of the hospice center?"

"It's on Glenn McConnell by St. Francis Hospital."

"All right," she said. "I'll rent a car and

get a hotel room near there and then I'll come to your house to visit the kids after I see Marney tomorrow morning."

"Okay," she said. "Thank you, Julia."

"Don't thank me." Julia bit her lip. "I'm not sure why, but I know I need to do this."

"Yes, you do," Aunt Dot said. "You most certainly do, my precious child."

The next morning Julia checked in at the front desk of the hospice center. They walked her back to where Marney was in a bed at the very end of the corridor. The hallway smelled sweet like an apple pie–scented candle, and it had several framed prints of wildlife and the salt marsh. One was even by her father. It was a print of his *Moon Rising Over Store Creek.* It showed an orange crescent above the live oak trees and the black glittering water.

She fought back her nerves and tapped on the door that read "Mrs. Bennett." A nurse opened it and nodded to her as if she knew exactly who she was.

"I'll come back in a few minutes," the woman whispered. "Buzz if she needs me."

Julia nodded and walked toward the bed where Marney was propped up against several pillows and reclining slightly back, her brown, graying hair fanned out around her as if she were floating on the surface of the water. Her lips had been coated with Vaseline and her face looked pallid and dry. She had a rattle in her throat that was eerie and her mouth was half-open, taking in air laboriously. When she opened her eyes, rather suddenly, she locked them on Julia in a gaze that was part resignation, part plea.

The tears rolled down Julia's cheeks, and her stomach felt as though it had caught in her throat. To see someone in their last days battling a disease that was winning over their body, devouring it cell by cell, was horrifying. Even if the person was your worst enemy. It suddenly occurred to Julia that in the end, your worst enemy was death, and it would have its way with you this side of heaven when the appointed time came.

"Jul-ahh," her voice spoke through the rattle.

Julia walked right up to her bedside and sat down. With a force that came from somewhere else, she reached out and laid her hands gently on top of Marney's. Though the sickly hands were nearly cold to the touch, they responded kindly but faintly by giving Julia's forefinger a meager squeeze.

Then Julia spoke with a voice that also came from somewhere else, a voice she could not stop and did not want to stop. She got right up beside her old friend's face and said, "What can I do for you, Marney?"

Marney turned to face Julia head-on. She breathed slowly until the words came to her and then she said, unblinkingly, "Love . . . me." She kept her gaze on Julia, and Julia knew full well what that request meant: it meant forgiveness, it meant being the presence of God, whose nature is love, to the woman who had hurt her most, and most of all, it meant sacrifice.

She must, Julia knew. She must *love* Marney. Even though it would be costly. Even though it meant laying aside everything that she had come to build and value.

"I will," Julia nodded, and she squeezed Marney's hand back as she met her eyes. "I will love you." Then Marney lay back and closed her eyes as if something in her had been released and the tenseness in her limbs seemed to relax and soften, as did the rattle in her throat.

"I . . . hoped . . . you . . . could," she said, then she turned back to Julia as if she'd saved a small reserve of energy for this moment. "Raise them well. And tell them that I love them. I wasn't the perfect mother by a long shot, but I loved them with all that I could, Julia. And so did your father. Please remind them."

"I will." Julia rubbed her enemy's hand gently and leaned in to whisper into her ear, "I know you loved them, and I promise not to let them forget."

Suddenly Julia became concerned about the legal issues and the details. "Is there a will? Is there something else we need to do?"

Marney shook her head and let her eyelids close completely. "Dot . . . knows," she said. "She will tell you everything." And then as she relaxed back into the mound of pillows, "Go . . . to the children. And bring them back . . . today . . . This is it."

At Aunt Dot's, Julia sat the children down and explained what was happening to their mother and that she would take care of them from here on out. She would move to Charleston and raise them.

Heath was nodding through tears, and Etta was so curled up that Julia sensed she was beginning to mourn in the only way she knew how, quietly and somewhere deep inside herself. Charlie was angry and threw his plastic fire truck at the Oriental rug. It bounced a few times and then the ladder broke off and he lost it, running into Julia's arms and weeping like a frustrated baby. She scooped him up and held him tight, rocking him back and forth as Heath bent down and tried to fix the ladder.

Then they filed into Julia's car and drove out to hospice where they saw their mother for the last time, hugging her and kissing her as she lay limp in bed, eyes closed, peaceful. She died early the following morning, days before anyone at hospice expected she would.

CHAPTER 36
MEG

Meg was racing the children from the Santa brunch at the Yacht Club to the Christmas pageant rehearsal at the church when her phone buzzed, flashing her mother's cell number. Just as she was reaching for it, she spotted Preston — in the rearview mirror — clocking Katherine over the head in the backseat with his long, wooden shepherd's crook. Meg let the phone ring and pulled over the car where Broad Street met East Bay and yanked him out on the sidewalk by the collar of his pressed white oxford shirt.

"You're going to bed at seven thirty tonight." He shrugged and she was so angry she was seeing spots. "And if I were you I'd be very concerned about the strong possibility of Santa erasing my name from the good list."

Preston rolled his hazel eyes. "I know it's you, Mom, and you've probably already bought the stuff." Yes, she had bought all of the stuff, and it was stored at the Toys "R" Us in North Charleston where she planned to pick it up during the pageant rehearsal. But she'd had just about enough of his smartness, and she was willing to pull out all of the stops to teach him a lesson.

"Everything's returnable, Preston. Santa's elves keep all of their receipts." She placed her manicured hands on his shoulders and put her powdered nose just inches away from his freckled one. "Now, I want you to be kind to your siblings and anyone else you're around all day, all night, and all week long, or the elves are going to trade all the good stuff in for coal and switches. Do you hear me?"

Meg glared at her firstborn son, waiting for his response. She didn't bother looking at the car honking behind her or the friends that passed by in their luxury SUVs on their way from the Yacht Club over to the church. And she didn't flinch when her phone continued to buzz and then blip, indicating her mother had left one very long message.

Preston looked down at his polished loafers as the brisk December wind sifted through Meg's thin hair, messing up her do. Had she gotten his attention? Did he have a conscience somewhere in there or at least a desire to behave in order to get the iPod

Touch and the BB gun he had asked for? Was she as terrible a mother as she felt?

Finally, he met her eyes and nodded slightly. "Yes, ma'am."

"Thank you, Lord," she uttered. Perhaps she had hit home somewhere inside of his heart and mind. She gently squeezed his dimpled chin as he began to shiver. How she loved him. How she loved each of them. How she hoped they would turn out all right in spite of her maternal shortcomings. In spite of their natural inclinations toward greed and control and, in Preston's case, violence.

You were loved. She heard these words in her gut. They were not audible, but they were clear and heavy as lead. *You were loved. You were loved.* And the thought crossed her mind that God had just answered her back with something other than, *You're welcome.*

Her son swallowed hard and she shook her head as if to clear it. Then he slipped back into the car where he quietly apologized to Katherine, who was still rubbing the top of her head.

"I forgive you," she said.

Once the children were dressed for the rehearsal in the parish hall, Preston in a

400

shepherd's costume, Cooper in an ox costume, and Katherine in an angel costume, Meg delivered them to the sanctuary for practice. Then she ducked away from the gaggle of mothers under the portico and dipped into a quiet corner of the graveyard where there was a bench and an overhang of thick, bare wisteria vines. She only had a few minutes to talk if she was going to make it to North Charleston to pick up the toys, hide them back at her home in Mount Pleasant, and pick the kids up downtown at the end of their rehearsal. Her husband didn't like it when she drove and talked on the phone at the same time after she nearly ran over a cyclist at an intersection a few months ago, so she crouched down on the bench, hoping not to be noticed by the chatty mothers or the pageant director, who was always asking for last-minute help, and found her mother's number on the call screen.

Her mother should be in Manhattan by now. She had taken the train up with her neighbor friend, Nate. The one she'd threatened to sue just a year before. She had somehow befriended him and they seemed rather tight. Meg had spotted them walking their dogs down Broad Street toward Berlin's for his tuxedo fitting just the other day, and her mother had even turned down a Thanksgiving invitation to Preston's mother's house because she was joining Nate's family at Charleston Place.

"Don't you want to spend Thanksgiving with the grandchildren?" Meg had asked her mother. It wasn't that she wanted her to come so badly as she was embarrassed to report to Preston's mother that her mother was on a date with her gruff neighbor from off.

"Well, of course I do," her mother had said. "I was hoping you all would come over to my house for dessert in the evening."

Meg had thought to protest: a day with Preston's family and then an evening with her mother was going to wear her out. But she softened momentarily and said, "All right, Mama. We can do that. I'll bring a pumpkin pie."

Now Meg called her mother back without listening to the message.

"Have you heard, love?" her mother said. There was an echo in her mother's voice as if she were in the bottom of a well.

"Heard what?" Meg pressed her other ear down with her index finger and listened hard.

"Marney passed away yesterday."

Meg pulled her red peacoat tighter around her and buttoned it to the top as a chill ran up her spine.

Marney. Passed. Away. Yesterday.

The words sounded otherworldly at first. As if they were foreign and impossible to decode. Then they felt like a pin pricking an enormous water balloon Meg had been carrying on her back, and Meg jumped slightly as a thick lump formed in her throat.

"No," she said. "I had no idea." She had known the cancer was back, but she didn't realize how bad it was. She had ignored Aunt Dot's call a few days ago. Christmas was a busy time, and she did not want to get bogged down in her old family history this time of year.

Now she thought of her half sisters and brother: Heath, Etta, and Charlie. She saw their round faces in her mind, their big, unblinking eyes. Then she pictured her father and the way he had danced with pregnant Marney at Meg's wedding in the back corner of the Yacht Club ballroom behind a potted plant. A place where he thought they wouldn't be noticed.

However, Meg had noticed. She was on her way to change out of her wedding dress into the strapless linen sundress for her grand departure on Preston's family yacht where the guests would shower the couple with pale pink rose petals as they ran down the dock and onto the grand boat. They would tour the harbor and eat a private dinner on the bow beneath the light of the moon before starting their European honeymoon.

Then Meg pictured Marney as an eighteen-year-old college freshman — in cutoff jeans and a bikini top and a frayed Georgia Bulldogs baseball hat — hopping in Meg's sailboat with an orange Fanta and saying, "You can drive this by yourself?"

Meg had nodded, proud to show her independence to such an older, cooler, womanly college student. "Yep," she had said as she shoved off from the dock, looking back to her mother and Julia who were waving to them as they headed out toward St. Pierre Creek.

"That's really cool," Marney had said. Then she offered Meg a sip of her Fanta, which Meg took for a moment as she told Marney to take hold of the main sheet rope. Meg took a large swig and handed it back to the girl who smiled and took off her hat and leaned back with her thick, dark mane nearly touching the water, the summer sun showering her face with its light. *Will I be that beautiful someday?* Meg had asked herself as she watched Marney soaking up the brightness. How she had hoped she would.

"Meg? Are you there?"

Margaret, she thought to herself, but she didn't correct her mother.

"I'm here, Mother." And then the words floated up from that same place in her gut. As if in response to it. "What can I do to help?"

"Oh, I was hoping you'd ask," her mother said. "I'm in Penn Station right now. We can't get a train out until tomorrow morning."

"Can you stay with Julia?"

"Well, yes, Bess can put us both up. She's got a couple of extra bedrooms, but Julia's not even here."

"Where is she?"

"She's in Charleston, love."

"Three days before her wedding? This is crazy."

"I know," her mother said. "I don't know exactly what's going on, but she asked me to plan the funeral reception, and since it will be a day and a half before I get home . . ."

"I'll take care of it." The words kept working their way up from the gut and out of

Meg's mouth before she realized what she was saying. Her family Christmas party, the pageant rehearsal, the trip to the Greenbriar they had planned just after Christmas, it would all need to be canceled, but it would be all right. Everything needed to be put on hold. She could be a help to Julia and Aunt Dot. And she wanted to.

"Oh, darling," her mother said. "I was hoping you'd say that. Are you sure? I know how much you have going on this time of year."

Meg brushed the tears away. "I'm sure, Mama. I want to do this."

"All right." She heard her mother exhale deeply, and Meg pulled out her notebook for the planning.

"Now, I think we need to order some finger sandwiches from Hamby's," her mother instructed.

"Chicken salad and pimiento cheese?"

"Precisely."

"Done," Meg said. "And I'll make the tomato aspic and marinate some shrimp."

"Wonderful," her mother said. "And would you mind ordering some mini coconut cakes from Normandy Farms? I remember that was her favorite."

"No problem."

"Oh, thank you, darling. I don't expect

there to be more than two dozen people, but I want it to be nice."

"Me too," said Meg as she turned to find her daughter, dressed as an angel with soft feathery wings and a white dress and a gold tinsel halo, behind her.

She held up her finger to indicate that she'd be just a minute, and the girl lifted up her dress to reveal two skinned knees.

"And I'll make some sweet tea and get Preston to handle the bar and bring some large bags of ice," Meg continued.

"I hope Dot's silver is in good condition. She's not the best polisher, you know."

"Well," Meg said, "I'll bring some of mine and you can bring some of yours so we should be fine."

"You're right." The roar in the background grew. "I'm out on the street now," her mother said. "I'm leaving it all in your hands, Meg. I'll be home late tomorrow night."

"Consider it done," Meg said.

"I will," her mother said.

"Oh, and, Mother? Do you need Preston to pick you up at the train station?"

"Yes," she said. "We get in tomorrow at nine p.m."

"He'll be there." Meg hung up the phone and turned to her little heavenly host.

"What happened?"

"I fell down on my way to the bathroom."

Meg sifted through her purse and pulled out two Band-Aids and some Neosporin ointment.

The little girl stepped closer and hiked up her gown, and Meg cleaned her up before looking into her full cheeks.

"You've had a rough day, haven't you, sweet pea?"

The little girl nodded.

"I'm so sorry." Meg opened her arms and her child stepped inside of them and hugged her mother.

"Thank you, Mama," Katherine said as Meg blinked back the tears and held her child tight.

"I better get back to the rehearsal," Katherine said as Meg pulled back and kissed her daughter's cheek before standing up.

"C'mon." She reached out her hand, which her daughter gently took. "I'll walk you back, and I'll stay with you."

CHAPTER 37
JULIA

They buried Marney at noon three days later. It was the Saturday Julia was scheduled to marry Simon. She had called him the day she met with Marney for the last time and told him what she had decided. And then she called the dean of the fine arts department at Hunter College and explained why she would have to resign.

The dean was dumbfounded, and Simon was somewhere between outraged and distressed.

"You can't throw it all away." He flew down the day she told him and sat with her on Aunt Dot's front porch steps as the cars whizzed down Broad Street. "It's your whole life." He had taken her hand and made her meet his gaze. "And our future, Julia."

"I can." Julia squeezed his hand back and let it go, returning it to his knee. "I'm sorry for the pain I've caused you, Simon. I'm really sorry."

He studied her face as if she were a horrible mystery. "You're not going to be persuaded, are you?"

She shook her head gently, then carefully pulled the sapphire off of her finger. He opened his hand to receive it and exhaled deeply, holding it up to the afternoon light before calling a cab to take him back to the airport.

As she watched him leave, curling his long body up into the small Prius taxi, she knew he thought she had lost her mind, but she wasn't bothered by that. She had made a sacred promise to Marney. And in a way, she felt that her entire life had been leading to this moment. To shrink back now would be to deny the unusual charge to which she had somehow been called.

Her mother and Nate spent one night at Bess's, then took the morning train back to Charleston, where they spent the next day helping Meg and Preston prepare for the reception at Aunt Dot's house while Julia took the children to the aquarium. They spent several hours wandering through the dark corridors peering into windows of jellyfish and sea horses and watching the fish and the sharks and the sea turtles in the enormous two-story tank glide round and round.

The burial was at Magnolia Cemetery in the Bennett family plot next to her father's headstone and below the headstones of Julia's paternal grandparents. Only a handful of people were there to say their good-byes: Skeeter and Glenda, Jane Ann Thornton, a few neighbors from Edisto, Brooke, the babysitter, Meg and Preston, some nurses from hospice and MUSC, and, of course, Jed.

Julia's mama and Meg set up the reception at Dot's house. Jed helped them in the kitchen. Then he and Nate threw the football with Charlie in the backyard when the little boy grew restless from all of the whispers and the clinking of silver on china.

Marney had made all of the arrangements. She had drafted a will last summer with an old attorney friend of Julia's dad's, citing that Julia would be the one to raise the children.

"She knew you would," Aunt Dot said when she explained it to her the evening after Marney's passing. "She believed you would. It was like a kind of faith she possessed. She put all her hope in it." Aunt Dot patted her hand. "And she was right."

In the three short days between Marney's

passing and the funeral, Julia had figured out what homeschooling curriculum the kids were using and she had ordered the updated materials. She would teach them through the spring and enroll them in school in the fall. And she had an interview at the fine arts magnet school for the visual arts director position. "You're a shoo-in," her former art teacher (who was retiring from the school this year) had said. "They'd be crazy not to take you."

The night of the burial, after the children were put to bed and the silver trays were washed and set on the drying rack, Jed took Julia's hand. He pulled her out onto the piazza where he lifted her chin up in the moonlight and kissed her tenderly.

She pulled back and caught her breath. "That was unexpected." Then she couldn't keep herself from falling back into his sturdy arms. She felt so very vulnerable. As vulnerable as the kids, perhaps, and scared. And while she knew she could count up her times with Jed over the last two decades on one hand, she was sure he was someone she could be vulnerable with. Be honest with.

"No, it wasn't," he said as he embraced her tightly. "You knew it was coming. And you also know I've been waiting twenty-five years to do it again."

She smiled through her tears and pulled back.

"I meant what I said, Julia." He gazed at her with his soft brown eyes. "I want to help you raise these kids. And I want to court you too. And I know that's a whole different event, and I'm willing to wait for you until you're ready." He rubbed her back with his large strong hands and continued, "And if for some reason you don't think we're right for one another, I'll understand. I don't want to push you. All I want to do is help and be a part of your life. No matter what."

She felt her heart pounding in her chest. And even though it was an unseasonably chilly night in Charleston with a low of thirty-five degrees, she felt warmer than she'd felt in a long time. As if there was a kind of heat radiating from her core, knocking off the chill and all the years of sadness she'd become so accustomed to lugging around.

"Why not?" she said. "This has been a year full of unexpected turns, but the truth is I feel more at home and at peace than I ever have." She squeezed his arms. "I just want to do right by the kids. I want to raise them well. I always wanted a family of my

413

own, and I guess this is the one I have now."

"It is," Jed said as he leaned down and kissed her once more. The warmth between them grew so strong she had to pull away and say good night.

"I'm heading out to Edisto this coming weekend," he said as he stepped down the steps toward his car. "Can I cook you all dinner on Friday night? And maybe wet a line with Charlie on Saturday?"

"Yes," she said. She cocked her head and tried to contain her grin. "That sounds great." And then she closed the door and stepped back into Aunt Dot's old house, which had hardly changed at all since her childhood. She turned off each lamp, gathered up the few linen napkins from the reception that had been crumpled up and discarded around the living room, and put them in the laundry room. Then she took off her pumps and padded up the stairs to check on each child. Both Heath and Charlie were sound asleep, cocooned in their thick comforters, but Etta was up with the bedside lamp on, drawing, and when Julia tapped on the door, the girl pulled the sketchbook to her chest and looked longingly at her big half sister.

Julia came in and sat on her bed and patted her legs beneath the covers.

"We'll pack up tomorrow and head home to Edisto, okay?"

The girl nodded gently.

"I know your heart is broken, Etta," Julia whispered as the child continued to meet her gaze. "But I'll be here for you, sweetheart. If and when you're ready to talk, I'll listen."

Etta nodded as she bit her rosy bottom lip. Then she stood and plopped down into Julia's lap, curling up each long and gangly limb of hers until she was a tight ball, a ball just the right size to nuzzle into Julia's chest. Julia held her this way, tightly, for a long time as she rubbed her knobby back and rocked her back and forth on the end of the bed. When she felt the child's breathing slow and then turn to a light snore, she lifted Etta up and laid her on the old mattress where she tucked her tightly beneath the covers.

Then, before she turned out the light, she lifted up the sketchbook so that Etta wouldn't crumple it in her sleep, and as she instinctively turned it over, she saw an image of a bowl with light emanating from it, ray upon ray shooting out far and wide to the ends of the page and beyond.

As Julia stared at the rays, she was struck with a knowledge that though there was much mourning ahead for each of these children, they would be all right. They would get through it. And she would be all right too. And the unlikely family they would form would provide healing and strength for one another, and most of all, a place for this light to grow. Then she uttered as she did when there was nothing more to say, *Lord, have mercy. Christ, have mercy.* And she leaned down and kissed Etta on the forehead before pulling down on the metal string of the old lamp.

READING GROUP GUIDE

1. Do you think Marney was a good mother? Why or why not?
2. Main characters need to be capable of change. Trace the journeys of Julia, Mary Ellen, and Margaret (Meg). In what ways have each of them changed by the end of the story?
3. This novel is told from several different points of view. What do Etta and Jed's perspectives add to the story?
4. Painting plays an important role in the novel. How do the images Julia and Etta paint mirror their inner struggles and/or reveal their hearts?
5. When Julia returns to Edisto for the first time, in what way does the setting itself soften her outer shell? How can nature impact our lives? How can it shed light on our confusion and push us out of our grief?
6. Etta, the secret keeper, has a condition

called selected mutism. What do you think brought about this condition? Is it healthy or unhealthy? Explain.

7. The idea for this novel was sparked by a question: What would be the most difficult thing to forgive someone for? Can you come up with some scenarios that would be nearly impossible to forgive?

8. Do you think Julia forgives her father and Marney by the end of the story? Should she forgive them?

9. Consider the impact Aunt Dot has on the characters in the story, especially Julia and Etta. In what ways has she helped them along their journeys?

10. Imagine the characters five years from now. What do their lives look like?

ACKNOWLEDGMENTS

Once again, I am thankful to my editor, Ami McConnell, my copy editor, Rachelle Gardner, and my agent, Claudia Cross, whose literary skill and support made this novel possible. And thanks to the Thomas Nelson fiction team: Allen Arnold, Daisy Hutton, Katie Bond, Becky Monds, Ruthie Dean, and Jodi Hughes. You make it all happen.

If I were to make a list of the folks who have taught, encouraged, and shepherded me along the way, it would take up several pages. Here are just a few of the names that would be on that list: Joe and Betty Jelks, James and Peggy McKinney, Jim and Libby Johnson, Al and Elizabeth Zadig, Peet and Jenny Dickinson, Rick and Annie Belser, Jean and Johnnie Corbett, Tim and Kathy Keller, Hamilton Smith, John and Carolyn Pelletier, Meghan Alexander, Bret Lott, Kelli Hample, Jeannie Lyles, Amy Watson Smith, Karen Turner, Meredith Myers,

Elisabeth Hunter, Rachel Temple, Avery Smith, Rene Miles, Rachel Barrett Trangmar, and Evie Cristou. Thank you.

I'm grateful to the belles I blog with at www.southernbelleview.com: Lisa Wingate, Marybeth Whalen, Rachel Hauck, and Shellie Tomlinson. Sharing conversation, stories, and life with you on the cyber porch each week is a downright delight.

Thanks also to the booksellers who hand-sell the stories every day, especially Jill Hendrix at Fiction Addiction in Greenville, SC, Jonathan Sanchez at Blue Bicycle Books in Charleston, SC, Tom Warner at Litchfield Books in Pawleys Island, SC, Christine Meredith at Saints Alive in Charleston, SC, and Karen Carter at the Edisto Bookstore on Edisto Island, SC.

My deepest gratitude goes to my husband, Edward, and to my children, Frances and Edward. Your love has made all of the difference.

And most of all, thanks to the One who continually transplants my heart. We've clocked a lot of hours in the operating room together. You are my lifeblood.

ABOUT THE AUTHOR

Beth Webb Hart, a South Carolina native, is the best-selling author of *Grace at Low Tide* and *The Wedding Machine*. She serves as a speaker and creative writing instructor at schools, libraries, and churches throughout the region, and she has received two national teaching awards from Scholastic, Inc. Hart lives with her husband and their family in Charleston.

414